D1359305

BAD NIGHT

IS FALLING

Berkley Prime Crime Books by Gary Phillips

VIOLENT SPRING
PERDITION, U.S.A.
BAD NIGHT IS FALLING

Bad Night Is Falling

GARY PHILLIPS

BERKLEY PRIME CRIME
NEW YORK

BAD NIGHT IS FALLING

A Berkley Prime Crime Book
Published by The Berkley Publishing Group, a member of
Penguin Putnam Inc.,
200 Madison Avenue, New York, NY 10016

The Penguin Putnam Inc. World Wide Web site address is
http://www.penguinputnam.com

Book design by Casey Hampton.

First Edition: July 1998

Library of Congress Cataloging-in-Publication Data

Phillips, Gary, 1955–
Bad night is falling / Gary Phillips.—1st ed.
        p.   cm.
ISBN 0-425-16302-4
I. Title.
PS3566.H4783B3   1998
813'.54—dc21   97–34988
                                                CIP

Printed in the United States of America

10   9   8   7   6   5   4   3   2   1

For my wife, Gilda, the coolest.

The idea that those who are most happily at home in the modern world . . . may be the most vulnerable to the demons that haunt it; the idea that the daily routine of playgrounds, and bicycles, of coping, eating and cleaning up, of ordinary hugs and kisses, may be not only infinitely joyous and beautiful but also infinitely precarious and fragile, that it may take desperate and heroic struggles to sustain this life, and sometimes we lose.

—Marshall Berman,
All That Is Solid Melts into Air

Prologue

BURNING THE DARKNESS DOWN

Efraín Cruzado's first sensations were of opening his eyes and coughing roughly. He awoke next to Rosanna with a vicious dry hack ratcheting from his body. Damn, he reflected sleepily, maybe he should get over to the all-night Sav-on over on Alvarado. Suddenly Rosanna too was coughing, and Cruzado realized their bedroom was far stuffier than usual.

"What's happening? Put on the lights," his wife said groggily, rousing herself from her slumber.

It came to him in the same moment he got to his feet. "Fire, Rosanna, there's a fire in our place." He tried to sound calm, he didn't want her getting panicked as he clawed along the wall for the light switch through the invading soot. His eyes began to cloud from fear and smoke.

The light from the fixture in the ceiling had a weird, otherworldly effect, illuminating the moist, oily fog rolling through their bedroom. Cruzado was already out the door heading for the girls' room. Behind him, he could hear Rosanna loudly coughing and stumbling about, her idea the same as his.

In the hall he bumped into a hurtling body and Cruzado crazily imagined that it was one of those *mayate* bastards, one of those blacks, who'd surely set the fire. Or, goddamn him, maybe it wasn't them. Maybe it was the others. Damn this hopeless city, and goddamn these Rancho Tajuata Housing Projects.

"Efraín, Efraín," his sister, Karla, exclaimed, latching onto his arm, "I can't see anything. Where are the children?"

He grabbed her shoulder and gently but forcefully pushed her to the right. "Stay still. Rosanna is coming this way, and I want you to hold onto her," he said in Spanish, moving to his left. The door to the girls' bedroom was hot and he knew what that meant, but what could he do? A father can't ignore his responsibilities.

He got the door open, the heat from the room literally sucking the breath out of him. He rocked back, sagging down against the far wall as the fire's fury overpowered him. A blur loomed before him and Cruzado, an agnostic, knew it was an archangel come to collect his children.

But the time for sweet music was not just yet. He could hear their wails. The girls, the girls had to be saved.

"Karla, please," he heard Rosanna plead.

He found some air but it hurt to take it in. His lungs were singed like meat on an open spit but he had to get up, he had to do something.

One side of the girls' room was a dance of glowing saffron and Cruzado could hear Olga screaming in that particular wail of hers. Normally the sound got on his nerves, but now it was a beacon guiding him in a savage terrain.

"I'm coming, *mija*, Daddy's coming," Cruzado promised. He was up, shuffling forward, his chest feeling as if an electric blanket were wrapped around his insides. He got to the girls' doorway, dazed, tired. Rosanna emerged from the burning whiteness eating away at their home and encroaching on their bodies. Olga was in her mother's arms, Lola had her arms wrapped around the woman's legs.

"Take them out, I'll get Marisa," Cruzado blared.

Her dead stare cut him off. "There's no need to go back in," she said gravely.

Cold iron poured over his knees and it was all Cruzado could do not to faint. He watched the tears silently travel the length of his wife's face, and he put his hand on her shoulder. "Mother," he said with a sick realization.

"I'll get the girls out." Rosanna clutched Olga tightly.

A whoosh of flame shot at them as if driven by a jet engine. The girls screamed and Cruzado beat at his arm, which was now on fire. "Yes, out, get them out into the yard," he desperately repeated. "I've got to see about Mama."

Karla had stumbled over. "I'll go with you."

"No." He pushed her and his wife toward the front. "You two must take care of the girls."

Smoke undulated behind the father. He'd stopped the fire on his arm, but the limb radiated a tremendous pain that intensified as he tried to moved it. "Mother," he called out, turning around and moving off. He was swallowed up by the mass of grey. "Mother," he called out as he found his way toward the small room off the service porch.

He could hear nothing as he got to the room. The door was closed and cool to the touch. Cruzado nervously twisted the knob and snatched the door open. More smoke, grey and glistening with malicious intent, came at him. He didn't bother to call her name as he bent down to her bed. She was warm, but she wouldn't be going anywhere in this world any longer.

The virulent pall congealed around him, gagging him and gorging into his watery eyes. Then it ebbed and parted to briefly reveal the carved rosemary wood cross he'd tacked over her bed. The cross for Christina.

Cruzado got up. The room was suddenly lit by a jagged flame that was billowing across the worn linoleum. A flame eating its way to where he stood. From somewhere he could hear the neighbors' voices and hoped that meant the rest of his family was safe. He removed one of his mother's blankets and wrapped it around himself. Since he wasn't sure what he believed in after this life, he assumed God would find it awfully hypocritical for him to start praying for deliverance now. He got the blanket about him as best he could, took a last look at his mother, and plunged into the fire.

One

Antar Absalla was not one who enjoyed having a finger poking at him. And he was particularly not fond of Mrs. Reyisa Limón, twice widowed. He was therefore hard-pressed to hold his tongue as the older woman hooked her talon at his face as she reprimanded him.

"Where were your security people, Mr. Absalla?" she demanded for the fourth time since the meeting had begun a long hour ago.

Absalla mentally centered himself before speaking. "At those hours of the morning," he began with a forced calm, "there is a thinner crew than during peak time. This was a financial decision that your tenants' association made, Mrs. Limón. As you'd be aware if you'd reread the minutes from past board meetings." He managed not to smirk.

"You don't need to remind me of the procedures of Robert's Rules, Mr. Absalla," she leveled. "It's your performance that's in question here."

"I don't think that's quite the case, Reyisa," Henry Cady, the president of the tenants' association, responded. The aging black man did that little self-effacing clearing of his throat and adjusted his black horn-rimmed glasses. "We've convened this emergency meeting to see what we need to do to make sure something like this horrible thing doesn't happen again."

Several heads around the square conference table indicated agreement.

Mrs. Limón leaned back in her seat, the chair creaking under her commanding size. The woman made a slight gesture, a slice of her palm like the drop of an axe. "I'm not saying we aren't. I am saying we hired a twenty-four-hour security force who are supposed to be ensuring the safety of our residents."

"And the Ra-Falcons were on the scene in less than three minutes," Absalla pointed out. "My team was helping put out the fire before the fire department got here. And two of them were taken to the hospital for smoke inhalation after trying to enter the premises to get free Mr. Cruzado." Indignation made his face warm but Absalla was determined not to lose his temper, and thus play into the scheme of this tormentor who sat across from him.

"You do have a point," Juan Carlos Higuerra said. "I think if we can discuss this so we can better the patrols, we can get something accomplished."

Limón fixed a gaze to seize hearts on Higuerra, silently damning him for his usual conciliatory approach. "We must also talk about how we're going to deal with this vicious gang element."

"The Ra-Falcons security are not the police," Cady asserted.

"But"—the long finger went to work again— "Absalla does employ those he admits are ex–gang members. They can find out who killed the Cruzados. If they don't know already."

"I've asked my people what they've heard, and no one

knew about any rumor to harm the Cruzados. And of course we will continue to ask around to see if we can find out anything.'' Then he used his index finger on Limón.

"Yes, some of the Ra-Falcons used to be gang members,'' Absalla continued. ''They come from these impoverished neighborhoods. They are also young men and women who have decided to turn their lives around, and give something back. This is not so-called, it is a fact. None of my crew are criminals. They wouldn't be on the patrol if they weren't disciplined and dedicated."

"Some of them used to be Scalp Hunters though, right?'' Mrs. Graves, who'd been quiet until now, asked.

"Yes,'' Absalla answered. ''Just as some of them used to be members of one or more of the Rolling Daltons set or the Del Nines.''

Mrs. Limón leaned forward again, her heavy breasts expanding against the edge of the table. ''What's important is that everybody around the Rancho says it was the Scalp Hunters who firebombed the Cruzados' apartment. The little bastards set the fire off in the girls' room. They broke the window and shoved their . . .''—she paused, searching for the word—''Molotov right in there between the bars.'' Her sunken face testified to the cruelty of the crime.

"How do you know that?'' Cady inquired.

"It's common knowledge,'' she barked.

"I don't mean the rumor about who set the fire,'' Cady clarified. ''I mean how do you know where the device went off less than two days after the incident.''

"I have friends on the fire commission,'' she said proudly.

She bestowed on Absalla a sidelong glance, which seemed to imply she also had friends on other commissions—like the one that oversaw the police department. He felt like backhanding her.

"I've already sat down with my sergeants to figure out how we can change our patrols to best cover the complex during the off-hours. But I'm afraid it's difficult without putting more people on staff."

Limón snickered but didn't say anything.

Cady said, "We're under the knife on this, Mr. Absalla. As you know, the owners of this property will soon be allowed by the Housing and Urban Development Department to place the Rancho on the private market. To counter that, we have to have a two-thirds majority of the families organized to agree to buy the property for themselves. If the residents vote to incorporate as a limited-equity cooperative, we can qualify for federal grants and loans to do so."

Cady removed his glasses. "I don't need to tell anyone here, the conservatives who control Congress are looking for any excuse not to allow those grants to be issued. These murders must be cleared up if we are to have a chance at realizing something for ourselves."

"I know we need results," Absalla said sincerely.

"Not to mention your contract comes up around the same time as the grant application," Limón needlessly reminded him. "And if the murderers of the Cruzados remain free, let alone if more horrible things happen to other Latino families, this body will take that as a sign we may need to do things differently."

"Blacks get attacked too," one of the African-Americans interjected.

"Nobody's saying different," Mrs. Limón blurted.

Trying to ease the tension, Cady said, "Let's stay together, people. This whole body must examine and discuss the facts. We have to set the example for the rest of the Rancho." He looked directly at Mrs. Limón. Surprisingly, she bestowed a deferential smile on him without displaying any of her usual combativeness.

Absalla promised to submit a revised patrol plan to the tenants' association by the end of the week. Leaving the multipurpose center, Absalla noted not for the first time the tranquility it was possible to find walking around the projects. Sure, all the cinder block buildings, lying squat and heavy and uninteresting-looking against L.A.'s lethal air, wouldn't be on the cover of *Architectural Digest* anytime soon. And yes, the taupe-colored apartments were in bad need of paint, having last seen a fresh coat sometime during the middle of the Bradley Administration.

But many of the residents took pride in keeping their plots neat, their stoops swept clean. Arrow shirts and prim little girls' dresses hung nonchalantly from clotheslines, and several dogs romped around, wagging their tails, their brown eyes gleaming with playfulness.

As he turned a corner on the row of apartments along Biddy Mason Lane, Absalla spotted several young black men lounging against the fender of a lowered '73 Monte Carlo, the front raised on jack stands. Despite himself, he instantly categorized the youth. Due, he reasoned as he confidently strolled past, to the blaring boom box at their feet and the ubiquitous forty-ouncer being passed around.

He purposefully slowed down. "You young brothers ought to put as much time into cracking a book as you do standing around bullshitting and drinking that piss."

One of the young men was tall with elongated muscles like an NBA pick. His shirt was unbuttoned, displaying a torso adorned with three California Youth Authority–type tattoos. He bowed slightly. "*A-Salam-aleikum*," he said, chuckling, and the others also dipped their heads.

"Got some pigs' feet if you want one, Minister Absalla," another one piped in.

The security chief didn't even bother to shake his head as he moved on. The offices of the Ra-Falcons were located on the second floor of the building housing the laundry rooms. It was a structure on the southwest end of the complex, some distance from the old, defunct Southern Pacific tracks that cleaved diagonally through the Rancho.

Originally, when the place was built in the waning days of FDR's New Deal years, the Rancho, located near the central city, was envisioned as an experiment in planned multiracial living. The Taj, as the old-timers called the place, along with public housing places like Nickerson Gardens and Imperial Courts farther south in Watts, had also been part of that vision. They were all part of a plan that was drafted by the progressives who'd burrowed their way into the local Housing Authority. It was an objective endorsed by the bipartisan reform forces at work in the city in those days.

But those people, and that dream of institutions playing a role in the engineering of racial harmony, had both long since been discarded like so many old bottles.

Absalla's reflections ended as he arrived at the Ra-Falcons' office. On its steel door was a colorful decal, which displayed a stylized profile of a falcon's head with a golden ankh prominent in the center of its ebon orb. Encircling the head was a border containing various African and Egyptian symbols of the warrior and the harvest.

Before he could grasp the knob, the door swung inward to allow a man with sergeant's stripes on his shirt's bicep and another man, a corporal, into the passageway.

"Brothers," Absalla greeted the two.

The sergeant, Eddie Waters, said, "Boss man, how'd it go at the meeting?"

"We got to get on this bad, Eddie," Absalla said, zeroing them both with a stern look.

"I know," Keith 2X, the other one, answered. "There's already been a retaliation."

Absalla didn't want to seem out of the loop in front of his crew, but he hadn't heard and so was forced to ask. "What happened? I've been so busy with the tenants' association that I didn't catch this."

"Old Mrs. Ketchum and her sister got a nasty note tacked to their door last night," Waters said. "The note said something about how the blacks at the Rancho bring down the place, and how maybe somebody's going to do something about it."

"Their apartment's near the Cruzados'," Absalla said. "I guess they didn't see who left the note."

"No, but it's a sure thing them Los Domingos did it," Keith 2X replied.

"We're on our way to check it out, and maybe get a little sumptin' sumptin' on them punk-asses," Waters added with enthusiasm.

"Don't be no provocateurs, you hear," Absalla warned them. "Just confirm it if you can, understand?"

"We ain't scared of them *mojados*," Waters spat with bravado.

"Restraint, black man, remember," Absalla retorted.

"It's cool," Waters said, and the two started to leave. "Oh yeah, there's an ese in there to see you." He grinned.

"Who?"

"Surprise." Waters tapped 2X on the shoulder, and the two departed.

The Ra-Falcons' office was one large room with two feeder rooms off that. A third area had been a walk-in utility closet, but the door had been removed. It now served as residence for a fax and a small refrigerator.

The larger area contained a black vinyl couch trimmed in ash wood with matching chairs scattered about. Several other chairs and desks, spanning various eras and tastes, were also present.

Hunched over the phone at the main desk was a woman who also had sergeant's stripes on the sleeve of her dark blue uniform, LaToyce Blaine. She made small circles with her free hand as she talked, her vermillion nails flashing like dry blood on shark's teeth.

"Hold on," she said to whoever she was talking to. "Five-O in there to see you," she whispered to Absalla.

The security chief didn't break stride as he went into one of the lesser rooms that served as his inner office. He came upon a Latino, who he made to be a Chicano, dressed in an olive green gabardine suit. He wore a bronze-hued tie, offset by a dark green shirt.

The cop, who'd been looking at a mounted photo of Absalla leading a contingent at the Million Man March, turned to greet him. "I'm Lieutenant Marasco Seguin," the man with the drooping mustache said. He handed Absalla a card.

On the card's left corner was a raised-relief image of a detective's shield in silver. Superimposed over that was a gold banner proclaiming his rank in blue lettering, City Hall in gold, and below that a bar in gold with his badge number in blue. The card stated that Seguin worked out of Wilshire Division on Pico.

Absalla put the card on his desk and stood looking at the clean-decked cop. "Look, Lieutenant, a couple of detectives from Newton have already been all over me about this Cruzado mess." He let his annoyance show. " 'Sides, aren't you out of your division?"

Seguin scratched at his chin. "This is an investigation the brass wants solved, with haste. I'm temporarily reassigned, and in charge of Fitzhugh and Zaneski's investigation."

Absalla was tempted to tell Seguin he'd found Zaneski particularly funky to deal with, but he wasn't sure this Chicano would empathize with a black man's plight. He moved behind his desk and they both sat down.

"Why is this murder so important to the LAPD?" Absalla asked.

"It's a little unusual even for the Rancho to have a triple homicide in one night." He paused a beat, and as he went on, a sour look contorted his face. "Especially when one of them was a little child."

"And the city wants the turnover of the Rancho and other public housing units to go through," Absalla observed. "No more matching funds the county is obligated to pony up if there's no federal program. The cost savings must look real good to the county supervisors what with the budget shortfalls we always have."

"Sometimes interests collide, Mr. Absalla," Seguin countered. "Some of your employees have records, don't they?"

"You know they do. I've asked all of them if they know anything, and they say they don't. These young folk who are the Ra-Falcons have demonstrated time and again they are no longer following the life, Lieutenant."

He put his hand flat on the desk like a distended creature. "I vouch for each and every one of them." His gaze didn't move off Seguin.

The cop said nothing and Absalla continued. "And it's still anyone's guess on who did the firebombing. I heard that Cruzado may have been mixed up in some kind of trouble back in his hometown in Mexico. That's why he came up here."

"I'd like copies of everybody's personnel record, Mr. Absalla."

"I don't think so without a court order."

"This isn't about you against the blue-eyed devil, man. This is about finding the guilty."

"A ten-year-old black boy named Troy was gunned down three months ago in what we gleefully call a cycle-by. Where was your special assignment then?" Absalla demanded.

"Sometimes it takes the deaths of one too many innocents to make things happen."

The right kind of innocents. "Uh-huh."

"I'll have the court order in the morning, Mr. Absalla." Seguin stood up, unconsciously fingering his tie. "I want to repeat that the department is looking for a slam dunk on this. Cooperation can go a long way."

"I'll bear that in mind."

"Please do."

Seguin left and Absalla sat looking intently out the grilled window at a cracked concrete walkway and one of those plastic tricycles designed to look like a rocket sled. After some moments, he got up and went back into the outer room.

Blaine was busy filling out her patrol report from last night. An oldies soul station played softly on the radio near her.

"Who was that brother you mentioned to me?" Absalla asked, moving about the room like a panther in search of meat.

The sergeant's braided head tilted toward the ceiling. "Ah, Pope or something like that."

"And he's a private detective?"

The young woman shook her braids. "I think so. At least, he helped a girlfriend of my friend whose boyfriend was shot to death."

He didn't bother to follow that trail. "Get his number, will you?"

"What you up to, Antar?"

"About not being put in a trick bag." With that the
stocky, shaved-headed Muslim went back into his office,
closing the door tightly against what he could feel was a
mother of a storm gathering.

van Monk used the end of his finger to get at some grit the wind off the Pacific had blown into a corner of his eye. Unlike his old lady, he was not big on the lure of the outdoors and all its wonders. That's why the good Lord created concrete and takeout for guys like him.

"So that's what's been going on since the murders about three days ago," Absalla said, taking another bite of his swordfish.

"I know Seguin. Is that another reason you want me to look into the Cruzados' murders?" Monk gulped down more of his delicious lemonade.

Three healthy, young women in jean shorts and taut bikini tops Rollerbladed past their outdoor table on the Venice boardwalk. Various men of differing ages and shapes gave them appreciative attention. Absalla was gauging his lunch guest. "I didn't know that." A halting crept into his voice. "You telling me this because there's only so far you're willing to go?" A forkful of swordfish and wild rice rested in his hand.

"No," Monk said casually. "I'm just pointing out

something that would come up sooner or later, and wanted to get it out of the way. Marasco and I are cool about working the same side of the street.''

The food slowly made its way to the stolid face. He chewed slowly and asked, ''You have a lot of friends in the police department?''

''Marasco's it.''

''How'd you two meet?''

Monk tugged at the underside of his goatee. ''A story only worth telling on a bar stool sometime. Have the cops questioned your Ra-Falcons?'' He finished his glass. He spotted a knot of people gathered on the sand. They were watching a man in a turquoise turban juggle two live chain saws. He shifted his gaze back to his potential employer.

''Been on them like white on rice since your boy subpoenaed my records. See, Monk''—Absalla pointed with the blunt end of his fork—''them cops are out to catch a case on one or more of my crew, and that ain't how it's going to be.''

''I'd like a copy of your records too.''

''You gonna take my money and not trust me?'' Absalla's voice went up half a notch over a piece of baguette in his cheek.

''It will help give me a full picture. And I'd also like a list of who's in the tenants' union. And if you would, I need you to introduce me to the members who can get me some play at the Rancho.''

Absalla worked the bread. He chewed like a man with loose bridge work. ''Black faces open some doors, brown ones others at the Taj, my man.''

''I assumed that.'' Monk tried to get their waiter's attention for more lemonade. As was the fashion at trendy restaurants, the kid who'd seated the two had told them what his name was, and what the specials of the day were.

He had told them that his name was Daniel, pronouncing the name like it was made of paper-mâché. He was a tall, dark-haired Filipino lad. He sauntered over to the table.

"Yes," he cooed at Monk.

He made his request and the waiter took off with his empty glass.

Absalla smirked. "Looked like he was hopin' you'd ask him for more than a refill."

"He's just doing his gig until the multimillion-dollar movie offer comes along."

"Oh, you one of them tolerant niggers, huh?" Absalla goaded.

"To a point," Monk retorted. Daniel returned with his refilled glass. "The possibility of you hiring me to find a killer or killers is to take the heat off you, Antar. Now there's nothing about that says I have to convert to do my job, right?"

Absalla held up his hands in mock deference. "Calm, my brother, be calm. I was only foolin'," he said unconvincingly.

"How long does the tenants' association have until they're supposed to have their application in to HUD?" Monk asked, eager to conclude their business.

"Well, it ain't no secret them crackers in Washington want to be shuck of as much public subsidies they can push through. What with time limits on welfare, creating workfare programs and all." Absalla stabbed at a piece of cauliflower like it was trying to get away. "The association's been told they've got about three months to apply and see if they qualify."

"That means most of the tenants want to stay and be owners together," Monk concluded.

The other man nodded. "That's right. Things weren't exactly 'we are the world' at the Rancho to begin with, then this incident had to go down. The tenant organizing has stalled, and the association needs at least another four hundred families or so to even attempt to apply. Plus,'' he added, pointing with the end of the fork again, ''the city housing people are also getting jammed up and want to see the Rancho conversion go through.''

''And if the tenants can't get it together then the housing project is sold on the open market.'' Monk ate some of his chicken fettucini. ''A lot of these potential signatures are to be found among the Latino population?'' Monk surmised.

Absalla grinned. ''You must study this housing jive in your off days.''

''It seemed obvious given the changing demographics of the Rancho.''

The other man made a curt sound that sounded like a semi's power brakes letting off air. ''That and every other part of the city. Even a liberal like you has to admit this city is turning into one big Tijuana.'' He gleefully attacked his vegetables once again.

Monk searched for an offhand comment, but couldn't find one. Presently he said, ''What are your theories about the murders?''

''I think it was those goddamn Domingos Trece. I think some of the Hispanic tenants living around the Cruzados know that, and are either too afraid to say it, or don't want to.''

''How do you mean?''

Absalla leaned forward, using his fork as teacher's tool a third time. ''Before the Ra-Falcons were brought in, the folks at the Rancho were catching hell, caught between the Scalp Hunters and the Domingos. Bricks through your car window to snatch a purse, muggings, dope dealin' on your front stoop. The security company they had wasn't doin' shit.''

"Your turning things around in other housing projects has gotten you a lot of press," Monk commented. "I guess the tenants' association at the Rancho had nothing to lose.''

The security chief got going, waving the end of the fork as he talked. "We take those that many have given up on and give them something to believe in. Now don't misunderstand me, Monk. I stand foursquare for my people, but I'm also the first one to come down on a brother when he's doing wrong. The Scalps ain't no Jehovah's Witnesses. We came in, and with the aid of the tenants' association, we put the squash on a lot of that action. At least as the Rancho proper is concerned. See, the Ra-Falcons don't joke, and people know that.''

Monk wanted to reel him in before he launched into one of the soliloquies he'd seen him doing at televised press conferences. Absalla would regale, to any who'd listen, his rise from car thief and dope dealer, then redemption as a convert to the Muslim faith. The successes his security services had achieved at several crime-plagued housing projects in various cities had received national press.

However, his hip-hop Horatio Alger tale usually skipped the part about him being kicked out of the Nation of Islam due to some questions about bookkeeping at the mosque he ran in Philadelphia. His exile had precipitated his move west.

"How does all that get us to Los Domingos?" Monk abrasively cut in.

Absalla seemed caught up short, like a pitcher called in just before throwing a no-hitter. "Sure, I was getting to that. Over the last year or so, there's been some shootings and retaliations between them Central Americans and the

Scalps. This despite the fact there's been an unofficial de-tente between the two sets for years.''

"I gather the escalation is over who will control the drug traffic in the area," Monk concluded glumly.

"Yeah, there's that. But there's also been threats against black residents who aren't in any way mixed up with the gangs." Absalla looked at him knowingly.

Monk was adrift. "What are you getting at?"

"I'm not the only one who thinks the Domingos are working for some others who want to make sure the Ran-cho doesn't get into the hands of the tenants. Black tenants anyway."

Monk rested his chin on his hand, his elbow propped on the table. "So the Domingos kill a Latino family as part of this conspiracy."

"Exactly. See, Cruzado was trying to organize some of the immigrant tenants into his own association. He claimed neither the Chicanos nor the blacks were responsive to his people's—you know, immigrants'—concerns."

"So he was disrupting the program," Monk said, trying to flow with Antar's reasoning.

"Something like that, yeah. I'm not saying I'm sure who's behind the Domingos, but whoever it is wants every-body to roll over and let the place get sold out from under them."

Absalla continued. "The African-Americans there are generally the longest-running residents. They want to buy the place." The man sat back, content that he'd given the initiate a few glimpses of the secrets of the keep. "Did I scare you?"

Monk willingly took the bait. "I'll start tomorrow."

"Here." With a grin, Absalla handed Monk a sheaf of papers from a soft leather portfolio he'd placed against the legs of the table. "These are the reimbursement forms."

"You mean I have to submit these before I get paid?"

A quick torque of his gleaming head. " 'Fraid so, my man. See, I can hire you through some consultant funds I can access, but it is federal money, and there is a bureaucracy to follow."

"Isn't there always."

The other man made a fist and began working it as if kneading on an invisible ball. "I hope you can get onto something soon, Monk. I don't expect you to go up against the Domingos, but find us proof so the law can move on them. Make your friend Seguin a big man downtown."

Monk worked on a wan smile then lost interest.

"If I didn't have to oversee two other housing projects we patrol, I'd get to it myself." He rose, placed some money down, and tucked the portfolio under one muscled arm.

"I'll see what I can do to fill in," Monk deadpanned.

"Right on," Absalla said guilelessly.

Daniel hoped they'd have a nice day. Monk walked with Absalla part of the way along the boardwalk. They parted company near the refurbished Muscle Beach area. Several buffed participants were going through their routines for the enjoyment of both the onlookers and themselves.

In particular, Monk noticed a light-skinned black woman with a back broader than a set of double doors. She was doing a set of behind-the-neck lifts with some serious iron. Monk watched her for several minutes, the fluid muscles beneath her coppery arms bunching and flexing like part of a timeless machine whose sole function was to provide chiseled, efficient beauty in a flawed and treacherous world.

Eventually he walked off, trying to pick out tourists from residents. His path took him past a jazz trumpeter he recognized sitting in a frayed chaise lounge. He was singing a version of "I Should Care" which Rodgers and Hart probably never intended. But when he got to the instrumental part, his horn proved he still had his chops.

Monk, his sport coat draped over his arm, came to Ozone then turned left past a clump of bleached-out apartment buildings. He reached the street called Speedway, where he'd parked his restored '64 Ford Galaxie. The thoroughfare had gotten its name in the late '40s from the hot-rodders who used the then isolated straightaway to run their milled-out Fords and Willyses.

He beeped off the alarm and got behind the wheel. A homeless man wearing a grimy peacoat buttoned all the way up stuck a Styrofoam cup against his window. Monk cranked it down.

"How 'bout a little change, trooper?"

He dug out some coins and plopped them in the cup. "There you go."

The man mumbled something while he jingled the cup, staring intently at the contents as if he were a sage rolling the bones. He started to walk away, looking up at the warm, clear sky. As Monk started the car he noticed that the man was talking to himself.

"Bad night is falling," Monk thought he heard the man say as he drove off.

Three

"That was the going-away dinner they had for me. Gilbert Lindsey himself handed me the certificate." Henry Cady beamed, touching a corner of the framed photo. In the shot, an obviously pleased Cady stood alongside the diminutive Lindsey, the late councilman who had represented the district of L.A. he'd called "the Mighty Ninth."

Lindsey had been the first black member of the L.A. City Council. He had been appointed to fill a vacant seat in January of 1963. He'd worked his way up from janitor in the Department of Water and Power to aide to the late liberal white County Supervisor, Kenneth Hahn. Hahn had attended Thomas Jefferson High School. The same school Monk had, decades later.

Next to that photo was another one of a younger Cady without glasses, in creased khaki pants and shirt standing at the apex of an inverted V of men dressed similarly. The other men, all black save for a couple of Latinos, were in squatting positions and some had floor buffers before them.

A small metal caption read: CITY HALL JANITORS, AUGUST 1965.

"This couldn't have been taken during the riots," Monk observed. Everybody in the picture looked relaxed.

"That was taken on the sixth, a Friday. Five days before everything happened on the following Wednesday," Cady said offhandedly, clearly having repeated the date often to visitors. "Man, we didn't get back to work for damn near a month after the streets blew up."

"I was too young then to understand the cryptic smile on my dad's face," Monk said, reminiscing for no one's benefit save his own.

Cady was still examining the photo taken in the basement of City Hall. "Worked thirty-two years there. Made swing shift supervisor and was five times the shop steward for my local."

"SEIU?" Monk asked.

"Yep," the older man replied, finally turning from the past. "You'd be hard-pressed to believe it, Ivan, but in them days the Taj wasn't such a bad place to live. Had us barbeques in the common area on Saturdays, women and kids got in their finest to go to church on Sundays. None of this knockin' people in the head by young men with pants down around their cracks and can't spell cat."

The two were standing in the spacious living room of Cady's townhouse unit. Being one of the veteran tenants had its perks even in the Rancho Tajuata. The apartment had two levels and a separate kitchen, not a kitchenette like so many of the other apartments Monk knew.

"Come on, take a load off." Cady indicated a chair as he eased his thin frame with its slight paunch into a worn and cracked leather lounger. The thing seemed to form around him like an organic exoskeleton. The chair stood at an angle facing a late-model color TV set. A VCR sat on top of the TV, perpetually blinking 12:00.

"I was hoping you might introduce me around to some of the residents, Henry," Monk said. "Not necessarily the ones living near the Cruzados, but the ones who knew them."

"You know there's been two LAPD detectives prowling around here already."

"Is one of them a sharp-dressed Chicano with a Zapata mustache?" Monk indicated either side of his mouth with his thumb and forefinger crooked in a crescent.

"Nope, I Spy team. And naturally the black one is even more of an asshole than the white one. Gotta do more shit to keep his job," Cady joked.

Monk chuckled. "They've been to see you then."

"Not yet, but being the old dog around here does have some advantages in hearing about a few things. But to get anything out of the Spanish residents who knew the Cruzados, you better know some lingo. A few speak English, but even they won't savvy when they don't want to. Although I guess among the black folks around here, I'm about the best ambassador you're gonna get. And trust me, that ain't saying a whole lot."

"I figured I'd have to deal with the language situation, and I'm working on getting an interpreter." He didn't elaborate that his possible translator was an alcoholic accountant named Andrade who frequented the donut shop he owned. The man often sat hung over at the counter for hours, working angles on a race form or, occasionally, a client's books.

"Are you figurin' it wasn't a gang thing?" Cady asked earnestly.

"I'm not figuring much right now; I just want to get a

sense of things. One of my ideas is of course to try and get a line on the Scalp Hunters.''

"Won't the cops give you that?''

Monk snorted. ''Not hardly, Henry. My one buddy in the department hasn't returned my calls from yesterday or this morning. I have the certain feeling the LAPD wants this to be their cotillion.''

''So what do you hope to gain?''

''I'm betting the immigrant residents will hold back from the cops,'' Monk formulated.

''But open up to a black because he's got a Mexican speaker go-between?'' Cady asked incredulously.

''You're forgetting my natural charisma,'' Monk advised.

''Oh, yeah.'' Both men laughed. ''But what does it get you even if they tell you something they won't tell the cops? Especially if Absalla's right and it's the Domingos and not the Scalp Hunters.''

''A lot of the immigrants in the Rancho work long hours on bullshit jobs in the garment trade. And others in those big hotels downtown and at the airport cleaning rooms for five and a quarter an hour, Henry. They didn't come here looking for the money tree, but a chance to work steady and buy a little something of their own.'' Monk stopped, considering his own words. ''I think I'll find somebody who won't stand for an injustice no matter who did it.''

Cady looked off momentarily, trying to capture an image that was no longer in focus. ''My folks came up here from Georgia in the thirties. My father got work at the GM plant in South Gate, even though we couldn't buy a house out there because of the housing covenants.'' The import of his words fell on them. His parents' experience was a telling aspect of the city's history.

Presently he spoke again. ''I'll see if I can get Mrs.

Limón to talk with you. She's the shot caller on the Spanish side of things around here.''

''I'd appreciate that, Henry,'' Monk said. ''What are the rumors floating around among the black folks as to who did the crime?''

Cady made a face before replying. ''Most everybody seems to feel it was some of them Scalps. 'Bout three weeks 'fore the fire happened, Cruzado was supposed to have had a set-to with a couple of colored boys selling that crack alongside the walkway next to his apartment.''

''These two youngsters got names?'' Monk had been making a few notes on his hip-pocket steno pad.

''No, leastways I hadn't heard,'' Cady replied. ''The way I heard this was down at the bingo I go to at the VFW on Broadway. You know the one next to Gadberry's bar-beque off of Slauson?''

Monk indicated he did. Gadberry's was a legend of brick-oven Q delight among the residents of South Central.

''It was Mrs. Hughes with her weekly gossip. She said she heard Cruzado'd run these two off. These boys weren't gangbangers really, just young wannabes. It was later, she said, that Cruzado supposedly got a threatening visit from the older Scalp Hunters.''

''Will you call Mrs. Hughes and ask her if I can talk with her?'' Monk asked. ''Over the phone, I mean. I don't want to get her in any trouble.''

''Sure,'' Cady said hesitantly. ''But you should keep in mind the old girl is known to stretch a story for the sake of making it more interesting at its retelling. But she does live in the building right across from where the Cruzados stayed, so it may not be all talk.''

Cady made the call and got Monk on the line with her.

First he had to answer her questions about what a private detective did and how much money doing it earned. Seems she had a twenty-six-year-old great-nephew who'd recently been laid off from the electronics section at Sears, and was thinking about going into telephone repair.

Monk promised to talk with him after he'd given her his office number. Eventually they got around to the reason for the call. The old lady confirmed what she'd said at the bingo game. She claimed she'd gotten it from Cruzado's sister, Karla, directly.

"You two were on a friendly basis?"

"Of course, child," the old lady responded. "I take everybody as they come, black, brown, or whatever. Long as they ain't in no mess, I can get along with anybody," she said proudly. "Karla and I used to talk when I'd be coming back from the store and she'd be out hanging up the hand laundry."

"Have the cops been to see you yet?"

There was an extended pause. "You ain't gonna tell 'em what I said, are you? Lord knows I want to see them dope sellers stopped, but I'm too old to be havin' trouble comin' on my doorstep."

The cops had to have canvased the area around the site of the murders. It may be a sad commentary on civic duty, but for an old woman living alone, a cop knocking on your door and being invited in was not a formula for quiet nerves in a fishbowl like the Rancho.

"No, ma'am. What you tell me is between you and me. I won't be telling any police officers."

"Thank you, young man," she said, relieved.

That second promise might bite him in the ass later, but it wouldn't be the first time. "Did the sister say who the boys were or know the Scalp Hunters who confronted her brother?"

"Seems I remember her saying one of the gang members was called Baby Blue or something like that. I believe she said her brother had words with him before, said he was a real hothead.''

"This Baby Blue," Monk determined.

"That's right. And I'll tell you one more thing, there was more to Efraín Cruzado than people knew."

"How's that, Mrs. Hughes?"

"He and I got to talkin' once and he went on about how the Rancho could be an example despite the politicians. But for that to happen, all of us would have to pull together to make it go. I tell you, sir, that Efraín Cruzado had more on his mind than people 'round here gave him credit for.

"And that's the problem with black folks. We all the time think we need to think less of others just 'cause we ain't gettin' nowhere. Instead we need to be settin' our sights higher. My layabout great-nephew ought to see what I'm talking about."

Monk gently interjected, "Thanks for your time, Mrs. Hughes. Now make sure your Gerald calls me."

Cady eyed him knowingly.

She repeated his office number and assured him Gerald would be ringing him tomorrow if she had a say in it. Believing that she did, he hung up and got up to leave.

" 'Preciate your help, Henry, and see what you can do about Mrs. Limón talking with me, will you?" Monk wrote his home number on the backs of two of his business cards and handed them over. "Keep one for yourself and pass the other one along to her. She can reach me at the home number usually after six-thirty on a weekday."

The other man also stood to shake his guest's hand. "I sure hope you or the cops can get something on this. If the killers can be caught, I think that will ease the minds of the immigrant tenants. They gotta see if their own dies, something comes of it. Somebody pays. If that can happen, we got a chance to get a number of them to go along with the HUD deal.''

''I understand. How about the Southeast Asian residents of the Rancho? Where do they stand with tenant ownership?''

''That's been a hard nut. I got a couple of prospects in line for the board, and I'm tryin' to get one of the Vietnamese on soon. Then maybe things will open up with them too. So far, we got about as many of them come to meetings as hookers workin' grade schools. We even had somebody translating for a while.''

The phone rang and Monk waved good-bye as Cady went to answer. He stepped out of the townhouse to a bright afternoon and the sound of Warren G's old cut ''And Ya Don't Slip'' winding around the buildings. Walking in the general direction of the eastern end of the projects, he looked north to the bold relief of downtown L.A.'s skyline.

The spires of iron and tinted glass were not far from the Rancho. The buildings seemed like the towers of an industrial magus whose secrets the commoners in the lowlands could barely comprehend, let alone attempt to master. The starkness of what those close, yet leagues distant, buildings cutting above the landscape represented to the residents wasn't lost on anyone. The populace of the Rancho didn't go to lunch over two-dollar fizzy water, wondering if they could catch that play at the Dorothy Chandler while trying to get the prospectus modemed to San Francisco.

The remodeled downtown L.A. was the virginal citadel, sleek, polished, and waiting to be deflowered. Sure the vacancy rate was high now, but that was in anticipation of the next boom, the next big infusion of capital. Twenty years of the Tom Bradley Administration, and the dotage of Cady's one-time fellow janitor, Gilbert Lindsey, had opened the city till for developers and multinational business interests.

Bradley, the liberal Democrat, had been the great black promise when he finally defeated the right-wing Democrat, incumbent Mayor Sam Yorty, in their second race in 1973. Monk had vivid memories of the elation his mother and her club members, who'd done volunteer work on Bradley's campaign, felt at finally having a black man in office. Here was a brother who would do something about the conditions of South Central, would work to make the schools better, and, they especially hoped, would do something about the notorious police department.

But Bradley, a six-foot-four-inch, athletically built man, had too long been Mr. Safe. Too long he'd had to bite his tongue at the racism he'd witnessed in his twenty years as a cop. Too long he'd been told by image handlers over and over how a man of his size and his darkness had to be careful not to intimidate white audiences. He'd chameleoned into a controlled, endearing candidate, deliberate in manner and speech.

And that manifestation did pay off for him. He got to be mayor, and he held the job for two solid decades. His was the candidacy that a coalition of blacks, westside liberals, and a significant Latino segment could rally around. Later, midway into his regime, with plant closures happening at an unprecedented rate, and immigration from Central America spiking, Bradley worked the magic again and resuscitated the flagging multiracial component of his electoral machine.

But reality caught up, and the promises of 1970 had for the most part gone unmet by 1990. And Bradley's departure from office was not met with fanfare, but a sigh of relief that he'd finally stepped aside—post the Rodney King/Daryl Gates roller derby. Nowadays, he lived in semiseclusion like an elderly chanteuse, his energy and verve drained by a minor heart attack followed by a stroke.

Lindsey, the self-appointed "Emperor of the Ninth," managed to stay in until only the Grim Reaper himself removed him from office. And it took Death's scythe a couple of swipes to do that. Lindsey's district stretched from downtown, past and including the Rancho, and on into the heart of the ghetto. Lindsey had the best of both worlds— the backing of business interests and the votes of church-going older sisters with pillbox hats tucked over rose-colored memories of life in the black belt.

The tall buildings of Lindsey's and Bradley's legacy filled the horizon to the north. But places like the Rancho stood for those parts of town too many politicians only noticed when election time rolled around. It wasn't as though Lindsey and Bradley, and others, didn't know the problems. It was just that both men, having fought the good fight to attain office, found that some of the same forces that had opposed them were now willing to bring them into the game. They had been convinced the best way to make change was to go slow, to have the money trickle down from their illusory barbicans to soothe the passions of the masses.

Monk had reached the unused Southern Pacific tracks that cut through this end of the Rancho. Beyond the tracks were a series of angular buildings designed with Objectivist-inspired charm. These structures had been a job training center and offices for Housing Authority personnel. On a metal sign, chipped and drilled in random target practices, he could still read the name the center had been christened with: THE A. PHILIP RANDOLPH ADVANCEMENT AND PLACEMENT CENTER.

A Cyclone fence engulfed the abandoned buildings, but there were several gaping holes at various intervals. Absalla had told him crack heads and strawberries—women, and increasingly men, who'd perform sex for a hit on the pipe— used the interiors of the place for their transactions.

He'd heard them approach from behind, but hadn't let on until they were almost to him.

"Hey, you from someplace, slice?"

The owner of the voice was shorter than the other two. All three were Latinos. The one who'd spoken couldn't have been over five-foot-four, Monk estimated. But he was broad in the upper torso, with thick, sinewy arms the obvious results of a strenuous weight regime.

"I have to be from someplace to be here?" Monk said.

"What you doing here, eh?" another one said, irritated. He was dressed in black jeans and a loose, Borax-white T that had a red skull with a black eyepatch over the right breast. He had a buzz cut and there was a vinelike tattoo crawling upward around his arm from the end of his thumb.

"Yeah," the third jumped in, "why you got to be so unfriendly?"

"I'm from the Housing Department in Washington," Monk lied, shifting slightly as two of them edged to his right. "We're doing a survey of the Rancho."

"What for?" another demanded.

"Find out things."

"Like what?" the shorter one said.

"All kinds of fascinating stuff."

The kid in the white T—he was about nineteen—said something in Spanish and the other two had a good laugh. Idly he scratched the side of his cheek with a pointed fingernail. "You gonna ask us some questions?"

"Yeah, we got all kinds of opinions on shit," the other cracked.

The short one didn't say anything, just stared, his jaw muscles bunching and loosening. "If you're doing a survey, how come you ain't got a notebook or something. How come you dressed like some homey and not in a tie?''

"How come you ask so much?" Monk quipped evenly.

The tallest member of the bunch lurched forward but came up short when Monk didn't flinch. "You some kind of fuckin' undercover hoota, ain't you?" There was fresh beer and stale weed on his breath.

"I told you who I was," Monk countered. "And if you gentlemen let me do my work, I'd be ever so grateful."

The loose-limbed one raised his oversized striped crew shirt to reveal a revolver tucked in his thin waistband. "'Sup, huh?" he hissed. The shirt went down, the hands hovering tense at his sides.

Monk had a polymer-case Ultrastar 9mm tucked in an ankle holster, but wanted to use his words to settle this test of manliness. "Look, I didn't come here to cause any uproar. Let me get my work done, and I'm gone."

"You gonna tear those fucked-up shacks down," the shorter one said. His head did a quick flick toward the Randolph Center.

"Maybe," Monk lied again.

"Been in there?" the young man asked.

"Maybe."

"Could be you hire us to be your bodyguards. It's rough around here," the one with the one-eyed red skull suggested.

"There's some real criminals roamin' 'round," the tall one chortled, his gaping mouth displaying discolored teeth set unevenly.

"I'll give it some thought," Monk replied seriously.

"Yes you will," the muscular one said with a crisp inflection. He walked past Monk and the other two followed. The one in the striped shirt brought up the rear, managing a baleful scowl that was both menacing and comical. He was mad-doggin' him with an ''I dare you to do something'' look.

After the trio had moved along, Monk crossed the tracks and tried to enter the main abandoned building. The door wouldn't budge. He walked around the corner and found a paneless window that had its security grill pried back. He went inside.

Monk found miscellaneous trash, old tires, and stove parts strewn about the spacious room. Incongruously, along one wall hung several engraved plaques that for whatever reason hadn't been removed.

One of the awards was from Mayor Sam Yorty to the Rancho Tajuata Tenants' Association for outstanding work, 1968. Two of the other plaques were from heads of city departments praising the Randolph Center's staff. A fourth was from something called Ingot Ltd. thanking Yorty and the job training center staff for service well done.

The last award was to the training center's executive director, a man named Olin Salter. It was from the then chief of the LAPD, Bill Parker. It read, ''In these times of travail, you have stood tall against the hordes.''

Monk lingered over that one, finding it interesting that Parker would have issued a plaque to this Salter. Possibly they'd been friends over a period of time. Parker, the mentor of his redoubtable heir, Daryl Gates, had been a stiff-necked, law-and-order and fundamentalist-values type who recruited white cops from southern cities so as to better keep the negroes down deep in the jungle.

For the chief to acknowledge this Salter, then, the latter must have been a genuine son-of-a-bitch. Despite the honorable name, Parker's plaque cast doubt on the worthiness of the A. Philip Randolph Advancement and Placement Center.

Off in one cleared corner were two filthy sheet-covered

mattresses and some used condoms laying about. In another room, the walls had first been spray painted with the Scalp Hunters insignia, then sprayed over by Los Domingos *placas*.

The doors to other parts of the two-story building were locked, and Monk didn't try to force them open. Moving back to the paneless window, he noted it was only this wall that had windows at mid-height. The rest of the room had high, rectangular windows running parallel to the line of the ceiling. Possibly the good directors of the facility had deemed that windows at a normal height would provide the center's apprentices a chance to stare at the outside world, and wish they were somewhere else.

He started back toward the tracks and saw a familiar car drive up from the south, along the gravel swath beyond the cluster of buildings. He stood still as the Crown Victoria parked close. Seguin got out slowly, his face a blank.

"Homey, don't you know me," the lieutenant said.

"Young blood." The two shook hands, Monk squinting at Seguin as the sun beat down behind the cop's head. "I hear you're riding herd on this one."

Seguin put a hand in his trousers pocket, and looked off toward downtown then back at him. "I've had some experience with the Domingos." He took his hand out, seemingly unsure of what to do with it. "The brass wants this to be their show, Ivan."

"So much for the social hour." They both let minutes hang. "So Parker Center needs a winner bad," Monk observed acidly.

"This ain't for play, man," Seguin went on. "The Rancho murders have to be solved efficiently and by the police. The mayor and the chief want to show this department has rebuilt itself from the days of disarray and low morale under the previous chief. Captain Reno wants reports every other goddamn day, and he don't mean late, and he don't mean skimpy.''

''That and the mayor is still hot to add more officers to the department,'' Monk added. ''A check mark on a case like this goes a long way in giving him political cachet to push the council to take money from other parts of the budget to hire more officers.''

Seguin didn't speak.

''But why the heavy bit with me, Marasco?'' Monk said peevishly. ''The department can't stop me from wandering around the Rancho or talking to whomever I feel like.''

''But you can be compelled to tell Reno information or he could press interference with an ongoing investigation if he tells the command you're stumbling after us.''

''Or pointing out your errors,'' Monk chided.

Seguin said sheepishly, ''Reno has made it clear I'm not to share any information with you either.''

Both men were aware of the trio of Domingos leaning on a nearby fence, pretending not to be listening to the two men.

''How the hell did Reno find out I'd been hired so fast?'' Monk could hear the testiness in his voice.

''I told you, downtown is on this like a sissy on a pogo stick,'' Seguin said tersely.

''They been on shit before, Marasco. Why is this time sweatin' you so hard?''

Seguin probed his tongue on the inside of his lower jaw. ''I'm bringing this up because we're friends, Ivan. I'm trying to tell you I have no room to move on this. I'm trying to tell you the operating idea here is the Scalp Hunters did it, and that's the nature of things.''

''If you're so sure, then you must have a witness,'' Monk speculated.

Seguin didn't respond again.

"All right," Monk said, "but I'll still earn a little of that fabulous federal salary I'm going to pull down on this if y'all don't mind. And even if you and your boy Reno do."

"I realize that."

No words lingered between them for a time, each man alternately looking at one another then somewhere else. "What is it, Marasco? What is it about the Rancho you got such a hard-on for?" Monk finally prodded.

"I'm just doing what I'm supposed to do."

"Sure," Monk said unconvincingly. He tried a new tact. "Everything cool at home?"

Seguin's brows descended sharply. "Wrong direction, bloodhound. But let me ask you a question. What do you think about working for a dude like Absalla?"

Monk's shoulders lifted and fell. "He ain't no Father Flanagan, but he does some good."

"For black folks," Seguin remarked quickly. "I've seen him on a TV news show where he said just 'cause California was once Mexican, that don't give them any right to come across illegally."

"He's not the first asshole I've taken a paycheck from," Monk answered defensively.

"You wouldn't work for a Christian Right nut or Pat Buchanan."

"Absalla's ignorant, not a hatemonger, Marasco."

Seguin got his keys out of his pocket, but didn't head toward his car. "You know, Ivan, sometimes I get the impression you think you're above all this. That somehow you move in and out of these"—his hand did a circle in the air as he searched for the words he wanted—"outposts of our city with each one having its own set of village chiefs who have no interest in trying to bring the people together. The eternal seeker, Diogenes with a pistol. A shape-shifter among the company he keeps. But none of us remain unstained, swimming in this muck.''

Monk was hot and embarrassed simultaneously, like a stage magician whose tricks had just been uncovered by some audacious interloper. To recover he said, ''If I find that it's members of the Scalp Hunters who did this, I'll be the first one to point the finger. Absalla can't make me hide the truth because I'm black.''

''I'm not questioning your integrity, Ivan.''

''Then what are you questioning?''

''Where does all this take us?''

''You mean you and me, or black and brown folks in general?'' Monk felt he was maneuvering on rocky ground with a sliver of a map. ''I'm not joining Absalla's mosque or whatever the hell he's selling, Marasco. I took the gig because I found it of interest and, unlike you, I don't pull down a steady income. You know the damn donut shop pretty much covers the overhead. But that also doesn't mean I spread my cheeks for just anybody who flashes me rent money.''

Seguin jingled the keys in his cupped hand and opened the cruiser's door. ''You're helping pay a mortgage these days.'' He cranked the engine, slamming the Crown Vic into reverse. ''Keep your head down, man.'' The car righted itself and a chalky plume followed it as Seguin drove away over the gravel.

Monk rubbed the back of his neck and walked back into the Rancho Tajuata. The downtown skyscrapers stood mute and colorless behind him.

Four

"**R**ecall criminal judges. Recall criminal judges," the woman chanted loudly as she marched in front of the Superior Courts on Temple in the afternoon haze.

"Hey, hey, ho, ho, Kodama's got to go," a man wearing tan loafers and an ostentatious NRA button on his suede sport coat joined in with gusto.

At least twenty protestors were spending their lunch hour marching in front of the courthouse. The group consisted mostly of middle-aged and older men and women but there were a few younger ones too. A smattering wore suits, and all of them were white.

Eight stories up, and looking out a hallway window, the judge the placards and enmity were intended for watched the gathered dispassionately. Superior Court Judge Jill Kodama turned from the window, absently gnawing on a triangle of tuna fish sandwich.

"Come on, Judge, you should be back in your chambers," her bailiff said quietly over her shoulder. "This can only be bad for your indigestion." His name was Mitchell, and he'd been a sheriff's deputy a little less than four years.

He was a tall, dark-haired wheat stacker who must have taken the wrong bus and got stuck in the wicked city.

"I'm alright, I always like to see our democracy at work." Her lips formed a thin line as she turned back to the window.

"Okay," Mitchell said reluctantly. "I'm going to grab a bite myself. I'll be back in about forty."

"No sweat," she replied as his fading footfalls echoed along the marble corridor. Kodama watched the scene down below for several moments and finally decided she had had enough of the Gumby and Pokey Show. She rounded a corner and into a hallway lined on both sides with waiting people. Kodama encountered Assistant D.A. Jamboni leaving a courtroom.

Kodama didn't slow down, her head not turning to look to the left nor to the right. It was too much to hope for.

"Good day, Judge Kodama," Jamboni said in his stentorious baritone as she moved past him.

"It would seem, Mr. Jamboni." She resisted the temptation to add, "you slick-headed cocksucker."

The assistant D.A. moved on, a hyena's grin stretching his lower face.

Nearing the door to her chambers, she wasn't too surprised to see a few bodies clustered in front of the unmarked entrance.

Glowering looks were aimed at her as Kodama, not breaking stride, closed in on the door and the relative privacy that lay beyond it.

"Judge, we'd like to speak with you if we may," a matronly type in red stretch slacks and a sweater smelling of Woolite said.

Tersely she replied, "To what purpose?"

"Your decision to let a murderer off," a stocky man in work shoes piped in.

"Mr. Wright was convicted, and he will be incarcerated for his act." Her hand was on the knob, and she almost had the keys out of her purse with the other one.

"You know damn well he should have received twenty-five to life for shooting that clerk," the woman added. "Good citizens like us voted for the three strikes law so trash like Wright would be taken care of properly."

She unlocked the door, but couldn't make herself go in without responding. "No, good citizens like you voted for mandatory minimums with the same rationale as you voted years ago to cap property taxes so you wouldn't be putting your precious public dollars into the upkeep of inner city schools. Places your kids weren't going to anyway."

"A radical," the woman said and sniffed disdainfully, as if talking about devil worship.

"I'm not on the bench only to punish, but also to make an attempt at justice when I can."

"I don't believe you understand what justice is," the woman shouted. "Maybe you shouldn't be on the bench."

Kodama shut the door in the woman's uncomprehending face. She crossed to her small refrigerator and pulled out a bottle of seltzer, twisting the top off with more force than necessary. She plopped down behind her desk, swigging down the carbonated water like a drunk on a binge.

Off to the side of her desk was a recent stack of letters she'd received in response to her sentencing of thirty-three-year-old O'Shay Wright, a two-time prior felon—armed robbery and grand theft—with a discolored eye and the ability to read on a fourth-grade level. He was black, stood over six feet, and his last real job had been four years ago working as a pizza delivery man. He'd have kept the job except for the fact his homies were always dropping by the business, trying to beg free slices of pizza or hitting on his woman boss.

His latest attempt at upward mobility had been to stick up a 7-Eleven, a stop-and-rob as the cops called them, on Alondra in the Athens Park section of the city. But the clerk, a burly Samoan by the name of William Atupo, began to beat the luckless Mr. Wright about his protruding ears with a bat signed by Hank Aaron. Naturally the gun went off, and Atupo was hit in the leg.

At his trial, there was some discrepancy as to whether Wright had intended to shoot Atupo, or the piece had gone off as a matter of reflex. Whatever, Assistant D.A. Jamboni was out to send a message to all would-be master thieves like Mr. Wright. And of course since he'd already made noise about running for the head D.A. slot next year, he could send a message about how tough he was to the voters.

Naturally Mr. Wright's attorney was an overworked public defender. So Kodama, on her own initiative, exercised her prerogative and reviewed Mr. Wright's past record. Seems the grand theft was a wobbler. The car had belonged to a girlfriend upset that Mr. Wright was also playing the humpty with a former Raiderette and current auto drape model. The conviction was such that the law allowed Kodama discretion to reconsider it as a misdemeanor, and not a felony. This she did. Thus the present case would count, she informed a puckered-lipped Jamboni, as a second strike.

Of course the assistant D.A. protested, and filed for a further review of the case and her sentencing procedure. Subsequently the item leapt from page three in a legal paper, the little-read *Daily Journal*, to a prominent position over the top fold in the *L.A. Times*'s Metro section. Thus Kodama became the object of microscopic scrutiny by the legal system and the public.

Spokespersons for a homeowners group in the northern end of the San Fernando Valley began to send in letters.

Interestingly enough, Jamboni also lived in that portion of the Kmart–strewn basin. The Lydia Homeowners Association stepped up the campaign from letters to the personal touch.

Over the past week, they'd been holding pickets in front of the courthouse demanding she rescind her decision. Jamboni had been barking on several local radio talk shows, and even his chief, a reasonable enough fellow, had to bend with the prevailing sombrous winds. The head district attorney had been quoted in the paper as saying that even though he'd been opposed to three strikes, he understood what the voters wanted when they'd passed the initiative during the Republican sweep a few years back.

Politics and posturing, Kodama thought, and grimaced inwardly as she perused a few of the scathing missives. There was a knock from the court side door and she said, "It's open."

Mitchell stuck his head in and asked, "Are you okay, Your Honor?"

"Fine. My friends still downstairs?"

"They were breaking up the road show when I got back." He came into the room, fumbling with the hasp on his gunbelt's cartridge case. "I realize you know what you're doing, but there's nothing in the law preventing you from going after Jamboni on one of those Sunday TV shows, is there?" He looked purposeful and awkward all at the same time.

"I couldn't until the review panel was through with its work, Mitchell." That wasn't true, but she wanted an out.

"I see."

"But I appreciate the thought."

"Sure." He went back out, slowly pulling the door shut.

*   *   *

"Is Mrs. Limón in?" Monk said in the most pleasant voice he could manage.

"I'm sorry, who did you say is calling?" the teenaged voice on the other end asked politely.

She knew who it was. He'd been calling since yesterday afternoon and his little chat with Seguin. He'd made nine attempts, five of which had been answered by the young woman now on the other end of the line. "Ivan Monk. I'm a private detective looking into the murder of members of the Cruzado family."

With false innocence, the voice responded, "Oh yes, haven't you called before?"

Kid's gonna make a fine bureaucrat. "Yes, I have," he drawled. "I would still like to talk with your mother about this incident if I could."

"She's very busy, sir. I did give her your last message though."

"Shall I leave my office and home number again?"

"No-o-o." The young woman dragged the word out for a good three seconds. "I gave that information to my mother already."

"Okay." He was going to try a new direction. "Let her know I'll be meeting with Mr. Cady and Mrs. Hughes, and they've told me they have some ideas on this thing."

"Ideas?" a suddenly interested voice responded.

"Yes, something to do with Los Domingos Trece that I'll be sharing with my friend on the LAPD, Lieutenant Marasco Seguin. He's the man in charge of the investigation." He measured out a few clicks before speaking again. "Do you have all that?"

"Ah, yes, yes I do," the young woman said flatly.

"Thank you." He hung up satisfied. Monk hedged that Mrs. Limón would want to put her spin on things if she believed he was only talking to the black tenants, especially if he was also going to see a pal on the force. It nagged at him to play the race card, no matter how subtly, but if it benefitted his investigation, so be it.

Delilah Carnes, the woman Friday he shared with the architect/rehab firm of Ross and Hendricks, came into his office. She'd been on a diet, and her naturally large frame had tapered in at the waist so that her full hips and healthy bosom were even more accentuated in the black skirt and light blouse she wore.

"Elrod was on the horn a minute ago and he wants to know if you've made a decision about the blueberry and banana nut muffins." She managed to say it seriously.

Monk stroked his goatee, twisting his mouth to one side. "Being the owner of a donut shop has more complexities than one might think, D."

"Has it occurred to you, you're a seller of vice who preys on the weakness of people like me."

"Donuts are nature's quick breakfast. I'm contributing to the efficiency of the modern world." He leaned back in his ancient swivel. "See, Elrod wants to expand our menu and add muffins and gradually phase in speciality coffees like cafè mocha and cappuccino."

Delilah knew the six-foot-eight, galvanized mahogany Goliath of an ex-con that was Elrod. And Monk could tell from her expression she was having a hard time reconciling that image with what he'd just told her. "Elrod's idea?"

"Man has expanded his horizons, D. Man can't get no-where in these times by doing what's ordinary."

"He said that."

"Yes, he did." Monk answered. The phone rang and his face brightened, as he pointed at her. "The big man's on it, baby." He winked and picked up the handset. "Hello."

Delilah exited, mulling over this new information about the buffed donut shop manager.

"Is this Ivan Monk?" the caller he had anticipated asked.

"It is." He all but gloated.

"I understand you've been trying to reach me," said Mrs. Limón with a hint of haughtiness.

"Yes, ma'am. Antar Absalla has hired me to see what I can find out about this terrible affair."

"You know that two days ago several black youths ganged up on a Guatemalan boy and kicked and stomped him, breaking his kneecap and causing him to have a concussion."

"No, I didn't," he answered truthfully.

"You see there's plenty of things going on down here that we have to deal with every day. The murder of the Cruzados has only . . ." Her voice trailed off, and he could hear her talking to someone. "The killings have only increased the tensions, the fear that already exist between the blacks, Chicanos, and Latinos around here."

"But that's why it's necessary to find out who's guilty as soon as any of us can, Mrs. Limón."

"Hmm," she mumbled. "I didn't see who did it, and neither did Henry or that Hughes woman."

"But you have the ear of the Latino residents," Monk countered.

"We don't all get together down at the washing machines and, what's the word . . . gab."

"I'm not suggesting you do, Mrs. Limón. But I know you're a leader among the Latino residents, and it's only natural you'd hear things that the black tenants wouldn't. Things you might not even want the cops to know."

"Or things I would go out of my way to tell them," she said pointedly.

"And have you?" Monk sought.

"Why should I tell you?"

"I'm not out to make imaginary villains, Mrs. Limón. Whatever you think about Absalla, and I know you voted in favor of the Ra-Falcons being brought into the Rancho, I'll let the facts decide."

"Even if it means it's blacks who're guilty?" she asked, skepticism evident in her voice.

"Yes," he said without hesitation.

"If we talk, I can't have you coming over here. Already there's a rumor going around about you being some federal man who's probably an undercover narc."

"That's interesting," Monk said. "Where'd you hear that from?"

"You know how these things get around," the older woman bantered.

He'd only laid that vague line about working for the feds on the three Domingos who'd tried to jam him. "What have you been hearing among some of the Latino residents, Mrs. Limón? Is there anyone you believe may have actually witnessed the crime?"

"A lot of people came out when the fire was going," she said tersely.

"I mean someone who may have seen the bad boys setting the fire."

"You ask a lot too damn quick," she barked.

"It's just you, me, and the phone line, Mrs. Limón." Monk was as soothing as a grave plot salesman trying to get a ninety-five-year-old to buy the one next to the mottled elm. "No one to know anything if you and I have a little conversation."

"You're working for that Muslim," she reminded him.

"You seem to mean I'm some kind of follower of his."

"He's paying you."

"That makes me a lousy convert, Mrs. Limón. Besides, I was looking for a job when I got this one."

"You're *sediento* then. Always looking for the next paycheck." Her assessment of him registered a triumphant tone in her voice.

"I get hungry enough," Monk admitted, his sporadic Spanish translating for him. "But not like you mean. Anyway, being lean in the hip pocket doesn't equal being a yes-man to Absalla, or becoming part of some cover-up. Yes, I took his money, because this is the kind of work I do. It's the service I provide, like a mechanic or a plumber."

"They don't look for criminals," the woman on the other end parried. "Of course the garage that did my alternator were definitely thieves."

"But the honest ones will tell you what's wrong, and go about dealing with the problem the best way they know how."

Mrs. Limón made a sound somewhere in her throat. "So Absalla is just your employer for the moment, not your *patrón*? You understand the difference?"

"I do. And if I find out something that makes the boss mad, then it wouldn't be the first time I was fired."

"Alright," she retorted noncommittally.

Mrs. Limón had more to offer and Monk wanted to meet with her in person to better press the woman for answers. "Couldn't you come out to my office? Or maybe I could meet you at a friend's house outside the Rancho."

"We'll see," she hung up, quietly severing the connection.

Monk got home around seven. Kodama, in jeans and rolled up sleeves, was already there, sitting in the study before the gessoed canvas she'd stretched over the weekend. Oil painting was a hobby of hers. Several of her pieces hung over mantels and couches in the homes and offices of friends. She was humble about her work, claiming her friends just wanted a conversation piece from the painting judge.

Her paintings did not have an amorphous, impressionistic quality, nor did they exude the studied calm of the landscape artist. Kodama's works were representational with definite line and purpose. Subdued under-colors gave way to strong colors, Prussian reds and Cyan blues. Her masculine stroke gave her subject matter a nearly tactile quality.

Kodama was currently doing street scenes. A recent piece depicted multihued party goers along Melrose Avenue passing a window where a solitary old-fashioned rotary phone resided with a cracked casing. Another, now residing in a legal services office up in Humboldt County, was of an old woman in a shawl feeding her parakeet on Alpine Street in Chinatown, an indistinct City Hall in the near distance.

Tonight, no such inspiration moved her.

Monk touched her lightly on the shoulder. "Your fans back at the courthouse today?"

"Like flies on stink." She made disinterested motions with a charcoal pencil over the blank plane. This soon ceased and she added, "And it's getting shittier every day."

"Want me and Elrod to pay a visit on a few of those Newt-lovin' burghers as they emerge disoriented from their tanning salons?"

She patted his leg, smiling without much feeling behind it. "Save your energy, baby." She got up and gave him a quick kiss and headed for the bar. She uncorked a bottle of Chianti and poured a measure for herself. She didn't look at him as she walked toward the archway. "I'm going to take a long bath," she said, waving the wineglass listlessly, "with a little something for comfort."

"What do you want for dinner?" Monk asked. "Maybe I'll try to do something from that *tapas* cookbook we got. Whip down to Trader Joe's to get the ingredients for potato and seafood *banderilla*."

"Whatever." Kodama was already moving toward the back of the house.

Monk stood before the canvas, tapping the charcoal pencil against the knuckle of his index finger.

Five

Burnt orange light permeated the room, a salmon color flooding across its walls. It was as if an unseen hand was swathing the room with ephemeral jelly. Monk turned from the shade he'd let up to look at the inert form of Kodama.

"Time to chop some cotton," he said loudly. "My mama's folks used to say that, being from Mississippi and all."

She didn't acknowledge his words by movement or sound.

Monk, clad solely in a pair of tan chinos, went back to the bed and gently rocked her hip with his hand. "We gotta move and groove, honey."

Softly from beneath the blanket: "My docket is clear for a few days. I'm going to rest today. Call in for me, will you, Ivan?"

He decided against the urge to shake her more vigorously. All he could do was stand there looking down at the fetal form and feeling about as wanted as a Hare Krishna selling flowers at a Pat Robertson convention. "How about some coffee, Jill?"

Her legs scissored slowly then stopped.

"Do you want some coffee?" He demanded more than asked.

"No," she stated with equal brashness.

Monk went and retrieved the morning *Times* on the lengthening lawn, snapping the string on his way back into the kitchen. Once there, he put on the radio beneath the sink's bay windows and tuned it to the all-news station. As the coffee got going he sat at the oblong pine table in the breakfast nook. He unfolded the paper, scanning the front page for a story of interest.

He settled on Boris Yeltsin still complaining about the pesky Chechens who kept pissing him off. Imagine their temerity after the last bombing raid he'd ordered on their territory? By the time he got to the interior pages, the brew was ready.

Monk got his cup and finished the piece on Russia, and another on electronic piracy in China's Hong Kong before traipsing back into the bedroom upstairs.

Kodama was still in the bed lying on her stomach, her face turned to the side. He wasn't sure, but it seemed her eyes were open.

"We'll get through this, Jill," he mumbled.

"Maybe. But I'm in a glass box where everyone can spit on me but I can't give them the finger."

"Did you read the information I had Coleman get on-line for you about the homeowners' group?" Coleman Josiah Gardner was the teenaged son of his divorced sister, Odessa. He was a B-minus senior in high school, but that wasn't much of a reflection of his capacity. The six-foot-four-incher was a nimrod of the hardwood and the outfield. And despite knowing the odds, he was of the opinion he was going to be the next ten-million-dollar flash in pro basketball or baseball.

When not out tossing the rock or batting, Coleman could be found attentively plying the cyberways on the Pentium computer his uncle got him last Christmas. It was the fourth computer the young man had received, but the first new one. Coleman's introduction to the electronic keyboard was not the result of a keen interest in the wonders of the computer.

When he was eleven, Coleman had gotten into a shoving match with a classmate and been sent to detention. Due to the fact that the principal's office was being painted that day—after thirty-two requests and five years of waiting—the two pugilists were sent to sit in a corner of the teachers' lounge.

In the room was Mr. Timmons, the seventh grade teacher. He was attempting to fire up an ancient Kaypro computer a parent had recently donated to the school. Beyond turning the thing on, he couldn't get the monitor to show him anything save a series of green dots.

Disgusted, the teacher had tromped out of the room muttering, leaving the computer running. The two battlers continued with verbal thrusts, each daring the other to fool with Mr. Timmons's machine. The harried teacher returned to find Coleman sitting before it, typing on the keyboard.

Snatching the child up from the Kaypro and threatening him with a suspension, Mr. Timmons noticed the book report the youngster had been writing.

"I looked through it," she said disinterestedly.

"There's some good stuff in there, Jill," Monk said, incensed. "Members of the association have ties to the Christian Coalition, some of 'em have gathered signatures on anti–affirmative action and English-only petitions. There's a menu of lovely items to blast them on. You could

challenge one of those yahoos to a debate and peck their
liver out. Or write an op-ed defending your view of what
the justice system should be about.''

''I don't need you to tell me what I should and should
not be doing.''

''Cool,'' he snapped sarcastically. He stalked into the
bathroom, shutting the door. After his shower, he got into
his chinos again and a loose-fitting polo. Kodama had left
the bedroom, but he didn't hear her moving about.

Walking to the front, he went past the sunken study and
could make out her form submerged in there. The blinds in
the study were still closed, the judge slouched on the couch.
She wore a robe with Aztec cut ziggurats lancing over the
folds like chain lightning. Her legs were open; one of them
swung back and forth like a gate in the wind.

''C'mon, Jill. You can't let these Valley bastards get you
up against it. You gotta start hitting them back.''

''You and Glenn think the same,'' she said dryly. The
leg continued to work like a motorized derrick left unat-
tended.

''Glenn Tsong?''

''He came to see me the other day, and gave me the
pitch that it was my duty as an Asian jurist to stand for the
cause. He didn't have to mention it was the APILA's PAC
and a few other organizations that are responsible for sub-
stantial amounts of the fifty grand or so they raise for me
and others to run for the bench.''

Tsong was a lawyer, and the president of the Asian Pacific Islander Law Association, a civil rights grouping of
fellow API lawyers. One of its functions was to watchdog
the legal system. But its main, its pragmatic, function was
to put their money where they saw fit.

''So what're you going to do, Jill. Go to work, come
home, bury yourself here until the recall goes down?''

She craned her neck to glare at him.

"You know that's what this is leading up to," he said.

"Goddamnit, Ivan, I'm just tired of feeling like everything I do I have to uplift the race." She sat forward, thrusting an open palm at him. "Get on the bench in my thirties, get feted and written up in the Asian and mainstream presses before I've even tried three cases. Then"—she began to count off on one hand using her index finger from the other—"I have all my so-called peers, the old white guys in the black robes, reviewing my rulings like they're ogling the latest *Penthouse*."

"You do be out there on the lofty tip, my dear." Monk amended warmly. "Considering the wolfish political climate in these times, you're making a hell of a statement every time you get up there swinging from the bench."

"Increasingly unpopular statements," she modified.

"You're woman enough for the job." He gave her a hug and kissed her on the forehead.

They separated, Kodama adjusting the material hanging formless on her. She seemed to fill it for the first time. "Very well, my dark and dangerous Balthasar, I'll get back on the horse. Or at least get dressed."

They parted, and Monk swung by his office and then got breakfast at the Cafe 77 downstairs. The eatery used to be located in its own tiny building on the lot behind his building—an edifice constructed as a mini version of the famous Flatiron Building in New York. But the market at the other end facing Venice Boulevard had gone through a remodeling, and exercised its option for the footage to increase available parking.

Cafe 77 was run by an older couple whose menu selections included crawfish and potato latkes. The two'd been together so long they'd taken on portions of each other's mannerisms and ways of speech. Each morning one could find both in their crisp white shirts, sleeves always rolled past the elbow. The woman forever wore a black skirt and the husband shapeless black slacks.

"Hey, Gorzy, did you check on those heads of lettuce?" The wife growled, moving behind the establishment's sole waitress taking Monk's order.

"Yes, Mrs. Gorzynski," the husband said deferentially as he made notations on a tablet, standing behind the register. "I'm taking care of it as you said, Mrs. Gorzynski."

"If only he would look after me as he does the asparagus," she said with genuine remorse.

Monk enjoyed the floor show while he ate his meal. He finished his second cup of coffee and paid Mr. Gorzynski, who clasped his arm, leaning over to him across the counter.

"You got plenty work these days?" The older man smelled like a produce section.

"Maybe, why?"

"Could be someone has something to be seen about." His watery blues were unwavering.

"You need me to look into this something for you, Mr. Gorzynski?"

He counted out Monk's change rapidly. "Why you think it's me?"

"You play poker, Mr. Gorzynski?" He pocketed the change, having already left the tip.

"What?" The watery blues gleamed with confusion.

" 'Cause you'd be lousy at it. I've got to be out most of the day, but come on up tomorrow morning if you want to talk." Off to the side, Mrs. Gorzynski was writing the lunch special on a chalkboard propped up on an easel. If she was paying attention to the conversation, she didn't let on. Now, she'd make a fine poker player, Monk reflected as he took the stairs up the four flights to his office.

"Good morning, champ," he said upon entering the rotunda and seeing Delilah Carnes. She was working at her computer, and waved as he crossed the space to her left.

"Hendricks wanted to see you, but she had to leave for an appointment." Carnes was moving the mouse, eyeing the monitor with malice. "Shit," she exclaimed.

"I hate when that happens," Monk said, going into his office to make a few calls. That done, he exited and found the office manager still boxing with the computer.

"What are you doing, D?"

"Trying to lay out this newsletter on Quark. Whoever said it was better than PageMaker can kiss my butt."

"I know several cats who would line up in the rain and spend the house rent for that thrill. I'll be down at the Rancho for a while. You have the number to the Ra-Falcons' office, right?"

"Yeah, but you don't want me giving it to anybody, do you?"

"If Jill calls, call me right away." He worked to keep the concern out of his voice.

Carnes's head tilted but she only said, "Okay."

He saluted good-bye and took Venice all the way east. Eventually Monk drove past the Rosedale Cemetery on the edge of the Central American/Pico Union section. The cemetery was an old-fashioned burial ground dating back to the last century. It had expansive green slopes and flats containing grave markers as big as tank traps, crumbling Agnus Deis, and various statues of saints Monk couldn't name.

He recalled that a distant cousin of his was interred there, and also remembered that a large plot had been bought by the once-thriving Los Angeles Typographical Union back in the late 1800s. Rosedale was the resting place for the original founders of this union dedicated to struggling for better work conditions and wages for typographers and printers in a town notorious for its open shop policies. The antiunion forces were led at that time by a paper still proud to this day of never having been a part of organized labor, the *Los Angeles Times*.

The printers had built a monument of polished granite shafts supporting an oxidized bronze tablet, which, if his memory was correct, had been commemorated sometime around 1910 or so to those pioneers. Monk spotted displayed on the graveyard's redbrick walls a spray-painted *placa* he recognized as belonging to Los Domingos Trece. Already another gang had splayed their mark over the Domingos'. In the post-modern age, one's memorial was as temporal as peace in Bosnia.

He got to San Pedro Street, turned left, and soon made a right into one of the contained roads that ran through the Rancho Tajuata, Gilbert Lindsey Lane. He was climbing the stairs to the Ra-Falcons' office just as a young man with a wicked fade and a crescent and star earring was entering the office.

"Hi, I'm Ivan Monk." They shook hands. The young man wore corporal stripes.

"I'm Keith 2X. Antar said you'd be by. He left some material for you."

They went in to the sound of beeps emanating from the message machine on one of the smaller desks. The midnight-to-eight shift was signing out and one of them turned some keys over to 2X. "I'll be with you in a minute. Have a seat." The younger man indicated the couch and Monk did as suggested.

The corporal cleaned the coffee carafe and got a fresh pot going. Then he took down the messages on the answering machine. The calls included one from Mrs. Limón asking in that stern way of hers for Absalla to contact her as soon as he got in. Afterward, 2X emptied the wastebaskets into one large garbage bag, and put paper in the fax machine.

Monk wondered if all the members of the security force were instilled with such diligence. "How long have you been on the patrol?" he asked cheerfully.

"It would be about five years now," 2X answered, arranging some papers on a desk into a neat pile, then walking off into the inner office. Momentarily he returned, handing two packets to the private eye. "Here's the files Antar left for you."

Monk rose and accepted the thick 9" × 12" envelopes.

2X added, "He also wanted you to know he's going to be out of town for a couple of days."

"Where'd he go?"

"Back to D.C."

"Is his reason for going there a secret?" Monk whispered playfully.

The other man maintained his pleasant, if unaffected expression. "Business with the HUD officials."

"You in charge while he's gone?"

"Not exactly. Though I'm responsible for making sure the shifts are staffed, and everyone is doing what they need to be doing. Eddie and LaToyce are the sergeants."

"Then you three know what I'm doing around here."

"Yes, Antar told us and Kelmont; he's kind of the lead man among the squad."

"Spiritual leader?" Monk said half-jokingly.

"More like the example, really."

"Yeah?" Monk encouraged.

"He was a hard-core Del Nine who got his life in turnaround after his two-year-old daughter was killed when a punk shot through his mother's house." 2X's face had remained impassive, but there was a somberness in his tone.

"How about you, Keith? If you've been in the Ra-

Falcons for five years, then you must have hooked up with Absalla about the time he left the Nation.''

"You aren't just asking to make conversation." He said it straightforwardly without rancor.

"Being nosey comes with the gig," Monk said unapologetically.

2X processed the information and said, "I can respect that. My introduction to Islam came through a study group I was in at Cal State Dominguez Hills. We were reading Carter G. Woodson's—"

"Miseducation of the Negro," Monk interjected.

"Exactly. John Henrik Clark, Fanon, Angela's writings, Huey's *Revolutionary Suicide*, and of course Basil Davidson's books on African history.''

"And from that you became a Muslim?''

The younger man touched his chest with a hand. "Technically, I'm not a Black Muslim. The Nation wasn't all that, yo? So beyond a few meetings, I never officially joined. Taking the name 2X stands for the rejection of my slave name and not eating swine, but I maintain my independence.''

"Your politics then are drawn from several sources," Monk concluded.

2X nodded appreciatively.

A woman in her midtwenties entered the office, crisp in her dark blues, her long braids flaying like living creatures.

2X introduced the two. "LaToyce Blaine, this is Ivan Monk, the man Antar hired to look into the murders.''

"What's going on," she said, eyeing Monk while addressing 2X.

"There was a call from Delugach over in Rita Walter's office, a couple of tips about what goes on in number 455, and one from our favorite supporter, Mrs. Limón. She wanted to talk with Antar right quick.''

Blaine rolled her eyes as she headed for the inner office. "I better call her 'fore she put a picket line around the office. See you around, Mr. Monk."

"Hope so." Placing his attention back on 2X, he said, "I was walking around yesterday and encountered some of the Domingos. You know any of them by name?"

"Sure." 2X moved to the main desk, picking up a clipboard and pencil.

"How about the leader. He couldn't have been over five feet four, but he was cut, you know?"

"That's Big Loco, the number-one hard boy of this set, yo?" 2X clarified.

"There's more than one Domingos set? I thought they were just here, in this part of town."

2X had begun to write some notations on the clipboard. He stopped and looked up again. "Trece is the biggest and best-connected of the Central American gangs this side of Oak Street. Most of them were originally Salvadorans, but I think there's been some Guatemalans and even Mexicans added in."

"Chicanos?" Monk asked.

"No, I mean those straight up from Mexico." He pivoted his torso and called into the inner office. "Hey, LaToyce, what's the name of the place in Mexico Big Loco and his bunch are supposed to be hooked up with?"

"Zacatecas—it's a state down there," she called back. "They supposed to be runnin' with some high rollers down there."

Keith 2X wagged the eraser end of the pencil at Monk. "What we hear now is that there's some new recruits into the bunch who are part of something called the Zacatecas Mob, or whatever that means in English."

Monk had read a *Newsweek* piece about the gangsters. "The Zacatecas bunch is supposed to be muscling into

L.A., having already taken over some rackets in Texas. Making money in hot jewelry, electronic parts . . .''

"And heroin," 2X finished. "All that just makes our work here in the Rancho that much more challenging," the young man said without sarcasm.

"Hear anything else I might find of use about these murders?" Monk shifted his packets from one hand to the other.

The other man seemed to consider his words but didn't speak.

"Like something the Scalp Hunters may be up to if their rivals are making all these big moves," Monk prodded.

The corporal tucked in his bottom lip, and watched other members of the Ra-Falcons as they moved about the office.

"We have to work together on this," Monk reminded him.

2X sighed. "There's supposed to be a meeting tonight or tomorrow among some of the Scalp Hunters' Ogs."

"These veterans gonna figure out how to vamp on the Domingos?"

A severe look finally broke through 2X's implacable demeanor. "I'm telling you this because Antar said to let you know what was going on around here so you don't make him look bad, you know what I'm saying, yo?"

"I appreciate that," Monk said.

"Awe-right then. I don't exactly know what the meeting's about, and it's not like any of us can go there and find out."

"Even the members of the security force who used to run with the Scalps?" Monk knew the answer but was curious to see what the young man would say.

Scoldingly he said, "Now you know especially those brothers won't be let into the meet, yo."

Thinking ahead, Monk asked, "This meeting supposed to happen off-site?"

2X looked at the wall clock, checking the time against his watch. "Look, I gotta get these people out and about. But yeah, it's supposed to be happening somewhere else, but we ain't heard where."

Monk made to go. "If you do, would you let me know?"

2X gave him a questioning stare.

"I'm not going to do anything stupid," Monk tried to assure him.

"Then why you gotta know where the meet is?"

Monk pointed at the falcon's eye on the door. "All-seeing, all-knowing."

"Yeah, right," 2X huffed. "If I peep anything, I'll let you know. But don't you tell anybody else, yo?"

"Dug, home." Monk tapped him on the side of the arm and left the office. Downstairs, several women, young and old, black and brown, were in the laundry room doing their wash. A tabloid talk show played on a TV secured in a mesh grilled box on an overhead platform in a corner of the room. A section of the metal was cut away to allow viewing of the images on the screen.

The subject of the show was ex-stripper mothers who were pregnant by their daughters' bisexual boyfriends. The women were vigorously discussing the issue in English and Spanish simultaneously as Monk reached Pio Pico Court. Harmony through salaciousness, he reflected.

Walking through the Rancho, he was struck by the almost diametrical contrasts the complex seemed to go through. For beyond the laundry room, the Rancho was tomblike in its quiet atmosphere.

When he'd been here yesterday the Rancho had been vibrant with Alpines beating out the hard raps of the late

Tupac Shakur and Westside Connection. Somewhere underneath those kronik-induced rhythms he'd also heard a scratchy LP playing. The tune was a melodic wail of stone chimes and the hollow tap-tapping of sticks on the turned tubes of a bamboo xylophone. Today, there was no gangsta rap or Southeast Asian music. Today there was only the chirping of birds.

As he walked in the vague direction of Henry Cady's apartment, the stillness pervading the housing project appeared odd to him. No young men lounged about, no chopped Caprices ripped and ran through her byways. The quiet was nothing of a sinister nature. Rather it had the quality of one of those old ships he used to find himself on in his merchant seaman days.

Monk had distinct memories of being on a hulk that had seen many a rough voyage, a ship that had served its crews as best it could. There was the comfort of lying in his bunk after his shift, feeling and hearing the thump and slap of the engine's pistons in worn cylinder walls, a lullaby supplied by diesel fuel and oil. Now he couldn't escape the notion that this lull was connected to the upcoming meeting of Scalp Hunter leaders.

He got near Cady's townhouse then thought better of going to see the older gent. Cady had said he wasn't worried about who might see Monk come and go from his place. But if the combative Mrs. Limón hadn't been jiving him, and a rumor had already started about him being some kind of undercover cop, then he wasn't going to be the one to bring grief on the nice man. Even if Monk's radar wasn't picking up any unfriendlies in the vicinity. Monk decided to ring Cady later to see if he'd had any luck getting other people to talk to him.

Eventually his wandering took him near the tracks, and the abandoned center across the way. Monk stood there for a moment, his hands in his pockets while he let his mind free associate. A woman walked around the corner of the main building from the direction the busted-out window was located.

Her hair stood out from her head like she was receiving continuous electric shock waves. It was in the peculiar state black women's hair achieves between straightening and going back to its natural texture. The woman was dressed in a conservative dark blue pants suit, bright silver buttons diagonal like a bandolier across her upper body. The only clue to its worn status was the large tattered hole over her left rib cage.

She seemed disoriented in the sunlight, as if she had emerged from labors in Erebus, the dark region. Her gaze eventually settled on Monk. She rocked on her heels, waved at him cheerily, then stumbled away. He watched her go, then concentrated on the buildings for several more minutes. Maybe a clue would manifest itself on one of the center's walls, like a profile of Selina emerging from a mound of mashed potatoes. Or at least that's what a supermarket tabloid Monk had glanced through in the checkout line last week had said had happened to a woman in El Paso. Alas, after several moments, he surmised no such divine intervention was to be.

The rest of the day brought nothing new, no call from Keith 2X, Cady, or his buddy Mrs. Limón. Around four he got over to his shop, Continental Donuts, on Vernon in the Crenshaw District.

The shop was an investment he'd made with the scratch earned as a ship's engineer, a bit of entrepreneurship he'd been talked into by Dexter Grant. Originally, the establishment had belonged to a cop buddy of Grant's, also retired. The buddy used the money to go to Burma. He'd gone there with some other ex–law enforcement and military types to hunt for some supposedly stolen caches of Chinese gold. Wisely, Grant hadn't gone along. The former owner of Continental Donuts and his expedition were never heard from again.

Monk's mother had also been an influence in his decision to buy the shop.

"You got to have property, boy. Black folks been struggling and dying for hundreds of years because of land, son. You ain't never without something to tide you through the bad times when you have a grant deed with your name on it. Especially if it's earning you an income," his mother, a nurse, had advised him. "Why you think I been keeping up the taxes on that plot we got down in Mound Bayou, near Clarksdale? We've had that family farm since right after slavery."

What little profit the damned place showed generally went for salaries and expenses, but he liked being a donut magnate. As he walked in, Elrod the giant was fixing one of the fryers. Monk went into the reinforced room where he kept hard copies of his files. He punched in Kodama's number, and the receiver was picked up immediately.

"Yes, who is this," the voice snapped.

"Monk. Is Jill there?"

"How'd you get this number?"

Fucking Mitchell. "I said this was Monk, you know who I am."

"Oh yes, I believe I've talked with you before," he replied, feigning only a fleeting recognition. "The judge is busy right now, I'll tell her you called."

The word "called" already sounded distant as the receiver was replaced in its cradle.

"Asshole," Monk cursed, backslapping the phone. Anxious, and with nothing else to do, he swept and straightened up the room. He finished, taking the files on the members of the Ra-Falcons with him.

Elrod the invincible donut shop manager resided in the kitchen. The former heister was six feet eight inches, three hundred and twenty-five trim pounds of prison-tested muscle. His squared-off head topped shoulders as wide as an aircraft carrier's deck, and three earring studs, in gold, silver, and turquoise, were punched into the rim of his left ear.

"Chief," Elrod greeted him. He was instructing a new employee on the fineries of making raised chocolate donuts just so. "This is Andre, he started yesterday."

The young black man, he couldn't have been over twenty-three, looked in Monk's direction but said nothing. He promptly returned his focus to rolling the dough. His coal black jeans were long in the leg and frayed at the heels of his white Pumas. He wore a heavily starched blue work shirt buttoned at the sleeves and at the collar. His hair was shaved very close to the scalp on the sides, with a modicum more along the top.

"Dre's been in CYA," Elrod said, confirming what Monk had been speculating. "He's the little brother of an old pardner of mine. Said he wants to do right, ain't that so?"

Dre nodded quickly that indeed it was so, and began to pull little plugs off the dough and roll them into balls.

"Righteous," Monk responded and moved toward the front. If the kid didn't work out, and especially if he tried to run a scam, he'd have to deal with the big fella. A fate to make grown men weak in the knees. The fact that Elrod could inspire such fear allowed Monk to sleep sound at night.

Out in the main section were three customers. Gloria was in her MTA bus driver uniform, playing a game of chess in one of the booths with a woman he didn't recognize. At the counter was Andrade, occasional accountant and periodic binger. A medium cup of coffee and an uneaten French cruller sat before him. He was dressed in a sport coat and open collar, his black hair uncombed, grey beginning to set in. He was going over the racing form, making tight, concise circles around his picks as he read through the upcoming heats.

"How're you fixed for some possible extracurricular work?" Monk poured himself a cup of coffee.

"You that hard up for a sidekick?" Andrade answered, never taking his eyes off his homework.

"I need," Monk began, making his way around the counter to sit next to the accountant, "a Spanish speaker for some translating."

Andrade put his red-shot eyes on Monk, blinking. *"¿Cómo?"*

Monk sketched him in on his case and said, "Basically, it might be needed for a meeting I am hoping to get together with a few of the neighbors. Or else several phone calls. Of course you'd be compensated."

Andrade opened the paper, folded it to another page, then folded it down to quarter size agin. "I suppose this would require me to be, oh, how should I say it, around?"

It suddenly came to Monk he didn't know where Andrade lived, but assumed it had to be nearby as he'd never seen him drive to the shop. "I'm at the mercy of other forces, Andrade." He refrained from making a comment on the *bruja* Limón. "It would help if I got your home number, so when something jumps, I can buzz you."

"No phone," he retorted, making another pick on his form. "No car, either."

"How the hell do you do business?"

"Badly." He made another find.

This was beginning to annoy him. Andrade wasn't the only Spanish speaker he knew, but he was the most handy. "How about I get you a cellular to hold onto for a while."

The red pen circled a horse called Distant Gloom. "Sure, I can come back here to get it."

Monk's curiosity about where the strange accountant lived was gnawing at him, but he didn't want to make an issue of it and tick him off. "Fine. I'll leave it with Elrod by ten tomorrow. Just so we don't run up the bill on the damned thing, for now just click it on between"—he consulted his watch—"eleven and three."

"On it." Andrade got off the stool, finally taking a bite of his cruller.

"Andrade . . ." Monk began, then stalled.

"What?" The man rubbed his unshaven jaw.

"Thanks, I appreciate your trouble."

He made a casual flick of his hand, took a few gulps of his coffee, and tucked his racing form into his jacket pocket. He departed without another word.

Elrod, standing in the opening leading to the kitchen, was wiping his hands on a cleaning rag. "If his Spanish is anything like his accountin', you might be peddlin' backwards."

"I've heard him speak Spanish more than once; as far as I can tell he's not some *gavacho*."

"Uh-huh," the giant remarked dubiously. "You just better hope he's sober between them hours you told him to be available."

"You ever been to his pad?" Monk enjoyed some of his coffee.

"Nope. As far as I know nobody knows where he stays. Wait." He held up the rag in one massive paw. "I think maybe Honest Abe took him home once. Way I hear it, Andrade lost his license for his second DUI conviction."

Abraham Carson was a carpenter and regular at the Abyssinia Barber Shop and Shine Parlor where Monk got his hair cut and the neighborhood 411. "I'll give him a call, thanks."

Sitting at the counter, Monk started to go through the files Absalla had left for him. From his stash underneath the Formica counter, he retrieved a compact Te-Amo number 4 cigar. He puffed on the ember and read, sometimes stopping to fill orders for customers who came in. He pretended not to notice the disapproval on some of their faces at the sharp smell. When he got to Kelmont Reeves, he finally found something of interest. It was an assessment Absalla apparently did of each of his employees.

As a member of the Del Nines street gang, Reeves had been known as Kid Blue. Taking out his notes and browsing through them, he found the reference to a Baby Blue that Mrs. Hughes had mentioned. Absalla's write-up stated Reeves had a cousin in the Scalp Hunters called Junior Blue. Monk was sure that was one of the kids Mrs. Hughes said Cruzado had confronted.

Monk put a Post-it on Kelmont's rap sheet and went through the other files. Nothing else jumped out at him, but he'd make another pass later. He plodded into the kitchen to answer the ringing phone attached to the wall.

"Continental Donuts."

"Ivan, you got a call from a Keith 2X down at the Rancho Tajuata," Delilah relayed over the wire. "He said you'd want to know this like yesterday, yo?"

The house was a toast-colored stuccoed bungalow with wide green trim on Trinity, off of East Adams. Sections of its aging paint had fallen away from parts of one wall. Someone had made a halfhearted attempt at repainting, giving the wall a blotchy relief effect with mismatched explosions of other shades of light brown

The block was full of similar homes, with other variations on the Craftsman style, and a couple of nondescript clapboard jobs too. Several of the houses had cars in various stages of repair and ruin placed at angles along their respective fronts. Tall palm trees dotted both sides of the street, and Monk could smell eucalyptus on the evening breeze. Big dogs could be heard bellowing indifferently, contemptuous of the need for peace among humans.

He could discern music playing nearby. It was an old number, whose tune he couldn't quite identify, but was pretty sure was a cut by the trumpeter Lester Young. Prez. Right out of Woodville, Mississippi, swaying and playing in that signature flat, broad-brimmed porkpie hat of his blowing grooves for the horn players before him, and setting the double-time pace for the cats after him.

Monk moved back into the recessed darkness between the patched wall and a stand of cypress trees as another car rolled past the house.

The vehicle stopped, reversed its travel, and coasted beneath the pale glow of a street lamp. The car drove farther down the street. It was a late-model Buick Regal, glossy black with shimmering gold trim. The Regal evidently found a parking spot, because Monk heard its doors open and close and footfalls approach along the cracked sidewalk.

Three men came toward the house he was spying on. Two were black, above average height. One of them was sporting a natty beard. The third was white, or a light-skinned Latino, of medium build. His dark hair was shaved close to his head with a thin, long braid swatting lightly down the center of his back.

Each was fashion-model sharp in coat and slacks, all of them wearing gold rings that dispersed flutters of light along their large hands. It was obvious from the way the one with the strand of hair and the black one with the beard flanked the man in the middle that they were his bodyguards.

They gained the porch, knocked, and a vertical shaft of light briefly striped the middle man's face. From his hiding place, Monk could see his features. The man was matinee handsome, his eyes horizontal slits that seemed to have been drawn rather than organic. The door opened wider and the three went into the meeting.

Keith 2X had told Monk he'd found out this house on Trinity would be the site of the OGs' gathering. He'd made him promise not to tell anyone else, or be discovered, as 2X had been told the information on the down low. Monk wanted to know who'd told 2X, but the Ra-Falcon corporal was not willing to give that information up.

He knew 2X wanted to follow Absalla's orders by letting him know what was happening, but he understood 2X also had to maintain his standing with the rest of the security force. The private eye liked the young man for standing up and doing the right thing.

Problem was, Monk had hoped to catch snatches of conversation from a cracked window. But the night was cool and no window was open. No sounds other than the occasional burst of raucous laughter could he hear by crouching alongside the wall.

He eased out of his hiding spot, checking to see if anyone was coming or leaving the house. He went for his car parked down the block to wait until the gents and their Buick left. The man with the smooth face had been older than the others who'd previously entered the house. Given the near seppuku existence of a gang member, being an OG usually meant anyone who'd managed to live past twenty-five. The man last to arrive was at least thirty-two or so, Monk estimated. His age and his dress set him apart as a man who doubtlessly held an emeritus position with the Scalp Hunters.

Time dragged, and Monk was losing the battle to stay awake. He hated stakeouts, hated them even if he had Dexter Grant along. Invariably the older man would relate a series of ancient battle tales derived from his days on the force. And plentiful they were, since Grant had made detective under that drunk Parker in the late '50s.

"Gates was an ingratiating little prick even then," Dex would regale. Not only could he go on forever with these stories, he could also sit for long stretches of time, just watching and existing. Monk had to believe Grant did it just to mess with him, as only a manic-depressive could enjoy sitting on his sweaty butt for hours staring like a loon out of a bird shit–splattered windshield.

He was working on naming the B sides of hits by Big Joe Turner alphabetically in his head when the door of the bungalow opened. Monk could only make out a knot of bodies gathering on the porch. He got out and did his best to become one with a palm tree's trunk. The door to the house remained open, the inner light bathing the clustered forms from one side, giving them the quality of a single, writhing entity. A compressed thing of pain and fury, soon to spin off its spirochetes in erratic orbits to zooming and then eventually faltering in a universe of chaos.

Some of the Scalp Hunters began to depart and the trio made their way to the Regal. Shots suddenly reverberated from the other side of the block. The remaining mass on the porch became numerous tendrils elongating into action, as several guns flashed.

Monk, his old man's .45 in his hand without his thinking

about it, hurtled along the street side of the parked cars. He ran in a crouch as his fingers graced cold metal. Gunfire, curses, and darting bodies filled his senses. A shotgun let loose, scattering its load into the fender of a cream-colored Trans Am inches from Monk. He fell flat, straining to see his assailant.

A Scalp Hunter, dressed in oversized khaki shorts and handling a semiauto, ran past a prone Monk, intent on finding a target. There was a large oleander bush in direct line from him across the street, and Monk was very aware of a squat dark shape disturbing its leaves.

"Get between the cars," he screamed at the Scalp Hunter in the shorts.

The man across the street let go with rounds from the weapon he held. It tut-tutted bullets in no discernable pattern, or at least that was Monk's perception as he vaulted over the trunk of the Trans Am, the back window blowing apart like tossed marbles. He banged his knee on the way over, gritting his teeth as he hit the concrete with his shoulder.

More bellowing of gunfire, running, and "Mother-fuckah" filled the night. As his heart jackhammered in his throat, Monk caught glimpses of the attackers. Body types and recent encounters collided in his mind like Polaroids spread before him on a table. He knew the broad, squat form of one of the assaulters was Big Loco. He was letting loose with whatever the hell his spurt gun was.

Not bothering or chancing to aim, Monk cranked off two shots in the wide little man's direction. More bullets tore into the sports car's frame, some of them penetrating to the other side.

"Goddamn, they popped Stake," a voice yelled.

"Get them wets," someone else exhorted.

More gunfire erupted, and the uncertainty of life on the battlefield was played out on Trinity Street.

Monk belly crawled onto an adjacent lawn, two sets of feet trampling over him.

"Watch out, motherfuckah," a voice belonging to one pair rasped. "Yo, they bookin'," the Scalp Hunter said to no one in particular.

Several members of the gang ran down the street to the sounds of car doors slamming and engines racing.

Monk tried to get up but a foot, shod in slip-ons, kicked at his head. Instinctively, he got a forearm up to block the movement. Utilizing the direction of his motion, he rolled on his back, coming up to thrust the muzzle of his gun into the crotch of the kicker.

"Hey, Pelé, want to go for the goal?" It was the white bodyguard of the older OG.

The face at the other end registered surprise, but was quickly jerked out of sight by a massive black hand. The other bodyguard had snatched him back. "Come on," he advised hurriedly.

The two surrounded their boss, hurrying him away, the largest one wielding a pistol proportionate with his large hands. The white man looked back, his right arm extended rigidly, the index like an arrowhead intended for the center of Monk's head.

A shot took out grass and dirt near him, and Monk scrambled for the bungalow's porch. By now the attack seemed to have dissipated, the Scalp Hunters having driven the Domingos back.

Monk was among several trying to get their breath back and nerves calmed down when a young man ran up. He wore a black eyepatch with a white Japanese ideogram sewn onto it. "Them eses capped Stake and Junior Blue. Motherfuck"—he threw down a gun—"they gonna pay."

Monk tried surreptitiously to remove his rattled six-feet-plus-off the stoop.

"Who the fuck is you?" A twenty-odd-year-old with hair dyed a bright blondish-yellow with a maroon streak demanded. The second color was shaped like the prow of a ship. A bright and shiny hoop earring dangled from each lobe. The Dennis Rodman of the gangster set. He underscored his question with a gun.

Monk held his hands out from his sides. "My name is Ivan Monk. I was hired by Antar Absalla to find out who firebombed the Cruzado family in the Rancho." Though there were holes in the front of the house, the porch light was untouched. Various sweating heads were inclined threateningly at the stranger.

Three Scalp Hunters brought a body into the light. It was the young man Monk had tried to warn. His khaki shorts were now drenched in red. They put him on the lawn, another offering to nihilism. Each week more and more bodies were stacked up on altars of recrimination and self-hate. The trio, moving like *mirzas* given a job at the beginning of time, moved off to collect the other corpse on their eternal rounds.

"These Mexicans follow you here?" The speaker stepped close to Monk, bringing his homely face almost to his nose.

A correction in ethnicity seemed inappropriate. "No," he said resolutely.

"Then how they be here, cuz?"

"How you be here?" The angry query was repeated by the first one who'd spotted him. This one swaggered over.

The ring was constricting, Monk's options of staying alive reduced to nil. "I told you, nobody followed me here."

"He did try to warn Blue, I saw it," a thin one offered.

"How'd you know about this meet, chump?" A hard shove to his chest accompanied this request. The ring tightened more.

The .45 was back in his shoulder holster, under his nylon jacket. Could he draw the weapon, take one or two out before they dropped him? As he gauged his next move he became oddly aware that the elbow on his right sleeve was ripped. The breeze felt good on his scraped elbow. "I told you, I was here on business," he said sharply. He was about to remind them their gang were suspects, but he let it pass. Where the hell were the goddamn cops?

"You gonna jump, frog?" Blondie taunted, waving the gun like a wand—a magician about to materialize him in the afterlife.

"I said what I said. If I led the Domingos here, why the hell would I have been shooting at them too?"

"Maybe they crossed you, sell-out." With his free hand, Blondie casually dug a finger way up his nose, searching and probing. "Let's take you somewhere so we can find—"

"Sirens," somebody yelled from the gloom just beyond the porch light milliseconds before they seemed to reach the others' ears.

"Take him," Blondie ordered to no one in particular, jerking his phosphorescent mane at Monk.

"Like hell," he declared.

Blondie swung with the flat of his gun, sending Monk staggering back. He faked more pain than he felt, doubling over so as to get his piece clear. Blondie stepped nearer.

"Straighten up, bitch, so I can hit you again."

Monk did so, jamming the automatic under the hitter's left eye. "This straight enough?"

"We gotta book," another warned excitedly.

Blondie snarled but said nothing, his gun remaining

trained on Monk, as Monk's gun was on him. The overhead light reflected hypnotically in his earrings.

Some of the crew were already running off. "Come on, B.B., we need to hat, man. We'll deal with this punk in a short minute."

B.B. the blond relented, backing off, gun still leveled at Monk. "We ain't through, bitch."

The Scalp Hunters faded away and in less than a minute, police cars careened across lawns, disgorging uniforms with the de rigueur shotguns and 9mms at the ready.

Monk stood with his hands visible on the pockmarked porch. The body of the one called Stake stretched before him on the uncut grass.

"We got another one behind this van," a cop bellowed.

Monk was ordered on his knees, a foot slammed hard into his upper back. He went down stomach first on the weather-beaten floorboards of the porch.

"Now, what's your story, Bo Peep?" A voice thick with malice said as muzzles were connected to his head like antennae.

Out on the lawn, just at the edge of the light, he could see the inert form of the boy-man. Another grave marker signaling one more bad night.

Six

"What in the fuck did you think you were doing?" Absalla worked his fist, opening and closing the hand like it was hooked to a generator.

"My job," Monk answered evenly. He crossed his legs, trying to give off a casual demeanor sitting across from the yelling man. Inwardly, he felt like notching it up several octaves himself. He'd already spent six hours with several fairly disinterested LAPD cops doing the "I'm innocent" tango. One of them, a hollow-eyed detective named Fitzhugh, was the cop Cady had mentioned as an extra-large asshole.

He and the compact number called Zaneski were the leads on the Rancho case. Fitzhugh promised to make a formal complaint to the Bureau of Consumer Affairs—the state agency that oversees the licensing of PIs. Yet even hardheaded detectives must give in to logic. They finally put out a pick-up order for Big Loco.

Those pleasantries out of the way, he had to fill out a firearms discharge report, and call Jill to pick him up. He'd been asleep for about an hour, after sharing a shower with the slippery jurist, when the phone call from the man shouting at him now had disturbed his slumber. Apparently Absalla had flown back from D.C. upon getting the news of the shoot-out.

"You supposed to be a pro," Absalla retorted.

"I was not followed." Monk spaced his words like flares around an accident. "I ain't no goddamn greenhorn."

"Oh really," the other man said condescendingly. "Aside from Keith, you was the only one who knew where the meet was."

"No," Monk corrected forcefully. "Whoever told Keith also knew."

Absalla tugged on an ear. "That floats like shit, Monk. What are you trying to get at?"

"Something that makes sense. If I wasn't followed, then whoever peeped Keith must have rolled over on the Scalp Hunters."

The Ra-Falcons' leader put a foot on the edge of his desk, leaning his chair back. "Naw, that don't wash, Monk. It could have only been another Scalp Hunter, and an OG at that. That meeting was on the high level."

"So what makes it such a lock?"

Absalla detailed, "Keith gets his info from a Scalp Hunter, who then turns around and tells them Domingos. Why should he? What the hell's in it for him?"

"Maybe Big Loco laid out some of the dinero he's rumored to be getting from the Zacatecas mob for the information," Monk speculated. "Or the real answer is easy to grasp. A Scalp Hunter gets followed to the meeting."

"The second part still assumes the Domingos would be following a Scalp around. And let me clue you, that's about as likely as Whitney Houston breaking down the door right now so she could sit on my face."

"In your world," he flared, "maybe blacks and browns

can get along.'' Absalla took his foot off the edge of the desk, letting the chair's legs come down heavily.

''But this here's the Rancho, Monk, the Taj, you dig? Black kids get popped at around here when they're doing nothing more than waiting for a bus out on San Pedro. Not 'cause they're in the Scalps, not 'cause they look like somebody who crossed some other dude's girl. They get shot at 'cause they're black.''

''It happens the other way around too,'' Monk noted.

''It does,'' Absalla conceded. ''But that's why I thought I was hiring somebody sharp, somebody who knew the deal and could maneuver around without stumbling all over the place like a chump.''

''I wasn't followed.''

Absalla did an apologetic gesture. ''You still looking like the bah, bah.''

Monk got up quick, his chair scooting back forcefully. ''I got your goat.''

The security chief also shot up. ''What it be, Monk?'' he yelled, ''we gonna redecorate the office?'' He worked his fist, kneading his unseen ball. The muscles along his arm bunched under the pressed cotton sleeve.

A vein in Monk's neck was pulsing like a gas hose fed too much fuel. He felt the intensity working its way up to his head and he welcomed the feeling. Each man gave the face to the other. Go on, prove how much of a tough private eye you are and leap over the desk at that self-righteous, self-appointed black leader.

The standoff ticked down; a baby's cry carried in on the breeze. Finally Monk exhaled, and calmly righted the chair. ''I guess I can submit an invoice for my expenses.''

Absalla looked down at his desk, his mouth working at words but not vocalizing them. He looked up with his eyes. ''Mail it in.''

He pulled open the door; Keith 2X and a Ra-Falcon he didn't know were making a show of being absorbed in some sort of paperwork. 2X went out of his way not to look at him. Something that wasn't a smile lighted on Monk's face as a rush of hot blood filled his forehead.

Crossing quickly to the main door he asked, "One of you mind telling me who were the two that got killed last night?"

The one Monk didn't know looked at Keith 2X. Absalla stood in the doorway to his office, his hands placed on either side of the doorjamb as if guarding against bad spirits.

"Junior Blue and Stake," 2X replied tersely.

"This Junior related to the Reeves who used to be called Kid Blue?"

2X's expression told Monk what he wanted to know and he left. He managed to make it to his car, feeling his height and esteem diminish with each step. He aimed the Ford over to his donut shop on automatic pilot. He went in, grunting hellos to Elrod and two of the regulars.

"Andrade came by and picked up the phone," Elrod informed him.

"Glad to see somebody's on their J." He disappeared into his steel-shuttered room. He used to keep a cot in the room, but was glad he'd recently replaced it with a futon. He put the radio on, sliding the dial left to KLON, the jazz station out of Long Beach State.

He pulled his shirt out of his trousers, unbuttoning it all the way as Chuck Niles queued up a cut from a Joshua Redmond album. Monk put out the lights, and laid on the futon as the saxman's tune blew.

It wasn't the first time he'd been fired. He'd been taken off jobs for being too independent, or for getting too close to uncomfortable answers. But he'd never been let go for being incompetent. Despite what he'd said to Absalla, he wasn't that sure he hadn't been followed. In fact, it made sense that this might have happened.

He'd piqued the interest of the Domingos leader when he and his boys had braced him at the Rancho. It hadn't occurred to Monk that the Domingos might have enough wherewithal to tail him. He hadn't taken any precautions, hadn't really made an effort to check to make sure he wasn't being followed once he got the tip from 2X.

"Shit," Monk said aloud, scratching his bare belly.

"Hey, boss, you want some coffee?" Elrod said through the door.

"No thanks, man." He could feel the manager's presence on the other side but didn't want to keep talking.

"Alright," the big man finally said, his footfalls resounding in the cement passageway.

Robert Cray's sharp guitar solo drifted to him from the radio, and Monk wished he could follow it as it transcended distance and walls. Several hours passed, with Monk lying on his back, hands behind his head, alternately staring at the ceiling and dozing off. Finally he got up, buttoned his shirt, and tucked it in as he quit the room.

It was getting on dark and Elrod was counting the cash from the register. Not being a chain, Continental Donuts was not a twenty-four-hour concern, and only stayed open late on Fridays and Saturdays. He zeroed Monk with a questioning gaze. "You need anything?" The big hands kept working as he talked.

The other man clasped him on his steel buttress of a shoulder. "Nothing to sweat, bro'. All my troubles seem like yesterdays." He poured some coffee into a Styrofoam cup.

Elrod totaled the day's take, and went into the file room to place it in the safe. When he came back, Monk was sitting at one of the booths, his cup of coffee held between both hands. The big man got in opposite. "How about a game of dominoes? I ain't beat your butt in a long time."

"No, thanks, I wouldn't be much good tonight." Monk started to sip the coffee and thought better of it. The brew suddenly tasted old and bitter. "I'll lock up. Go on home, man."

"Okay." Elrod delayed getting up, his silence indicating he couldn't find the words he wanted to try and pierce the other man's funk. He raised his muscled frame out of the bench seat. The booths were old-fashioned, and each had a coat rack attached on the outer end. The big man lifted his leather coat off one of the hooks, draping it over a thick forearm. "Good night, boss."

"Take it slow, El-D." Monk said quietly, his head resting against the padded bench.

In the silence of the room, the phone rang twice, two separate times. Monk didn't bother to answer. The coffee in his cup had long since grown cold.

Seven

The Airport Casino was designed with Eisenhower-era coffee shop-futurism in mind. The building was composed of two-story-high angular bronze planes of glass on the front and left sides. The rising reflection of aircrafts skimming across their opaque surfaces from nearby LAX created the effect of an endless film loop. The panes led up to a series of curved trusses that in turn held up an undulating roof line.

The sunken entrance itself was flanked by purple Doric columns topped with brass saucer-style capitals. A wide red carpet led straight from the massive glass and chrome double doors, then curved off toward the sprawling blacktop parking lot. The whole effect was of something designed by the masters of the form, the architect firm of Armét and Davis.

The lot, which was patrolled by blue-grey–uniformed security personnel in white Cherokees, was intermittently landscaped by low shrubs and spiky philodendrons embedded in concrete islands of gravel.

The casino and its grounds sat on a hill west of Sepulveda Boulevard. Directly south lay the airport, and beyond that the unimaginative office buildings of El Segundo, once known as the "aerospace center of the world." Nowadays, with the collapse of the Cold War, some of the displaced engineers who used to spend hours hunched over bluelines of satellites and MX missiles were equally intent on the outcome of a hand of stud or Texas Hold 'Em. In California the law dictated that players play against one another—that is, jackpot poker—and not the house as in Vegas or Atlantic City. So the antes tended to be smaller, but the incentive to stay longer at the table even if you were losing was greater.

Monk got a ginger ale for $2.50 at one of the bars and strolled across the three-level expanse of the Airport Casino's football field–sized main gambling area. The inside was tasteful in comparison to the exterior. Las Vegas red velvet walls mixed with beaux arts chandeliers and wall sconces. Waitresses in short, tight black skirts, with wide gold belts, medium-high heels, and black garrison caps stitched with a gold lightning bolt along one side flowed through the place like blood cells.

He passed a table where several middle-aged white women, including one in a dark pair of sunglasses, were playing a furious hand of draw poker. Overhead, a soothing version of "Simply the Best" poured quietly from the hidden speakers. This table seemed to be the most lively; many of the other ones were only half full. At the surrounding tables, the players looked haggard, disoriented, like vampires who forgot they shouldn't be out in the day.

Monk made a circuit of the front part of the large room but didn't see the man he'd come to find. He got some chips and sat in for a few hands, losing a quick twenty-five. However, he did discover a ginger ale ordered from one of the girls of the Order of the Jetsons only cost $1.50

if you were playing. Having established his bona fides as a bad poker player, Monk left the table and wandered toward the back, where the real action was.

This section of the main floor was demarcated by an overhead neon sign in royal blue lettering. Hanging perpendicular to the industrial fixtures webbing the ceiling it stated: ASIAN GAMES. This part was the boomtown to the front's rural subdivision.

Men and women, mostly Asian but with a smattering of whites, Latinos, and a few blacks, were laughing, shouting, cursing, and slapping cards on the green felt as they gamed earnestly. Examining one table, Monk could see two-inch black tiles similar to dominoes being put into position. Pai gow was a game of chance from China which had become very big in Los Angeles and Vegas.

Monk, keen on differentiating Asians by ethnicity, noted the majority of people in this part of the casino were Chinese or Chinese-American. There was a kind of possession gripping each table, as players—young and old, well-dressed and decked out like pensioners—held their respective tiles facedown. Each player rubbed a finger over the hidden red or white sunken dots as if reading braille to discern the value of the tile. It was considered a weakness if an opponent saw your hand. But it wasn't considered cheating, and attempting to see another's tile was part of the pleasure of the game.

The object of Pai gow is to make nine or as close to it as possible. A player is initially dealt four tiles. Then a frenzied state of betting and bluffing ensues. Like poker, there are low and high stakes tables. This Monk knew from past observation. But as to actually playing the game, it seemed to him learning to fly a 747 would be easier.

A fog of cigarette smoke hung in the room like old moss. Unlike at typical poker games, here the consumption of alcohol was kept to a minimum. "Bombers," he knew, referred to players who lifted the tiles of other players who'd gotten too drunk or tired. If players got too inebriated they also risked miscounting their dots with their gin-oozing fingers.

Several dialects of Chinese were being spoken as tiles were slapped down. A few of the tables in this part of the room were also engaged in poker. One in particular held some men, aged fortyish, in off-the-rack suits playing anaconda. Their eyes were more intent on a table near them of Pai gow players using black and white chips—big money chips—than on their own game.

Sure enough, in a corner table sat Isaiah Booker, the man Monk had spotted three nights ago on Trinity Street at the disrupted Scalp Hunter summit. Booker was adeptly making bets with blue and white chips. At his table English and Chinese mixed, and the cofounder of the Scalp Hunters was going with the flow.

Nursing his soda, Monk took up space on a far wall, next to a Hockney print in a cheap frame. Searching online through numerous reference and news sites, Monk had produced several listings of the Scalp Hunters' deeds: drive-bys, strong-arm tactics, drug dealing, including amphetamines, moving stolen vehicles across state lines, busts for automatic weapons, etc. The gang had evolved from mere street thugs to a multitiered underground capitalist enterprise.

The most recent piece was about the ambush. In the article, the reporter mentioned a rumor that Isaiah Booker had been in attendance on Trinity. A sidebar was a capsule history of the founding of the gang. It seems that Booker and fellow Manual Arts High School dropout Tony Tyler established the Scalp Hunters in the early '80s after each had finished his sentence at the California Youth Authority.

Monk had also found an archived article from the *Atlantic Monthly* on the lives of L.A. gangsters. The piece included a profile on Tyler. Tony T, as he was called, was discovered one bright and sunny morning in 1995 with five bullets in him in his office at the rap record label he'd started.

Pulling up additional info, Monk had found an article from the *Times*'s now defunct *City Times* Sunday supplement that described how a remorseful Booker supposedly went straight after Tyler's murder. Timeslink offered re-keyed text, not the actual typeset articles. But at the downtown library, using the date he wanted to view, Monk went through the right section of microfilm, finding the article from the fall of 1995.

The article mentioned that Booker had been supplying ex-gang members to his construction project in the Crenshaw District. Brooks was described as a retired former Raider and a prominent brother who had grown up in Watts, who was now a partner in building a movie theater complex and music/video superstore. It was the first first-run theater to be built in that part of town for over forty years.

The former NFLer had also hired Booker to be a kind of independent consultant on the project. A photo taken at the grand opening of the theater accompanied the article. It showed Booker, along with the football great, city councilwoman Tina Chalmers, and Mayor Riordan, each with a hand on a bifurcated prop movie ticket.

There was a quip from Booker saying his only vice these days was going to a card club now and then for relaxation. Taking his lead from that quote, Monk had spent three days trawling from the City of Bell, to Commerce, and other junctures located in the southeastern end of the county. These were towns where once the steel, auto, and rubber factories had run double shifts. But those days, and those industries, were long gone. Now these bereft municipalities chased the chimera of gaming dollars, gambling on sustainable economic development.

Monk's search inevitably brought him to the Airport Casino. The newest and shiniest citadel of chance. He again showed Booker's photo to employees and clientele. That and a few pretty little green ones got the confirmation that Booker frequented the club at least once a week, and that he had a penchant for Pai Gow.

The PI hung back for an opening until one came forty minutes later. A young woman dressed in middle management style tossed her remaining chips onto the felt and departed, disillusioned, from the table. He took a seat at the so-called reformed gangster's five o'clock.

Two Asian women, both heavy smokers, assayed Monk as if he were a bumpkin come for the fleecing. He put his four hundred and fifty dollars' worth of chips before him, trying his best not to show his panic. This was on his dime, goddamnit. There would be no reimbursement of expenses on this go-round.

A large-bellied white man in a cap and with a Pat Buchanan for President button pinned on his lapel shook his head from side to side at the sight of the newcomer's meager chips.

Monk was dealt four tiles, and he concentrated on counting the dots with his fingers. One of the Asian women made it obvious she was trying to see his hand. He subsequently lost the first three rounds, the play moving too fast for him. But he found if he paid attention to the calls of the dealer, he could at least keep track of the respective bets.

Booker hadn't looked at him once, which Monk hoped meant he hadn't gotten a look at him the other night. Every now and then, one of the black-heeled hammers would come by, giving Booker a drink, offering a sandwich, and even a towel to dry his moist fingers. At one point, he signaled a hostess to come over. Booker penned his name on a card, and she returned with some black and white chips. About a thousand dollars' worth, Monk estimated. He also noticed neither of his bodyguards were around.

He got into trying to keep up. An hour went by, he lost three hundred. He'd have to come up with a cleverer—and less expensive—way to approach Booker. Amazingly, once he got down to seventy dollars, he won a hand. The two Asian women became his cheering section. They laughed in unison, and the sneaky one leaned over and patted him on the shoulder. She was still trying to get a look at his tiles as she blew fumes from her Chesterfield in his face.

Booker finally acknowledged Monk's presence with a quick sidelong glance, then resumed his focus on his own tiles. The player between the two men, a woman in a stretched car coat, left the table. She'd been betting heavy, and was down to five red chips. The dour-faced dealer began again after everyone anted.

"Is it true that Acuras are very popular?" Monk said softly amongst the chatter.

Booker flung a white chip into the middle of the table. He remained mute.

Monk lasted another twelve minutes, got wiped out, and left to the applause of his two buddies. He checked his watch: four-twenty. Time enough for something with more grab than a ginger ale. He got a scotch rocks and threaded about the place some more. Waiting and calculating. Booker finally took a bathroom break.

Monk stood next to him at the urinals. "I understand the overseas market for Toyota Land Cruisers is fairly lucrative."

Booker analyzed the pores in the tile's grouting, finished, then rinsed his hands in the faux black marble sink.

"You don't like meeting new people, or what?" Monk cracked, still at the urinal.

"What the fuck is with you, man." Booker's voice was thin and insubstantial. It seemed that stringing several words together was an effort for him like walking up flights of stairs.

"Just interested in doing a little business."

"Oh, what would that be?" the hollow voice said. He spritzed some cologne from a dispenser onto his manicured hands and patted his cheek.

"Cars."

"I got a car." He started to walk out. "Three in fact."

"You so phat you can't get rid of a few more primo rides like an Infiniti or two?"

"And you the man to supply them, Mr. Officer?" he said with interest as they stood in the hallway, patrons ebbing by.

"Ain't no cop."

"I'm gone." Booker made his way to another table, chips appearing before him as he sat down.

So much for the infiltration plan. Monk wandered back outside, idly considering waiting around and trying to follow Booker. But he knew the man was too street savvy to let that happen. He walked to his Ford, a splatter of bird droppings on his window and hood greeting him. The capper to a less than fruitful day.

Eight

Kodama took the private elevator to her floor and stepped out into the quiet corridor. It wasn't quite eight in the morning. She carried the *Times* and a cup of mocha grande she'd purchased at the Pasqua stand in the courtyard behind the Superior Court building. Her docket for today only had a prelim in the afternoon, and she was determined to maintain her normalcy. She was going to sit in her chambers, drink her heavenly brew, and read about the further troubles of the cash-strapped county. Bigger problems always put your own in perspective.

She said hello to a passing bailiff and undid the lock on her door. Kodama got the light on and entered the office. Putting her paper down, she read the words "Nip bitch sucks black dick," spray painted in brilliant orange across one walnut-paneled wall. She then saw the other phrases splayed across her desk, another wall, and the carpet.

She removed the lid on her cup of mocha grande and drank, methodically rereading the hateful words. The judge didn't move; she just stood in the office, her door open to the hallway. Calmly she used the phone to call down to the second floor where the sheriff's bailiff's station was. Mitchell wasn't in yet, but she got another deputy she knew, a black woman named Larson, to come upstairs.

Larson got things in motion as Kodama sat in the hall, finishing her coffee. After the LAPD people were through dusting and taking their photos, and had gotten her statement, the photographer from the legal paper, the *Daily Journal*, was allowed to take some shots. He asked Kodama a few questions.

"Do you think this has something to do with the recent controversy around the Wright matter?"

"It would seem."

"Being a strong proponent of free speech, Judge Kodama, do you find it ironic this kind of thing has happened to you?"

"Somewhat."

"What sort of society do you think this act represents, Judge Kodama? Where the discourse of ideas is too often reduced to inflammatory rhetoric on talk radio that slyly winks at this sort of behavior."

"Messed up." She drained her cup.

"Thanks for your time, Judge."

"You betchum, Red Rider."

By the time she got home after six, she found Monk working on the rotisserie wheel in the microwave. Parts, needle-nosed pliers, and several long, slim screwdrivers were spread before him at the kitchen table.

"Hey," he muttered, concentrating on getting a small gear back into place.

"Hi. Wouldn't it be simpler to just get a new one rather than have you fixing it every month or so?" She didn't wait for an answer as she wheeled about, cadet smooth, tossed her attaché case with its over-the-shoulder strap onto one of the chairs, and left the room.

Monk watched her but said nothing. He continued to work on the motor.

Presently Kodama returned, barefoot, in jeans and a cotton shirt, its tail hanging out. She crossed to the refrigerator and poured herself a glass of pineapple juice. "My office got broken into," she said conversationally.

"Shit." Monk gingerly set the motor down. "What happened?"

"It got broken into, didn't you hear me?"

"Fine, if you want to be shitty about it." He fiddled with the motor.

Moments built up, the emotional temperature rising. Kodama dissipated it with, "I'm sorry, baby, this goddamn thing is getting to me." She moved toward the table as Monk held out his arms. He hugged her around the waist as she clasped his upper body, tight. She sat down and told him about what she'd encountered.

"Mitchell has another deputy assigned to watch just the office for the next few weeks," Kodama said.

"Helpful motherfuckah," Monk chimed in.

A defensive alignment set her mouth. "He's just trying to be sweet."

"Oh, he's being sweet all right."

She got up and poured more pineapple juice and handed the glass to Monk. "It absolutely frosts my left tit that these yahoos think they can fuck with me, and because I'm a judge I have to walk the line."

"Debate Jamboni," Monk said, his voice rising with indignation. "News shows would step over each other to have the both of you on."

Her mouth twisted. "Ideas and reason are not the wont of most of those venues. We would only wind up shouting at one another with me looking shrill and unyielding because I'm the woman."

"We keep having this same discussion, Jill. You said yourself the review process is loaded from the get-go. Ideas and reason can't be your only weapons in this battle. These fools out in the Valley are willing to play to fear and handily use half-truths to make their point, namely, the elimination of any semblance of liberalism from the bench."

"I stand for something more than that, Ivan. The law isn't some village idiot to be paraded along main street to be pelted by the rubes."

"This ain't about the law, Jill, it's about perception and who shapes it."

"So I must become a propagandist."

"If that's what it takes to win, yes."

"I refuse to do so."

"Then you've already lost," he said harshly.

"Maybe you're just tougher than me, Ivan, you want me to say that? You came in here the other night depressed about what went down on Trinity and being fired. So you wallow in your self-pity for a while. But being the hard-headed man I know you to be, you say fuck 'em, I'll show them they can't sucker punch me.

"But I don't sit on the bench because I want to get some payback so I can turn down invitations to be on Johnnie Cochran's cable show.

"The law is like this old, hand-carved wooden box." She leaned on the kitchen counter. "The catch on the lid sticks, and it has to be pried open now and then. And inside are these pieces. These pieces don't gleam, nor do they fit just so in the big mosaic. Some of the pieces come out warped and grimy from being pounded and shaped by rough hands.

"Pieces like the law that threw nisei into camps, while their businesses and land got expropriated, in the forties. Or the restrictive housing covenants that forbade homeowners from selling to black folks in this town until the sixties. Or Lemon Grove in the twenties when Mexican-American families demanded the same education for their kids as the white parents received for theirs. Separate and unequal. Laws upheld in court case after court case until some jurist said enough bullshit, enough with the con job and let's put an end to it.''

"That's also because there was pressure from civil rights organizations, and actions in the streets,'' Monk added.

"True. But you still needed a judge, Ivan. You still needed somebody like Brown in the Scottsboro case who stood up to his peers, the stump-sitting, cigar-chawing pals of his who'd just as soon see a blue gum nigger die as give him an adequate defense.

"Not because Judge Brown worried about making himself look good in the press. Hell, he got ostracized from the civilized Southern circles he used to be part of for his efforts to clear those innocent boys.''

Monk balanced two small screws in his palm. "Then what are you going to do, Jill? You have to stand up to these pinheads, and you might just have to come down off your soapbox to do it.''

"I'll decide what I need to do.'' Kodama left the kitchen, humming a tune to irritate Monk.

Again he stared after her, then got back to his work. Later, he got the rotisserie back together and tested it by heating a cup of coffee from the morning's brew. It rotated in a halting manner like a one-eyed rat trying to navigate a circular maze. Getting a new one was easy; it was making what you had work that was the real deal.

His coffee warm and cheery, he read through the newspaper, which he hadn't had the chance to do in the morning. When he got to a column Left in the Metro section, he read it with studied interest. Kodama came back.

"Can I buy you a drink, soldier? Say, at the Go Room?"

Monk folded the paper to display the article. "Throw in one of their swell roast beef sandwiches."

"Okay, and the paper towels to sop up the grease. And to keep things kosher, no talk about my work, right?"

"No, ma'am."

Driving in her Saab parallel to the reservoir, the couple let the reasonably clean air in through rolled-down windows. It was a balmy night to make the Chamber of Commerce proud. The palm fronds made their particular overhead music hacksawing in the lax breeze. A comfortable silence took hold of them, neither feeling they had to fill the void to keep the other's interest. Betty Carter's voice played from the dash CD unit, her singular style touchingly precise in its incantations.

Near the Hollywood Memorial Cemetery, perpendicular to the Beth Olem Cemetery containing the bones of Bugsy Siegel, the Saab came to a halt at a light. Up on the sidewalk, a dark-haired chickenhawk lolled against a mailbox. Clad in faded cutoffs and no shirt, he rolled a leg muscle, enticing potential clients.

Monk bit Kodama playfully on the shoulder. "You ever hear of somebody called Fletcher Wilkenson?"

"Is this some kind of kinky game, baby?" Her hand touched the area between his legs.

"Wouldn't think of it in public."

"Prude." She took her hand away and shifted. "The name is familiar, but I'm not sure. Why?"

"He was the most dangerous Lutheran in Los Angeles."

"The deuce you say," she replied, genuinely impressed.

Nine

The road flattened out across an expanse of dirt which abutted a pale green adobe-style house. There was a wide, covered porch partially hidden by spreads of bougainvillaea, box shrubs, and creosote bushes. Rising off to the left from the house was a hillock saturated with various types of ascending growth including cacti, bonsai trees, and corn stalks. Pieces of Spanish tile were missing from the roof, and several cats lazed about, indolently flicking their tails.

None of the felines bothered to move or look at Monk while he approached the porch, walking around an old Scout II parked in the driveway. The ratty screen door swung out, causing several of the cats to become suddenly active.

"Mr. Monk?" The speaker was an older white man clad in work pants, hiking boots, and a black long-sleeved shirt rolled past the elbows. He was of medium build, with a slight paunch creeping over his belt. About an inch taller than Monk, he wore rimless, oval glasses that accentuated his arctic blues. The effect, combined with his neatly combed white hair and white mustache, bestowed a scholarly air on the man. A number of the cats were encircling his legs, meowing and purring to catch the delight of their master.

"Yes. Thanks for seeing me, Mr. Wilkenson."

"Fletcher will do if you don't mind, Ivan."

"Absolutely." The two shook hands, the older man's grasp firm and direct.

The inside of the house was subdued but not gloomy; entering it was like finding a comforting cave, an escape from the heat amidst an expanse of desert. "Here, let me get some shades up. Living alone I cater to my own tastes too much," Wilkenson said pleasantly.

He let some light in to reveal a sparse living room with out-of-date, but serviceable furnishings. Incongruously, there was a well-preserved Persian rug laid over the scuffed hardwood floor, peeking past the edges of the carpet. "Come on back, I was just finishing the dishes."

They went into the kitchen, an old-fashioned number done in white and yellow tiles with cabinets whose doors no longer closed flush. Wilkenson poured Monk a cup of coffee and returned to washing and drying his dishes. "So you read my editorial the other day in the *Times*?" the older man began.

"I did, and wanted to talk with you because frankly I'm stalled on this Rancho Tajuata business." The anxiety in his voice surprised him. The circumstances of the case were closer to him than he cared to admit.

Wilkenson scraped at a piece of dried food on a plate with his fingernail. "You only gave me an overview on the phone—why don't you give me the details?"

By the time Monk had filled the other man in, they were out on the patio, at a round table of sun-bleached oak, seated on matching hard-backed chairs. Dropping away from the patio a thick grouping of apricot trees descended the hill. Beyond the grove more houses sat on the other hills that made up the Mount Washington area. And in the distance could be seen the edifices of downtown L.A. A sheet of brown air hung like dirty laundry between the houses and the skyscrapers.

Wilkenson had listened carefully, asking questions at several intervals. "Why do you want to go on with this, Ivan?" he asked at the end of the recap. There was melancholy in his voice.

"I like to think it's not just ego," he answered frankly, thinking about a similar conversation he'd had with Kodama. "But there is something about getting fired for screwing up which really rides my mule, as my dad used to say."

"I can appreciate that," Wilkenson said noncommittally.

Monk continued. "And particularly since I think I'm on to something with Isaiah Booker."

"His getting comped at the casino, you mean," Wilkenson said.

Monk was impressed with the older man's attention to the pertinent facts. He reminded him of Dexter Grant, the ex-cop he'd gotten his PI license under. "That's right."

"You may have something at that," Wilkenson observed. "The casino is owned by one of the men who got me fired, H. H. DeKovan." A grandfatherly smile lifted his full mustache. "From the look on your face, I guess you didn't know that?"

"I came to see you because of what you wrote in your op-ed piece, about your past association with the Rancho."

"And maybe I could be your entrée back into the Taj?" Wilkenson said guilelessly.

"You've busted me," Monk admitted good-naturedly.

Wilkenson shifted his gaze toward the pall and what lay behind it. "As I said in the commentary, I was one of the regional directors of the Housing Authority from the mid-fifties through the sixties." He paused, propping his arms on the table and leaning forward. "The Rancho, the planned projects at Chavez Ravine, Nickerson Gardens, and the others"—he waved his hand in no certain direction—"were to be our experiments in urban interracial living."

"The rap they used against you was your ties to the Civil Rights Congress," Monk recited from the passage he'd found on-line about Wilkenson last night. "Not only did the Congress have Communist Party members and other progressives as its members—"

"But I was a fellow traveler," Wilkenson finished, "not just some liberal dupe. The CRC was a successful coalition of blacks and whites who stood against police brutality and housing restrictions, and which regularly observed Negro History Week. Hell," he went on as he got up and headed toward the kitchen, "what really got in Yorty and Parker's craw was the Eugene O'Neill and Countee Cullen plays we'd do down in the projects with interracial casts."

Through the open back door, sounds of cabinet drawers opening and closing could be heard. This faded out but presently Wilkenson returned with a tray containing a pitcher of orange juice, two glasses, and a thick 10" × 13" envelope.

He set the items on the table, and poured them each a glass.

"Your memoirs." Monk tipped his full glass at the packet.

"The truth as I experienced it or, at least, the past as I reconstructed it." Wilkenson settled into his chair, a benign look on his open features.

"Not to be selfish, but how does this help me?" Monk asked, a lightness in his voice.

"Even nonfiction books need a solid ending, comrade Monk. You agree to give me that, supply information for my book, and I'll see what I can do about getting you plugged back into the Rancho. I'm still in touch with a few of the old-timers there. It'll be in my interest to see you finish the job." The older man quaffed a good portion of his glass, winking at Monk over the rim.

Monk eased the manuscript out of the oversized envelope. "City of Promise: A Slightly Red Memoir of L.A." was typed on the title page. There were some five hundred pages to the work. "Before I agree, I'd like to take this home and skim through it." He hefted the pages.

"I want you to. There may be something there in the past you'll find of use in this current situation."

"Which leads me back to this DeKovan you mentioned. Who was he?"

"Is—he's still around. Though I understand he's taken to more of the hermit lifestyle these days. Harwick Henri DeKovan got his start in garter belts and seamed nylons. Actually, it was a business his father began. There were rumors back then the old man had some doing with black market pharmaceuticals in Italy and France after the Second World War, but such is not the topic at hand."

"For another time over small takes of whiskey," Monk said, warming to the older man's style.

Wilkenson touched his forehead with two fingers and extended them in a mock salute. "The younger DeKovan had a feel for things to come. He invested some of the hosiery profits in would-bes that seemed too odd to be understood by the money makers of yesterday."

"Like?" Monk asked with interest.

"Fast-food joints, plastic trash bags, aluminum cans.

Stuff that from today's perspective make sense, but in the early sixties were iffy propositions.''

''A visionary.''

''A capitalist visionary,'' Wilksenson said, bitterness tainting his voice for the first time. ''DeKovan was a wheel in the Merchants and Manufacturers Consortium. It doesn't exist now, but in those days they had offices in the Richmond Oil Building. Which also ain't around these days. DeKovan, the mayor, and some others had a significant meeting some months after the riots. It finalized the course of this city.''

''When was this, Fletcher?'' The orange juice in his hand felt heavy.

''Nineteen sixty-six, the spring after Watts went up on that godawful hot August eleventh in sixty-five. I have a chapter in the book about the meeting. I've written it partly through speculation based on what I know about the participants, and partly from an eyewitness account. Kind of a Capote approach à la *In Cold Blood*.'' He smiled like a papa with new twins.

''And you've kept up with DeKovan's activities.''

''Research,'' he clipped.

Monk wasn't going to pursue the matter. He needed Wilkenson to get him back into the Rancho. ''I'll call you in a couple of days after I've looked your writings over, and we'll talk.''

Wilkenson was sitting rigid in his chair, his hands lying fallow in his lap. The big buildings out there seemed to be leering at him. ''That'll be fine.'' Abruptly, he got up and walked Monk to his car. ''Seems the Rancho never lets me go. Not a year's gone by since I was driven out of the Housing Authority that the Taj hasn't called me back for one reason or another.''

''An albatross?''

"A duty." Wilkenson clapped him on the shoulder and waved him off. Driving away, Monk watched the former bureaucrat trudge up his hillside arboretum with a watering can. A trover in baggy pants.

That night, Monk decided not to start "City of Promise" from the beginning. Instead he read the chapter Wilkenson had written about the historic meeting that took place after the Watts Riots since, frankly, it sounded so juicy.

The traffic down below on Sixth Street was audible through an open window at the end of the polished hallway, brilliantly viridian in the failing light. Los Angeles Mayor Sam Yorty felt his stomach gurgling thick and gooey like air pumped through melted Velveeta. He stepped from the elevator, his two bodyguards before him. Goddamn Cardinal McIntyre always insisting on rare steaks at the Pacific Dining car for their charity prayer lunches. Just like a goddamn Irishman to be contrary, even after he'd suggested to him to vary the menu.

"You guys stay put," the short, going-to-stout mayor ordered his men. "And for God's sake, Markham, don't you go chasing any big-hipped red-lipped secretaries who come sauntering along."

Markham, the tall ex-investigator for the D.A., looked recalcitrant but said nothing.

"Letting that goddamn Examiner *reporter in like you did last time," Yorty mumbled as he unlatched the rosewood doors to the boardroom on the twelfth floor of the black, art deco Richfield Oil Building with its gold chevron, spiral and frond fretwork. "That's why I brought a good German boy like Miller along to watch you," the mayor finished as the door swung shut on his bouncy frame.*

Yorty groaned again as his stomach bubbled with force, and again at the sight of that high-horse-riding and always ahead-of-time Police Chief William Parker. You could tell the cocksucker was tight; he'd noticed the number of double bourbons he'd knocked back at the luncheon. He was also sagging in his skin from the heart surgery he'd had last October.

"Chief," Yorty said, almost screwing up the word with a laugh he had to suppress.

Parker gave the mayor a half-salute. A quick, mocking gesture Yorty assumed was lost on no one else in the room. He eased into a chair on the opposite end, toward the rear of the room, away from Parker. Yorty poured some water from one of the offered decanters and drained the cup greedily.

Thompson McCain and Elias Toombs entered. Both men were members of the Golden State Realty Association. Each of them was dressed in a crisp double-breasted grey suit. Toombs's suit was a bluer slate than his chunky associate's. On Toombs, the cut of the cloth fell away gracefully from his Greek statue shoulders. As they sat down next to each other, Yorty once more had to hide a laugh. In the file that Parker had shown him, there were several mat prints of a swim-suited McCain with his head between the spread legs of the naked and muscular Toombs. The shots were blurry, but the intent was clear.

"Mr. Mayor," McCain greeted him, fingering the chain mail loop on one of his gold cuff links.

"How's the game?" Yorty asked him, knowing the show-off would only have something good to say about himself.

"Shot a twelve over par on Monday at Wilshire," McCain reported in an impersonal teletype voice that masked his vanity.

"Now that things are starting to calm down," Yorty

replied in his nasal twang, *"I'll see if we can get a foursome going again."*

"I look forward to it." He gave his boyfriend a look the mayor of Los Angeles couldn't interpret. Yorty took in the rest of the room. He nodded to several members of the M & M Consortium seated about the large oval table. All save one of them had been contributors to his last campaign. The holdout, the one who hadn't shown yet, was that dimestore libertarian, Harwick DeKovan.

Naturally, the smooth cocksucker had managed to get himself elected president of the M & M in the beginning of the year. Yorty knew from past experience he'd make his appearance after everyone else was in the room. Sure as shit, Yorty was working on his second glass of water when the rear door to the boardroom swung inward and DeKovan glided in like a preening swan.

He was dressed in one of those Botany 500 sleek-silhouette numbers favored by pretty-boy actors like Tony Curtis, Yorty reflected bitingly. DeKovan augmented his suit with a blue shirt, a gold collar stay, and a black silk tie and matching pocket square. Yorty realized he was staring at DeKovan too much. He knew Parker was watching him, had seen him stop drinking his water to assess the fine dresser. Well, he reasoned, maybe Parker didn't mind not taking care of himself, but Yorty could remember a time when he used to animate a set of clothes as DeKovan did. Okay, he didn't have his height, but he'd always fantasized himself in his early days as a compact, George Raft kind of guy.

"Gentlemen, given the onset of evening, may I offer something stouter than water?" DeKovan held his six-foot-plus frame in the doorway, one hand on each knob. His pale eyes flitted over the gathered, a baron taking stock of the nobles under his sway.

"You okay, Bill?" Yorty said, digging at Parker. This was May, and the chief was scheduled to return to work in June. But the operation, and the heavy shots he'd grown accustomed to after years in the top spot, had ravaged the once-dynamic man.

"Fine," the chief laconically managed. His hand was gripping the crown of his cap, pushing it back and forth on the table in short strokes like someone getting his arm ready for a shuffleboard match.

"Have a seat, H.H.," McCain intoned flatly. "Let's save the drinks for after the meeting, and see if we indeed have something to celebrate."

"As you say, Tommy." DeKovan made sitting down look like a command performance.

Yorty, smiling, patted the side of his greying, but still wavy hair. McCain couldn't abide his blue-blood name being butchered.

"Yeah, I've got to be out in Gardena by six," Parker growled. "I got a speech to do before the Satozo Block Club Association."

"Maybe you should take Lindsey with you," one of the Merchants and Manufacturers reps cracked. Over a cigar he was lighting he added, "Bad as he likes Oriental pussy, you might have to take that little bastard in handcuffs, Bill." That brought a round of laughter, except from Toombs, who looked uncomfortable.

DeKovan allowed a proper pause for the guffaws then raised his hand imperiously for attention. "Alright, this is one more in a series of these meetings the committee has had since the unpleasantness in Watts several months ago." A few more laughs punctuated his statement.

Before DeKovan could continue, the hallway door opened, and a medium-built, bespectacled man with a jiggling stomach entered, handling a thick file folder. He was wearing a plain suit with a checkered bow tie. "Apologies, apologies," he rushed out, taking a seat near Yorty. "Mr. Mayor," the hurried man acknowledged.

The mayor nodded briefly at the newcomer. He had a suspicion who he was, seems he'd met him somewhere recently.

"We had just begun," DeKovan said for the benefit of the late arrival. "In case everyone here doesn't know him, I'd like to introduce Davis Shaw, producer of the 'Mannion Forum' radio program."

There were the requisite hellos, and Yorty watched Parker for his reaction. The chief grunted something but otherwise made no other sound, nor did he turn his head in Shaw's direction. Parker was a frequent guest on the show, a program sponsored by the Birchers. Especially in the weeks after the riot last summer, Parker had stepped up his rhetoric about outside agitators and Mao-spouting intellectuals as the instigators of the burnings.

"So the Committee of Interests has been meeting and mapping out various strategies in the wake of this"— DeKovan waved vaguely in a southerly direction—"and other matters. Last December, with some discreet input from us, and of course the, how shall I say, camisado participation of the chief—a recovering chief, I emphahsize—the December 1965 McCone Commission report offered a palatable version of the causes of the Watts riot."

"Yeah, it blamed the coons for causing the ghetto," the man puffing out cigar smoke cackled.

Unfazed, DeKovan went on over soft laughter. "This summer our city will be hosting the fifty-eighth annual governors' conference. A little more than a year ago, it looked as if Pat Brown was a given for reelection as governor. Now, following the riots—and the handy defeat *of Roosevelt's son by our mayor to retain his post—the continued regime of the liberal Brown seems precarious.*

"I start with the long view to zero in on the particular. The hot winds of last August have been sniffed by the patricians of the Valley, and they don't like the way the wind is blowing."

"Now we're getting to it," Parker groused.

"Yes we are, Chief," DeKovan placated. *"With our aid, and the aforementioned anxiety from the homeowners and parents who were in World War II or Korea, we can foresee a conservative rise. Indeed, specific to our interests, we can predict an ushering in of a business-friendly climate."*

"But we have to give them preachers and professional Negro agitators something," Yorty said irritably. Goddamn DeKovan always had to belabor the obvious. *"With them kow-towing, or at least satisfied that changes are happening, they become the political buffer against the rock throwers and mau maus.*

"And don't you all forget," he added, pointing east, *"down here across the Fourth Street Bridge, them Mexicans are taking note. This instability isn't confined to just Watts."*

"The Black Panthers have already opened an office on Central Avenue," Davis Shaw blurted with impatience like a hyperactive child. *"We have unimpeachable documentation that proves they're receiving $4,000 a month from the Soviet Politburo."* Shaw started to assemble some papers from his file.

"We'll get to that in its proper time, Davis," DeKovan said, eyeing the Bircher hard.

He heard, but continued to collate his *"facts."*

"Anyway," DeKovan continued, *"as the mayor has reminded us, we're here today to map out the next steps for the following four months. For as we know, not only*

is there a continuing yammering from the likes of those living south of the Coliseum, there's the incessant demand from the members of the Johnson Administration to have some of these New Deal/Great Society policies implemented in Los Angeles.''

''I don't give a rusty fuck what bone we throw the wooly-heads or the beaners.'' Parker reared back in his chair, his face an unhealthy hue from anger and alcohol and sickness. ''I got my ass over here today to tell all of you there's some heads to be put on the spike in front of City Hall if we're going to make sure things don't get out of hand again.''

''But we have to be subtle,'' Toombs warned.

Parker snorted. ''Like you, huh?''

Toombs's face became wood, his hatred for the man evident. ''Everyone here doesn't think like you, Parker. Some of us actually believe there's some valid issues raised by responsible negro leaders like Bayard Rustin.''

''You would use him for an example,'' the man with the cigar piped in, snickering.

DeKovan made a cutting gesture with the flat of his hand in the manner of John Kennedy as he talked. ''Nonetheless, Mr. Toombs is on point. We want what's good for business and the law wants order. Conversely, pragmatic negro leadership knows change will come, but it has to come at a pace to accommodate the will of the majority. They, like us, also realize as business blossoms, so do opportunities for black workers in blue-collar, factory situations and public sector employment. And many of this deliberate leadership agree that progress will only happen by excising this radical element. An element that ultimately holds the negros' aspirations back while advancing a foreign philosophy antithetical to their culture.''

''Wilkenson,'' Parker barked.

"*Easy, Bill,*" Yorty soothed mockingly.

"*Fletcher Wilkenson,*" DeKovan echoed. "*Somehow, Mr. Wilkenson escaped the spotlight during the realignment of forces that took place here in the late fifties when our friends in the real estate concerns helped get the good mayor elected.*" DeKovan made sure the gathered saw his pale orbs float in the direction of Parker, then back to center.

The LAPD chief, beads of whiskey sweat collecting on his temple, hadn't missed the slight. "*Wilkenson was small potatoes in those days. A greenhorn college boy who was little more than a file clerk.*"

"*So was Hiss, before he became head of the Carnegie Foundation,*" McCain reminded everyone.

"*Exactly,*" DeKovan interjected, forestalling further verbal tangents. "*The reality of 1966 finds Fletcher Wilkenson as a regional manager in the Housing Authority. He's got an office down in the Rancho Tajuata Housing Projects not five miles from this boardroom.*"

"*Sumabitch's been all over the place since the riots,*" Cigar Man said derisively. "*Cover of* Look, *interviews with goddamn Walter Cronkite, debating Joe Pine—hell, making Pine seem like a loon on his own radio show. All the time talking about changes he wants to institute in the public housing program in bettering the status of poor people. On-site job training centers, vouchers to encourage hillbillies down in Maywood and Bell to come live there in interracial harmony. Goddamn,*" the man finished, as if the very notion of such a thing was blasphemy.

"*He's also taken members of gangs and put them to work in various projects.*" Shaw leaned forward earnestly. "*He's got coloreds and Mexicans painting and plastering in a couple of those projects like they were meant to be working together. And afterwards, he has them attending classes at these projects supposedly for reading and writing and discussion of community issues.''* Shaw spat out the words like a bad taste. *"But it's really indoctrination sessions like King's Southern Christian Leadership Conference did down South.''*

Toombs said, *"Not all of his ideas come out of Moscow or Peking. Hell, I've heard some of you talk about instituting similar efforts after the riots. Harwick here''*— he pointed at the sharp-dressed man—*"has talked about the need to train workers for the future to stay ahead in the world marketplace.''*

"And I stand by that,'' the other man emphasized. *"The question is, can we tolerate a crimson pirate like Wilkenson being in the position to raid our ideas, twist them, and get credit for them?''*

The sepulchral smiles on the men's faces provided the answer.

"Then what's the plan?'' the Merchants and Manufacturers representative asked, stubbing out his smoked cigar.

"Graham Greene wrote, 'Any victim demands allegiance.' Wilkenson is popular, inside and outside of Los Angeles. His removal must be seen as a desire on his part to go. Our hand in this must, by necessity, be nigh invisible.''

Shaw erupted excitedly. *"Through our media contacts, we can leak his membership in Communist front organizations, the Civil Rights Congress, his board position with the ACLU, and his strident support of school integration.''*

Yorty disliked—and distrusted—eager overachievers. His climb had been steady, if somewhat distracted in his brief fling as a New Dealer in the thirties. Sure, he aligned himself with the right crowd, rode the strong horse to ford the too-often dangerous waters of big-city politics. He'd done alright for himself since those hardscrabble times growing up in Nebraska. He spoke for the whites who'd worked hard to be part of the God-fearing, mortgage-paying, middle-class Valley stock. His own group, the Lydia Homeowners Association, were a concrete example of his aspirations and fears.

The Birchers may have their use, but to his Midwestern soul, they were just a bunch of armchair conspiracists who'd never had to dig an aqueduct or weld mufflers to make ends meet. And what if he took a helicopter to work now and then, or headed out after lunch to his "retreat" apartment on the Strip? Hadn't he earned such perks? Hadn't he stared down the professional negro agitators and Che Guevera–spouting long-hairs? Los Angeles was a provincial city, and under his watch it would remain so. He was the one standing between order and chaos, he was the one holding all these forces together; Sam Yorty was doing the thankless task no one else would or could do.

"Is that right, Mr. Mayor?" DeKovan was saying.

"Yes, Harwick, we need to apply the pressure on the back end against Wilkenson," Yorty opined, not having missed the flow of the conversation. "We move on him, and at the same time institute some safe, measured programs to keep things happy below Crenshaw, and we've got a successful formula.

"But"—and Yorty rose for attention—"it's important we ring in the colored moderates to endorse these programs. They have a stake in this too. They want calm like we do. Those are the people we can work with in the black community. Those are the cool heads who know the course is slow, but their ship will dock one day."

The men in the room gave the diminutive mayor

questioning looks. His sincere expression squelched rejoinders.

"Not to mention you might help them with a federal grant or two. Next to sniffing after white poon tang, there's nothing like feeding off Johnson's tit for some of these Cadillac-drivin' bos," Cigar Man added sagely.

"Wilkenson's not the only wild card we'll need to deal with down in the dark side of town. You got some bleeding heart allies," Yorty cautioned. "Just look at that New York writer Schulburg going down to Watts and opening up a writers camp or some such thing. That free expression shit is the kind of thing that leads to these younger bucks inciting others with that Zulu, bushy-haired poetry, how bad Mr. Charley is, and all that hoorah."

"He's just doing that because he still feels bad about ratting out his little Hollywood Commie pals to that faggot Cohn," Parker observed coldly, slightly shifting his bloated face toward Toombs, who remained placid.

"And we have documented files that the Watts Writers Workshop is a front for radical thought that is luring susceptible white girls, free-love types for the most part, to join up with them," Shaw remarked, the fear palpable in his voice.

Yorty felt like slapping the paranoid, ass-kissing bastard. "Chief, it seems Wilkenson is in your bailiwick at this point." He sat down. Deferring to that shifty Parker was a political pill he'd learned to tolerate, even if he always found the swallowing bitter.

A kind of sobriety mutated the color in the head cop's face. He sat erect, finally stopping with the business of pushing his cap back and forth. "Wilkenson's got his pious dick in more than one doorjamb over the years." A predatory glee modulated his voice. "My G-2 has got a couple of file folders on the life and loves of this gee. Going back to the days when he was studying for the ministry back in the synod with the Lutherans.'' He snickered, adding, ''It doesn't surprise me he was spawned from those reprobates.''

''This isn't a battle between your Vatican and his church. Nor is this Missouri, Chief,'' DeKovan needlessly reminded him.

''But illegal in Missouri is illegal in California, Harwick,'' Parker replied, baring crooked teeth. He waved a hand derisively. ''But we got something on him from here,'' he said and jabbed his blunt finger on the table. ''I'll have a couple of my men go over to see him. Thursdays and Fridays he's at his field office at the Rancho, seeing to the needs of his flock.''

''Not patrol officers, I presume,'' DeKovan intoned. He leaned into the intercom and ordered a tray of drinks to be brought in. ''This matter is too sensitive for some of your wetback-beating recruits from Alabama to go around taking care of.''

Parker had his hat back on, his head lowered and tucked down like a ram getting ready to charge. ''Don't you concern yourself, Mr. DeKovan.'' The words were shoved out with confidence. ''I passed the bar when you were still figuring out which silver spoon you were going to dip into your mushed peas that day. I got just the two detectives to handle this. Homicide boys, they work out of Southeast.''

''The Rancho's in the Rampart Division,'' McCain corrected.

''But Wilkenson knows these two. Remember, he also has an office down in Nickerson in Watts. This pair met him when they worked a murder down there. It'll go smoother if these two do it. Grant and Jakes know the score.''

*   *   *

Monk read the last paragraph again, saying the names of the detectives out loud. He put aside the sheet of paper from the manuscript Wilkenson had passed along to him the other day. Skimming through the next chapter, Monk read how Wilkenson described the encounters he'd had with Parker's envoys. One he described as a silk suit–wearing plainclothesman who wore a squared-up pinky ring. He'd favored a thin mustache—which attested to some odd position he'd enjoyed, as facial hair of any kind was verboten in those days under Parker.

That would have been Perry Jakes, alright. Monk had run into the man several times when he'd gone to work for his old friend. He read further.

The bigger cop, Grant, smelled like Old Spice and displayed a less serious suit than his partner. Jakes's was meticulously tailored; Grant had barely taken the trouble to get the cuffs and hems done when he'd bought it off the rack at Silverwoods. Jakes sat on the edge of Wilkenson's desk. He worked a toothpick between his side teeth. Outside, the sounds of children enjoying a water balloon fight could be heard through the open transom.

"We got to tell you the bad news, Fletch," the nattily dressed cop said with mock remorse. "Downtown says you're holding up progress. Downtown says you need to get your head on right, catch me?" The pencil mustache went up, revealing more of his too white teeth. He looked at his partner. "Ain't that so, Dex?"

"Sure is," the other man said, looking stern.

There Wilkenson took the narrative out of the third-person re-creation of the past and segued into first-person recollections. Monk stopped reading and stood up from his desk. He dialed Wilkenson but got no answer, not even a machine. Then he paced, a worrisome feeling winding him up. He picked up the phone again to call Grant, to berate him, to demand his teacher refute the old leftist's claim, but he ran out of energy and will. He didn't think Wilkenson was making it up. Nor did he want to know the truth.

Monk replaced the handset, put his feet up on the desk, and didn't do anything for some time.

Ten

It was a drive he'd done repeatedly, like sleepwalking. This time the effort seemed to drain him more each mile he took from L.A. Eventually he pulled the Ford off the 15 and found his way to Dexter Grant's house in Lake Elsinore out in Riverside County. It was a tidy ranch-style home with faded wood slats, windows with shutters loose on their hinges, and a dusty stone portico. Grant's prime deuce and a quarter, a '67 Buick Electra, was in the driveway. The hood was up, the ex-cop's arms were working on the innards.

His silver-white hair was uncombed, and a couple of days' growth canvased his creased features. "Ivan," he greeted warmly, looking up from the solenoid he was screwing onto the inside of the fender.

"Dex." Monk looked over at the house. The wood screen door still needed to be reframed, and the rain gutter off the front was twisted like a huge stick of licorice. He looked back at the Electra. It was showroom sweet.

"What brings you out?" Grant pushed back a clump of

hair with the edge of a greasy hand. The name tag on his overalls read: SAL.

"Ghosts."

"Huh?"

Monk pushed out his bottom lip, circling Grant like an uneasy wrestler.

"What the hell is with you, Ivan?"

"Fletcher Wilkenson and the Rancho Tajuata."

Grant had been cleaning his hands with a rag, but he stopped working it when Monk quit moving. A blue jay flitted onto a maple whose lush branches overhung the driveway. The bird made rustling sounds prowling through the foliage as the two men faced each other. "The Rancho," the older man echoed. He looked at his hands.

"How come you never told me about it, Dex?"

"What was I going to tell you, Ivan?" Grant mouthed. He threw the rag onto the Buick, walking away from the car at a clip. He went around back, whacking the back door open with a jerk of his hand. Monk followed, anger and disappointment welling up in him like a fever.

Grant snatched open the beat Frigidaire and plucked out a bottle of Beck's. He popped the cap and began drinking. Monk stood in the doorway, waiting. Grant finished the beer, chucked the empty into the sink, and retrieved another one. He sat heavily at the kitchen table, his arms resting on the red-checked plastic covering. His hands, their knuckles the size of quarters, bracketed the bottle. "That was so goddamn long ago," he rationalized.

"It doesn't change what was done." Monk said as he leaned against the cracked tile counter. "And getting tanked at two in the afternoon won't cover it over either."

"Drinking never hurt no one," Grant sneered sarcastically. He massaged the middle of his forehead with the heel of his hand. "It's not fuckin' simple as right and crooked,

Ivan. You know that.'' An imploring cast settled on his face. ''What do you want to know? How Yorty and Parker had a hard-on to get rid of Wilkenson? How me and Perry had to carry their water like a coupla Gunga Dins?'' Grant drowned his own words while guzzling beer. He tilted his head back and killed the contents.

Monk said, ''I want to know why, Dex. I want to know why you had to be the one to do the deed.''

Grant hitched the chair around in his accuser's direction. His arms made motions. ''And what, Ivan? Make a hero of myself and get busted back to patrol for insubordination? Or better, get assigned to Thad Brown's command. That's where all the fuck-ups found themselves. All the on-duty drunks, the burnouts, and the assholes who could only get their shield 'cause their father made contributions to Yorty's campaign.'' A defensive shame contorted his face as he blinked at Monk.

''What else, Dex? What else don't I know about your time as a cop?''

''You mean what else will embarrass you?'' his friend countered. ''Is this about me making atonement or you making sure the untarnished rep of the proletarian peeper ain't dirtied by the old cracker he used to work for?''

''Ain't nothing wrong with a little integrity, Dex.''

Grant's arm shook as he pointed at Monk. ''Don't you come into my house and play the padre, Ivan. You know too goddamn well I at least kept black suspects from getting the go-round from clowns down at the Seventy-seventh Precinct when I was working out of there. You know goddamn well I caught hell for my views when the lines were being drawn when Bradley ran against Yorty in '69.''

''Swell. That makes you a vicar compared to the gents Parker cultivated.''

''It's so easy for you to pass sentence on me, isn't it?''

Grant was getting to his feet, his voice also rising. "You ain't never been in that kind of situation."

"This going to be the wife, kids, and mortgage bit," Monk replied bitterly.

"You fucking right it is, Ivan. Here you are pushing forty, living in a house that belongs to your old lady. What do you have tucked in the bank? Three, four thousand maybe? Your only asset the donut shop."

Grant went around the opposite side of the table, putting distance between him and Monk. "Well, what did I have, man? Then I had about thirteen years on the force, a second marriage, and two young daughters. A man's got responsibilities, Ivan. It's not like I took some Mexican kid down below the Gage off ramp and gave him a correcting lesson."

"Shit, Wilkenson wasn't no kid; he knew the deal. He was just a casualty of war."

"The Cold War."

"Nothing that sophisticated, not like you mean it. But yeah, that was part of it. But I'm talking about the war that's always gone on in L.A. Over school integration, housing, where the jobs were, where the money got spent. This ain't right news to you, Ivan."

"Like it isn't right news the cops danced to the monied boys' tune. Were you in DeKovan's pocket?"

Satisfaction gleamed on the other man's sweating face. "That's what you really want, me to be some bent bastard you got the goods on. Somebody you can feel superior about."

"No."

"Bullshit, I can hear it in your voice."

"You're ducking the question," Monk countered.

Grant suddenly got hot again. "I don't have to justify my existence to you, Ivan. I didn't for my two wives."

"I guess that's why they're exes."

Grant's body became rigid and his mouth and eyes were straight lines. ''Take you and the horse that don't shit you rode in on and get the fuck out of my house.''

''Sure, boss.'' He opened the refrigerator and gently placed another Beck's on the table. ''Have some more, but it still won't wash away the answer.'' He turned and left by the back door.

Grant, sitting sullenly at the kitchen table, silently watched him go, a sentinel enveloped by the sins of the city he was supposed to guard against. He backhanded the unopened beer onto the floor.

Eleven

"Oh hell." Kodama put down her glass of wine.

Monk had another mouthful of chicken satay. He alternated looking at the tablecloth and chewing slowly.

She reached across and touched his hand. "Everyone's got something chasing them, Ivan. None of us are chaste."

He held onto her fingers, massaging their tips. "Should I be looking for the secrets you got locked away?"

"You can try," she teased.

He let go of her hand and ate again in silence for a while. "You think I'm making too much of this?"

"It's not for me to say how you and Dex should deal with this," she managed evasively.

"I don't mind giving you my opinion about your troubles with Jamboni."

"No, you don't," she responded pointedly.

Monk poked his tongue in the side of his mouth and sampled his wine. "Well, goddamnit, what would you do?"

"About Jamboni?"

"Don't be cute."

"I can't help it, baby. What's there to do, Ivan?" she asked rhetorically, changing her tone. "Make Dex crawl over glass and bricks for his transgressions? I mean, it's not like you haven't been known to do what's expedient on occasion." She leaned back, enjoying her Chablis.

"I stand accused," Monk acknowledged. "But that's because there was a greater good."

"The same might hold true for Dex. It was the best he could do given the situation."

"What was the trade-off?"

"For Dex or for the Rancho?" Her voice was clear, her eyes unyielding in the smokey light of La Faucon, the Burmese-French restaurant on the outskirts of Monterey Park, a city referred to as the Chinese Beverly Hills, given the influx of striving immigrants and Asian-Americans.

"He saved his ass, Jill. There ain't nothing else to it."

"I read that part in Wilkenson's manuscript. But he also states later this DeKovan made good on his promises. He financed the construction and supplied the staffing of the job training center."

"Ingot Limited." Monk visualized the citation inside the now useless shell of the center.

"So you did read more."

"Not exactly. When I first went to see Fletcher Wilkenson, he told me briefly about DeKovan, the Merchants and Manufacturers Consortium, and the rest. After I saw him, I talked with Henry Cady, a longtime resident. He said the construction of the center was some kind of public/private arrangement; federal money covered the continued overhead. DeKovan's company bought the land the center was on in eighty-one—it was belly-up by then, the Reagan years you know—in a lease back arrangement. Then he sold it off to some recycling company as far as he could tell. Not too much later this outfit went bankrupt before it could set up its recycling plant.''

Monk bit on an end of his chopstick with his front teeth as if attacking prey. ''But it was in reading that part of Fletcher's manuscript I learned of Dex's little, ah, ethical indiscretion.''

Kodama plucked a clump of broccoli and a sliver of beef off her plate with her chopsticks and worked the pieces in her mouth. She finished and answered him. ''Wilkenson states that he got a call from DeKovan when he first told Dex and his partner Jakes to go to hell. See, if you hadn't been so worked up, you would have known that.''

''You got me, prof.'' Monk's teeth glistened.

''Anyway, Wilkenson recounts how DeKovan knows he's been trying to get the job center set up, and all the roadblocks to getting it done, how can he help.''

''At best that makes him a rich, condescending, noblesse oblige prick. Really, it means DeKovan was the grand master, Jill. Dex and Jakes his puppets.''

''Dex is the one who told DeKovan about the plans for the center.'' She kept a steady gaze on him.

''Wilkenson say that?''

''No, I called Dex and asked him. Or rather it came up.''

Monk put down his chopsticks. ''So you are a meddler.''

''I stand accused.'' She extended her arms at ninety degrees and bowed slightly.

''So Dex knew DeKovan was a limousine liberal. I'm sure as a way to assuage his own guilt he threw that bone to the rich boy.'' Monk did a passing imitation of Grant's coarse baritone. ''See, Fletch, everybody wins. Sure you gotta make a sacrifice, but the Rancho gets the center you want, and, well . . .''—he used his own voice—''you get the shaft, baby.''

''You should ask him,'' she said confidently.

"Maybe I'll go to the source."

"Do so, my dear." She worked her sticks, raking more steamed rice onto her plate.

"You're so hep on my situation, huh?" Monk smiled knowingly.

"Jamboni and me is not the same thing, Ivan."

"Really," he said through a sigh.

"Yeah." Her head thrust forward with a bull elephant's brashness.

Monk let moments tick by before he spoke. "It's about unfinished business, Jill. It's about do we let bastards like DeKovan and the assistant D.A. set the agenda or do we."

Kodama's eyes glittered with a quality Monk couldn't identify. He suddenly felt as if he were drifting in a glossy ether with no point of reference.

"Jamboni wants this to be not just his launching pad into the head D.A.'s seat," she leveled. "There's rumors he isn't even going to waste his time with that if he and his allies get a win by getting me unseated. I understand he's interested in the governorship."

"Your point being."

"I don't want to be part of the opéra bouffe he's staging. I won't be this year's pincushion for the media and the spinmeisters."

"And you'll accomplish that by doing nothing. By sitting it out and letting the system take its course. Or is that, its *toll*?"

"There's no way my decision is going to be overturned. I'm standing on solid case law in California. Several conservative judges have done the same thing I've done."

"To repeat myself, this ain't about facts, Jill, it's about perception. You want logic and reason to prevail, and that's really swell, you know? But you got to work those facts to your advantage, 'cause you can be damn sure Jamboni is going to work overtime on the perception angle.''

"Look, it's not like I don't want to fight to keep my job. And not because I have to be a judge, but because I think I do make a contribution on the bench.''

"Sure, you're right,'' Monk agreed.

"I just don't want this to become''—she hesitated—"out of control, I guess. MFs like Jamboni think judges are just lawyers who couldn't cut it in the marketplace,'' she added self-deprecatingly.

"He's on the public dole too,'' Monk noted.

"But he's got bigger goals, Ivan. I can see it in his insincerity when he gets close to me. He's of the opinion the only reason I ride the pine is because I'm a mediocre lawyer. No guts, no heart.''

"I know different.''

"You're just trying to get in my pants.'' Kodama smiled, wriggling a sliver of chicken between her front teeth.

"That still leads you back to jumping in. But you take the high ground. We set up some interviews for you at various ethnic presses. While the homeowners attempt to mine white anxiety, you build support in the 'hood, and tap what remains of the liberal west side, or wherever the hell it is they moved to. You can talk about that Chinese honors student the cops tried to slam as a gangbanger, and how you lambasted them last year for that.''

A goofy smile twisted Kodama's mouth. "Somewhat self-serving, wouldn't you say?''

"We get the story tactfully leaked,'' Monk conjured.

Kodama laid her chopsticks on her empty plate. "Where do you want to go for coffee?''

Hand-in-hand the two strolled along the refurbished Old Towne section of Pasadena. People thronged about eating cups of frozen yogurt, discussing the latest mile-high salary commanded by the most recent mumbling, moody acting sensation, or stopping to gawk at bald-headed female manikins in clothing store windows wearing studded leather skirts with slits and feathered-ankle work boots.

Kodama moved her hand up and squeezed Monk's arm. "What's the word, thunderbird?"

He kissed her on the forehead. "I was thinking about you."

"Liar."

He chuckled softly. "I was thinking I don't want any more surprises between me and Dex."

"I understand." They walked along, passing by a store with a pyramid-shaped blue canopy over the entrance. A crowd snaked out from the front door, and Monk and Kodama slowed to see what was the attraction.

On a blackened picture window in machinelike gold lettering the name read: VIRTUAL EXCURSIONS.

"I heard about this place," Kodama said, as they stood to the side of the line. "It's a virtual reality salon where you pay for the goggles and a kind of cockpit you sit in to plug into a space trip, a Polynesian beach, or whatever."

"Want to wait and go in?" Monk asked.

Before Kodama could answer, a young white woman in black shorts and cowboy boots who'd been in line pointed at them. "Hey, aren't you the one who let that killer out of jail?"

Monk tightened his hand on Kodama's arm, but she wasn't moving. "I didn't let him out of jail, he's doing his time."

"Yeah, but he, like, raped somebody, right?" She turned her head from looking at the couple to her friend, similarly dressed.

"Didn't he rape the wife and kill the husband?" the misinformed friend added.

"Why don't you two get the case straight?" Kodama admonished.

The friend put her hands on her ample hips. "Well, honey, I'm not the one going around getting murderers off with a little pat on the rear."

"Yeah," the first one jumped in, "you people think you're above the rest of us, with your big expense accounts, and hanging out with people like that Leslie Abramson."

The other one uttered a distasteful "E-uuuuu."

Openmouthed, Kodama stared at the young woman. "What is it you think I do?"

"Huh?" the friend inquired, also openmouthed.

"How is it I was involved in this case you two know so much about?"

"You're the—What do you call it?" the first one rattled, looking at her friend to complete her sentence.

"Defense attorney, right?" the friend offered, looking at others in the crowd for confirmation. "Like the one that got T- Dog, or whatever that rapper calls himself, off for murder."

A visceral snarl of disapproval materialized from the crowd.

"Shit," Kodama bleated, guided forcefully away by Monk.

"At least they didn't think you sold used cars," he quipped, looking back to see if some righteous-minded citizen was bearing down on them. No one was coming; though a few had detached from the pack they didn't travel far. They were like radical cells whose encoding had suddenly been lost in transition from the main stem. The bodies moved about aimlessly, but not forward.

"We were going to get some coffee," Monk reminded her edgily.

Kodama said nothing, staring ahead, lost in another time zone. Warm air coiled around them, embracing stork-limbed palms and tear-shaped cypress trees along a ventricle off the main thoroughfare, Colorado.

In the near distance, another funnel of heat moved off the barren San Gabriel Mountains. Monk only had a sensation of tines of cold working the base of his cortex. They approached a coffeehouse with several people huddled in earnest over caffè lattes and carmel-colored cappuccinos sitting at white lacquered wood tables along the sidewalk. Monk slowed, but Kodama kept on. He fell in step.

"Fuck it, people sometimes get the karma they deserve."

"That's rather profound, my dear," Monk said evenly.

She stopped, her tongue sliding across the tips of her teeth. "You're fucking right it is. It's those kind of dickheads back there that Jamboni and his sycophantic homeowners are playing to."

"That's what I've been saying."

"And you honestly think I can change those kinds of minds?"

"Not change necessarily, but engage the discussion. Plus you know there's always going to be a certain percentage on the sidelines. That's the segment you can sway, Jill. The real truth is, babe, in the era of terrorist bombers getting their manifesto printed in national dailies, everything is the media and how it gets carved up in it."

"So no purity of law? No pursuit of an unfettered balancing of the scales?" She sounded sad.

Monk pulled her close. "There might be; I wouldn't know. What matters is you believe in the pursuit of it, the chance that this thing, this justice, or something like it may be out there.''

She snickered, tugging on the lapels of his sport coat.

''And I know you're too good, too valuable to get pushed aside like an empty bottle,'' he added.

Her hand touched the corner of Monk's trim goatee. ''Kiss me, you fool.''

Twelve

Monk lay on the couch watching a rerun of "Starsky & Hutch" on WGN. Kodama had gotten up early, pumped and focused. He was happy to have been useful getting the judge out of her entropy. They'd stayed up till past two discussing how she would go about launching her counteroffensive, first by calling a friend of hers who worked in public relations for some ideas.

Monk was so elated for her, he managed to avoid thinking about his blowup with Grant. Concentrating as they both were on her situation, she hadn't brought up the ex-cop again either. But once Kodama had departed, he suddenly felt like a gnarled gnome trapped in a house of mirrors. Regardless of which way he turned, he had to face the twisted visage.

Yet putting his mind on his mentor seemed to deplete his resolve. A protective torpor attempted to overtake his psyche. It was much less painful worrying about what was going to happen to Huggie Bear as the bad guys threatened him with knives and crowbars, the two heroes burning

rubber in that ostentatious red and white Torino on their
way to rescue their snitch buddy.

The phone rang as Huggie Bear's apple cap flew off his
head after he was hit upside it.

Monk coughed hello after the third ring.

"Is this Ivan Monk?" the recognizable voice asked.

"Yes, is this Fletcher?"

"That's right. I tried your office, so I thought I'd try the
other number you left me." There was an uncomfortable
silence, then he proceeded. "Have I caught you at a bad
time?"

Monk, aware that Wilkenson could probably hear the
TV going, became embarrassed. Tonelessly, he said, "No,
go ahead, Fletcher."

A gust of hurried breath carried his words over the line.
"Have you heard what happened at the Rancho yesterday?"

"What?" He took a swallow of his tepid coffee.

"Two members of Los Domingos were gunned down in
that little park they hang out in over on Union."

"Payback from the Scalps," Monk concluded unhap-
pily.

"That's the kicker, Ivan. The word is the shooters were
Latinos."

"Another gang moving in?"

"I think it was a message from someone else," the other
man said cryptically. "One of the youths was shot in the
upper thigh, the other much worse—the stomach."

"Christ, what's the kid's prognosis?"

"If he lives, he won't be eating cheeseburgers anymore."

"What the hell's going on, Fletcher?"

By way of a response, he said, "You heard of Jaguar
Maladrone?"

"The boss of the Zacatecas Mob. They've been linked to some sort of smuggling operations as I recall."

"Jaguar called me this morning," Wilkenson said huskily.

"Why'd he call you?" Huggie Bear's plight got shoved to the bottom of his list.

"I used to train him," Wilkenson tendered, as if the explanation would make everything clear.

Thírteen

Somewhere along the drive his left foot fell asleep. It was tingling as if gnats were crawling around inside his skin. The van hit another rut in the road, which only served to remind Monk how badly he wanted to relieve himself.

He estimated he'd been lying on his side, a blanket thrown over his head, for at least two hours. He hadn't bothered to try and raise up since he assumed the two gentlemen in pointed boots and straw cowboy hats were still seated near him. Their semiauto Ingrams handy and greased.

There was a swerve, and Monk's spine slid into the cool metal of the '73 Dodge van's side. More travel, then the wheels squealed to a stop. Words were exchanged in Spanish and one of his guards removed the serape from his head.

"Come on, my friend, the man wants to see you," the friendly face said. It belonged to the one with a deep incision running from his hairline to his eyebrow on the left side of his hide of a face. He was crouching near Monk's prone form, pointing toward the rear swing doors with the barrel of his weapon.

Because the interior was dark, Monk's eyes didn't require readjustment as he sat up, rotating his foot in an effort to get the circulation going. The other straw hat had been sitting up front next to the driver, an individual in a cutoff Levi's jacket and bedecked with arms like the girders on the Terminal Island Bridge. This man looked at Monk unexpressively, one of his eyes clouded over from either disease or past violence.

The one who'd taken the covering off him went out, and Monk scooted after him. The day itself was overcast, and an unblinking Monk found himself standing on ground layered with a chalky dirt. His foot continued to bug him, and he was about to wet himself any minute.

"Hold up, huh," he grunted. He turned, unzipped, and peed near the rear bumper. The two guards looked bored as he did so. The driver was already walking into the house.

The van had parked before a large Spanish Colonial structure done in muted hues of off-yellow trimmed in deep brown. There were bracketed balconies around the second story, and a rooster walked along the fringe of the tiled roof. A satellite dish poked into the air adjacent to a hexagonal turret slotted with rectangular windows running lengthwise. Monk watched the driver disappear under an archway bordered in white and blue tiles.

"Feel better?" the first one asked, again pointing with the barrel. Behind the man in the near distance were power lines, and beyond them the landscape was broken up by low mountains. A few houses were planted here and there in the manner children sprinkle pieces on a Monopoly board.

The three marched into the archway, the rooster looking down at them. Monk self-consciously came down hard on his foot in an effort to get the circulation going. Their brief trek through the house led to a darkened patio with a bench swing suspended by rusting chains. On the swing a fat Siamese lazed, stretching its corpulent body. The animal didn't acknowledge their presence as they passed and entered tall double doors of heavily paneled rosewood with silver ring knockers on each side.

Inside was a circular foyer that opened up to the second floor. Several carvings and paintings hung in the entranceway; Monk recognized an Orozco and a Braque. They looked like originals. The carvings were faces of what he presumed to be ancient gods of some sort in feathered headgear over broad brows and sunken eyes. Off to the left were stairs, but he was led the other way into an area that in other houses would have been the living room.

The room served as the repository for a man in an iron lung machine. The steady whir of the artificial breathing chamber's motor could be heard between the breaks of Santana that came from a stereo unit in a corner. The cylinder was etched with various symbols and designs that Monk took to be either Aztec or Toltec in origin.

The driver sat in a high-backed medieval chair near the machine, reading the Business section. Another man, in a cobalt blue suit and grape-colored shirt, sat in a rocking chair near one of the windows. Outside, the power lines stood like unfathomable metal totems.

"Fletcher says you're straight."

It took Monk a moment to realize the strong and clear voice had come from the man in the machine.

"You're Jokay Maladrone?" he asked, stepping more into the room.

"I used to be." The man laughed.

In the mirror angled over Maladrone's head, which

poked out of the machine like a turtle's head, Monk could see the eyes flick to the side, then settle on his own reflected image again. Following the line of sight, he read a laminated poster on the wall, done in black block lettering printed on aging paper. It was the kind made to be stapled to telephone poles and fences. This piece of preserved history announced a boxing match between Jokay "Jaguar" Maladrone and Terry Wallis at the Olympic Auditorium in 1962.

"Ever see me fight?" Maladrone seemed to ask no one in particular.

"Like lightning in a room, he mowed down everything," the man at the window said, rocking and looking out at the Martian landscape.

The driver didn't join the amen chorus so Monk spoke up. "A little before my time, Jaguar."

The head moved sideways. "Oh, I thought you were one of Fletcher's buddies from the old days. Shit, you're still young enough to get your dick up."

The driver snickered and turned to another page in the newspaper.

"What can I get you to drink?" Maladrone asked. Discordantly, Maladrone's face was healthy looking with its bronze color and the fullness of his cheeks. His eyes were clear and his hair, though greying, was full and combed back from an unwrinkled forehead.

"Water or juice would be fine," Monk responded.

"And a chair too," Maladrone added.

The man in the rocker got up and retrieved another leather and oak medieval-style chair from a row of them under an aquarium sunk into one of the walls. Numerous colorful fish inhabited the darkly lit tank, including koi and cichlids.

The suited man placed the chair near Maladrone's tank and went off to another room.

Monk sat down. Maladrone stared at his mirror. Monk had thought of several questions to ask since Fletcher Wilkenson had called him back to tell him to be at the southeast corner of Soto and First this morning. Wilkenson had been calling around about Maladrone, the kid he used to train in his boxing program. Apparently, when the gang leader contacted Wilkenson he said that he had information about the Cruzado murders, and wanted to know something about Monk. Word was the Zacatecas Mob heard a lot about what went down in the Rancho. Maybe another point he'd get to.

"Why not just tell Fletcher what you knew, Jaguar? Why'd you bring me out to your house?"

"To see if I had to cap you or not," he said easily. The face remained static in the mirror. The driver kept reading the Business section.

The man in the suit returned with a tray stocked with a tall glass of lemonade, a plate of sliced roast beef, Ritz crackers, and some cheddar cheese. A good-sized knife was embedded in the block of cheese. He put these down on a serving cart and rolled it near Monk. The man took his place again in the rocker.

Monk played unfazed and sliced off a portion of cheese and popped it in his mouth. Imperceptibly the driver shifted, the muscles along his arms knotting like molten iron being cast. Calmly, he replaced the knife on the tray.

"I guess I appreciate your invitation even more. At least it wasn't a bullet in the belly."

"At least," Maladrone quipped. "How tight are you and Absalla?"

"You know he fired me." Monk tried the lemonade.

A raspy laugh, the first hint of what had put the former

boxer in the iron lung, escaped from the unsmiling head. "Sure, sure. Then why're you still interested in finding the killers?"

"I don't like getting bounced."

"Or letting go," Maladrone said appreciatively.

"So what have you got, Jaguar?" Monk tore off some roast beef and made a cracker sandwich, munching on it loudly. He figured the best front with this powerful man with the infirm body was to pretend his balls were as big as grapefruits.

"I was born here, in L.A., off of Chicago, near the big hospital, you know?"

Monk nodded.

"At eight my old man left me, my moms, and my two sisters. No particular loss 'cept the weekly beatings from his drunk ass and the paycheck he brought home every two." Maladrone made a clicking noise with his tongue. "Moved to the Rancho after that."

The driver folded up his newspaper, got up, and took some crackers and meat off the plate. He went to sit near the man at the window who continued to rock softly.

"I don't know if you know how it is coming up hard, man, but it tells you something about yourself," Maladrone continued. "Ran with the Furys at eleven, overlord by the time I hit sixteen."

"You must have started to box around then," Monk guessed, thinking about his own serious foray into athletics via high school football.

Maladrone pushed out his bottom lip. "Fletcher was the first white guy I'd met who hadn't raised a baton to my head, or showed up at my mother's door sucking after the payment on the refrigerator. He'd grown up in Boyle Heights and knew more hiding places than me and my boys.'' He quit talking, his eyes flicking back and forth from the mirror to somewhere else.

"He was stand-up, you understand. He really tried with us. Didn't matter they said he was a red and agitator and all that. I didn't see no baby's blood hanging from his teeth or some dude named Boris with a beard and a trenchcoat.''

Monk grinned and said, ''Way I hear it, you were on your way to a sweet little career as a middleweight. But you still walked in the gang life, and got hung up in a robbery of the Olympic. Supposedly you'd planned the rip-off to take place on the night of your title fight.''

Maladrone breathed into his mirror.

''Shit went bad,'' Monk went on. ''Somebody got caught when they were high on glue and ratted. You split to Zacatecas where your mother was from, and where she had gone back to with your sisters. There you were supposed to start a franchise with the Furys. Only you had other plans.''

''Fletcher tell you that?'' The music had stopped, the steady humming of the iron lung's electric motor providing a hypnotic rhythm the fish and the men responded to.

''Yeah,'' Monk said, ''he's still disappointed.''

A flinty look set the other man's face and Monk was worried he'd overdone his bit. The driver was pretending not to look at him and the rocker had stopped moving. For several hot seconds, he was wondering how far and how fast he could get if he ran for the power lines.

''You make choices, you make decisions,'' Maladrone finally breathed. ''The Pandilla Zacatecas grew out of disorganization and misdirection, blood and paybacks over bullshit. I gave it purpose, I gave it heart.''

Even as the machine that gave him life hummed on, thereby reminding all how fragile Maladrone's hold on existence was, Monk had the impression that though his vision was corrupt, it nonetheless sustained him, made him something other than an ill gang chief in an iron lung.

"But the past leads us to this time, this moment," Maladrone said.

Monk was holding two Ritz crackers between his thumb and two fingers as if they were priceless doubloons. He shifted them around as he talked. "What do you want, Jaguar?"

"Peace, my brother." He showed oddly spaced teeth. "What I want—what the organization wants," he quickly corrected, "is order and discipline. The Scalp Hunters and Los Domingos Trece ain't getting with the program, and that's not good for any of us."

"What is good for business?" Monk put down the crackers. The two pieces seemed to rattle louder than possible on the plate.

"This is the goddamn end of the century, Monk. This is about moving forward, moving my people forward together." His head jerked and he said, "See that *traje* over there—he's a fuckin' C.P.A., see? We're about goals and timetables and balance sheets."

"The new mob," Monk said.

"Old story, I know," Maladrone stated flatly, "but new for some of us, eh? No more bullshit drive-bys, popping meth, and eight-ballin'. *Orale*, the millennium is upon us."

"Why am I here, Jaguar?"

"I'm going to give you the murderers." The diaphragm under the machine went up and then down. The rocker squeaked. the driver had started on the Calendar section.

"How do you know who did it?"

"Big Loco saw them."

Monk let that gestate for a while. "If you two are tight, then why did your boys shoot members of his crew after they lit up the Scalp Hunters?"

"You want this, or you want to get in my business?" he said truculently.

"I want it alright. But I also know you're only telling me this because it fits in your plans."

The head said nothing. The eyes flicked in time with the respirator as the man in the rocker rocked. Monk munched on another Ritz. The driver kept reading his newspaper.

"This is about what's good for the Rancho, Monk." Maladrone's etched face, like earth scarred by harsh winters, was solemn.

There was a sincerity in his voice Monk fought hard not to admit. "Who does Big Loco say did it?" Monk said, breaking the impasse.

"Two brothers," the gangster said solemnly. "One's called Junior Blue, and the other works for Absalla."

He wasn't expecting that. "How do you know this is true? And how convenient it is one of the names you give me belongs to a recently killed youngster. By Big Loco's crew in fact."

Maladrone moved his tongue around inside his closed mouth, his eyes clouding. "I didn't realize this Blue was one of the ones killed on Trinity. Anyway, what's in it for him to make it up?" He asked too effortlessly.

"This kind of thing could discredit Absalla, get the Ra-Falcons run out. Wide open territory for you working through Los Domingos Trece."

Maladrone snickered. "You ain't been listening too good, peeper. We ain't about the criminal life these days. We about being on the square. It is our return to what is natural."

"This is the second coming of Tlaloc, the time for fire and harvest," the driver drawled matter-of-factly while he folded his paper to another page.

Monk wasn't sure, but judging from the decor, he had

to believe the name invoked was some Aztec or Maya deity. "So this is about purification?"

"Right on," Maladrone replied earnestly.

Wonderful. Religious fanatic gangsters. "So you believe Big Loco?"

"He knows better than to lie to me," Maladrone warned.

Or to disobey, Monk ruminated. "And you want me to be the one who does something with this knowledge?" He couldn't shake the impression the gang chief's velvet trap was starting to unfold just for him.

"It would be better if it's a black who does it, yes?" Maladrone declared. "Absalla would be compromised if he knew this. He has too many pressures, too many he has to appease. But you, the outsider, could move on this, and maybe in such a way as not to jam up the Muslim."

Maladrone's empathy for Absalla surprised Monk. Maybe it was religious fealty, or maybe one more way to hook Monk into an intricate plot. He ate another piece of cheese. "Who's supposed to be the other hitter?" he finally managed.

"Eddie Waters, one of the sergeants in the Falcons," Maladrone said.

He remembered hearing the name before, but couldn't put a face to it. "So I'm supposed to go after him?"

"We have interests that benefit each other."

"I'm not looking to cleanse my soul."

"Is that right?" Maladrone asked skeptically.

The driver got up and came to stand near the two. Monk gazed at the symbols on the iron lung. Was it technology or an otherworldly power keeping Maladrone going? Or did it matter, as long as he believed in one or the other? "So you give me these names and I'm supposed to scamper back to L.A. and bat cleanup for the Zacatecas Mob."

"Knowledge is a burden, brother Monk," Maladrone rasped, his vision fixed on the face glaring at him in his overhead mirror.

The driver lightly touched the private eye's upper back, indicating his audience with his boss was over.

"What if I did nothing?" Monk quipped, walking away.

"What if you did?" Jaguar Maladrone replied obliquely.

Outside, the rooster was now pecking for bugs on the ground around the van. As Monk and his escorts got closer, the bird flapped its useless wings and crooked its neck upwards. Thinking the cock was going to charge him, Monk was prepared to kick it with his now fully awake foot. The creature strutted toward him then abruptly turned away from the threatening foot. It managed to clamber onto the front of the van, perching there as if it were a live hood ornament.

Monk climbed in back. The rooster still perched on the hood, looking off at the omnipresent power lines. Settling into what he hoped would be a more comfortable position, Monk lay down. He saw the bird pivot its head sideways. As the blanket was dropped over him, and the driver bent down to adjust something, the last image he had before darkness was the ruby red eye of the rooster taking the measure of him.

Fourteen

Cut off from the Ra-Falcons, and not exactly wishing to crawl to Seguin to ask a favor given his funky attitude, Monk was working overtime to find out the real name for the gangbanger known as Junior Blue. The record on Kelmont "Kid Blue" Reeves, the recently deceased youngster's older cousin, had been expunged because his conviction had been when he was a minor. California law allowed for ways to unseal the record. But the young man had impressed many in turning his life around, notably councilman Wilsson O'Mera. The councilman had interceded on the young man's part to ensure the file would forever remain closed. Therefore getting a look at it would constitute a full-time job. Time Monk didn't have.

So that was a useless endeavor insofar as looking up the elder's rap sheet to find out the deceased one's name. And Absalla's notations in Reeves's file hadn't bothered with Junior's actual name either.

Monk had tried a couple of the reporters he knew who covered the crime scene, but they came up with diddly. Then he asked Elrod, but the big man was too much out of that scene, and most of his contacts were among the Rolling Daltons anyway.

He could put an ad in the classifieds, but that seemed beyond desperate. He'd previously turned in the files he'd gotten from Absalla, and hadn't made copies since he didn't expect to be fired. The possibility of approaching Eddie Waters was also looking thin, even assuming he gave credence to what Maladrone had told him.

Monk was sitting on the couch in his office, feet out, beneath a shot of the last merchant ship he'd served on, the *Achilles*. As he half dozed, he heard the intoxicating tum-tumming of the inlet valves of the grand diesel engines opening and closing in a unison borne of human sweat and the ship's oily blood. The old freighter, still reliable in its rusting dignity, had made the Murmansk run during World War II as a Liberty Ship. It was a relief mission organized by the leftists within the maritime union to aid the then–U.S. ally, the Soviet Union. The image of the prow blading aqua green waters flooded dark by Antigua's sunset skies filled his memory as Delilah entered.

"Did you want those changes in the Medallion Insurance Company contracts done today?" she asked, shaking him from his daydreaming. "I've got a balance sheet Ross wants done if you're not in too much of a hurry."

Monk was leaning forward, elbows on his knees like a player used to riding the pine finally called into the game. "Tomorrow's fine, D."

"Why you looking so eager? You been dreaming about Jill in here?" she teased.

"No, your black outfit"—he indicated the pleated skirt she wore—"reminded me about a funeral coming up."

"When it's my time, try to have a little more reserve, will you?" She left and Monk got up to dial one of the freelance writers he knew who did work for the *L.A.*

Weekly. The newspaper was an alternative newsweekly published on the west side, but given to covering issues from Watts to El Segundo.

"Hey," Monk said to her after a few general amenities, "hear of any gang funerals coming up?"

"That's on the regular," the woman, Mari Sicorro, answered. Beneath her words, he could hear the muffled click-clack of computer keys being vigorously worked.

"But you'd have paid attention to this one. It would have been about two young soldiers killed after a nighttime shoot-out on Trinity Street last week. It was a meeting of OGs from the Scalp Hunters."

"Riddle me this, Batman. How'd you know about this shoot-out? The cops are more closemouthed than usual, and I heard the supposed payback involved other Latinos shooting at Los Domingos." Sicorro had once been a civilian employee of the police department and she continued to work contacts. She couldn't get away from cops, criminals, and the nadir of human existence.

"You get the scoop if there is one."

"Liar," she giggled. "Nobody's used the word 'scoop' since *The Front Page*."

"I ain't lying."

She stopped tapping. "What if I did get something across my desk?"

"Junior Blue is the one I'm interested in." Saying it, he realized how cold it sounded, not mentioning the other one killed. A young man whose street name he couldn't even remember. Had he too become so inured of youthful death it made no dent in his psyche any longer?

There was a motion of papers on the other end and Sicorro said, "Yeah, yeah, here it is: 'There's a graveside ceremony tomorrow at ten out at the Masonic Moor Memorial Park in Compton.'"

"How come that place sounds familiar?"

"It's on Bullis Road," Sicorro illuminated. "The place is done in the style of Moorish architecture with plaster minarets and tiled archways. It was in the news about a year ago when there was all that ruckus when the owners were discovered to have been digging up older bodies to bury the new ones."

"That note of yours don't happen to mention the real name of Junior Blue, does it?"

"No," she drawled. "I got this from Danny."

Danny Fine was the managing editor; he'd interviewed Monk once for a piece on L.A.'s underbelly. "Anything else?"

"His note mentions their gang names—and peep this," she added excitedly, "Minister Tariq is supposed to be doing the eulogy. Glad you called and had me look at this again."

"No shit," Monk exclaimed.

"On the real," she said. "I guess I will cover this after all."

"And maybe I'll come with you." The presence of the controversial black Muslim leader Stanis L. Tariq was definitely an interesting turn of events. He was the man who'd personally denounced Antar Absalla for wrongdoing. Yet Tariq, who was situated in Philadelphia, was apparently going to preside over a funeral that happened in Absalla's backyard.

"How come you're so hep on keeping a low profile?" Sirocco asked, wanting more information.

"I'll make sure it's part of your story, okay?"

"So you want this Junior Blue's name?"

"Yes, dammit," Monk proclaimed.

"Don't be snotty, or you won't get jack, jack."

"Yes, ma'am," he breathed in a falsely contrite voice.

"That's better," she laughed. "I like obsequiousness in a big-shouldered man. How 'bout you pick me up around nine tomorrow?"

"Bet."

"Later."

He hung up and opened up the book on Aztecs he'd checked out from the Culver City Library on Overland that morning. Earlier, he'd been reading a passage about their history. The Aztecs came after the Maya and the Toltecs. Their city-states grew out of the Valley of Mexico, Anáhuac as it was called, around the fourteenth century. Apparently there were seven Nahua tribes who had carved out fiefdoms in a divided Mexico as the Mayan civilization came to an end.

Of those Chichimecas, barbarians, the last of the seven were the wandering mercenaries, the Aztecs. As the other tribes had each usurped the previous one's rule, the Aztecs came to Anáhuac. There they staked out territory on two islands in the middle of Lake Texcoco. In 1325, the warriors built the city of Tenochtitlán. They had been guided to the area by their deity, Huitzilopochtli, who had told them to settle where they should find an eagle standing on a nopal, a prickly pear cactus, gorging on a serpent. But this god was not their supreme being, Ometeuctli, the creator of some sixteen hundred other, lesser gods.

Monk's interest was centered on Tlaloc, the lord of fire. The Aztecs believed that the present-day sun was the fifth sun. Tlaloc, the legend goes, periodically brings about the eruption of massive volcanoes, which cause billions of cinders to fall from the sky, consuming the world in smoldering ash—a kind of no-options recycling plan. Now, ol' Tlaloc could be appeased if his suns were shown the proper respect.

The Aztecs believed that blood, the most important element of life, coupled with faith, is what sustains the fifth sun. Captives of war were routinely sacrificed so their blood and hearts could be offered up to Nanahuatl, the sun, so that he would rise each morning.

Running his fingers over a photograph of a stone carving in the book, Monk was sure he'd seen the likeness embla-zoned on Maladrone's iron lung. He was positive it had been Tlaloc. Maybe Maladrone had the image painted there as a sign of strength, or maybe the Jaguar wanted to rain down some heat on a few select people. And maybe stop a few hearts from beating in the process.

He read for a while, then went downstairs to Cafe 77 on the first floor for lunch about half past twelve. Inside were a couple of studio types—the Sony/Columbia facility wasn't too far away on Washington—and several blue-collar workers. Mr. Gorzynski, a waitress who was a stu-dent at West L.A. College, and the cook were on duty. The wife didn't seem to be about.

Monk took up residence at the counter. Mr. Gorzynski—Gorzy—behind it, glared at him over the glasses shoved low on his nose. He ambled over, an assortment of break-fast receipts in his hand. "Lunch, huh?"

"Ah, yes," Monk said, waiting for the pinch.

Gorzy shuffled the receipts like a gambler in search of a full house. Head down, he whispered, "How's your time?"

Monk was fantasizing about the catfish and fried rice he was going to have. "What?"

"Your time," he repeated clearly.

"You think—" He paused as the waitress, Gina, walked past. "You think the old lady's tipping out on you, Gorzy?"

"No, she's not drinking on the job."

Monk sighed. "I mean, do you think she's seeing some-one else?"

Gorzy rubbed a cheek with the middle knuckles of a half-closed fist. "Were that it was merely love on the side." Abruptly, he canted his head toward the cook, "Catfish and beef fried rice, double on the rice for Ivan." He turned back, smiling. "I hope you don't mind me presupposing."

"Not at all," Monk allowed.

"I want to show you something in my office," Gorzy said too loudly.

"Sure."

The two went into the cramped office. No papers were carelessly thrown about nor was anything out of order. What made it crowded were the twin ancient schoolhouse desks, two Ivar chairs covered in red velour—one before each desk—and a large, free-standing lamp with a Tiffany shade. Gorzynski stood in what little open space his office afforded, the receipts bunching and unbunching in his long, malleable fingers.

Monk put his hands in his pockets, playing with some pennies and quarters in one of them. "What can I do for you, Mr. Gorzynski?" he asked quietly.

"It's not another man, I know." He blurted out with finality.

"Then what's the problem," Monk prodded.

"This." He shoved the receipts toward Monk.

"Her addition?"

Gorzynski didn't say anything, but shook the slips of paper.

"You mean money?"

"Yes, worse than if she had a lover." He lowered the receipts; his slim build slumped. "I think Mrs. Gorzynski is cooking the books, I think you detectives say."

"You have evidence of this." Monk was anxious to get

this over with, worried that his food would soon be growing cold on the counter. "The wife does the accounting, right?"

"Correct. Food is my area, and the organization of things is her worry." Gorzynski studied the receipts once more. "But I know something's been up for at least three months now. Short on the produce bill, short on payroll at least twice."

"Maybe it's just business, Mr. Gorzynski. Sometimes it's up, sometimes it's down, you know?" Monk could taste the Louisiana hot sauce peppering his corn meal–breaded cat. The older fella must be imagining this situation. "That's not much in the way of proof, Mr. Gorzynski."

He tapped his forehead with his index finger repeatedly. "I may be the food partner, but I keep enough in there to know when we have good weeks and when there are not-so-good ones. I know what I'm saying."

Monk was already edging toward the door, the catfish calling him. "Let me have lunch, and then why don't you see if you can get me a look at the ledger later."

Gorzynski huffed, "I can add. I can tell the money at the bottom isn't figuring out to the money I need to pay the bills." He jammed three fingers of one hand into the bundle of receipts in the other. "There's a difference, small but the same over the days, see what I'm saying? I want you to find out what the hell she's doing with the money."

Maybe the missus was getting even for what she rationalized was hers for years of unrecognized service. Maybe she was using the money to stuff the crotch of G-strings at some male strip joint. Whatever, it sounded like something he wanted no part of whatsoever. "We better get back out front."

"A man can get another woman; he can't always get more money," the other man theorized.

"I'll see about it, alright?" Monk was eager to succumb to the siren of food.

Mrs. Gorzynski had returned, and was busying herself with her own tasks. The newly arrived plate of fish and rice steamed on the plate as desire overtook him. The food's aroma made him light-headed.

The mister appeared momentarily, carrying a small crate of tomatoes. He took them into the kitchen, nodding at his wife as he walked past her.

Monk ate his tasty meal, chasing it with two glasses of tart, fresh lemonade. Sated like a bear after ravishing a stocked pond, he ascended the stairs back to his office. The book on the Aztecs could only hold his interest for another hour, and he felt restless. He'd called Wilkenson after returning from his meeting with Maladrone, but had got no answer. Trying him again this morning, he'd been on his way out. The old agitator had promised to call Monk later.

Until Wilkenson called back, it was just downtime. The judge was going to her folks' house tonight, so intellectual or physical stimulation would be nil. He glanced longingly at the inviting couch, considering a short nap to restore his investigative juices. But he would remain disciplined. And yet not all physical activity would be denied.

He'd make a run to the Tiger's Den in South Central. The emporium was a combination gym, sauna, and training ground to once and future Evander Holyfields and Oscar De La Hoyas. The Den was run by former welterweight and Korean War corporal Tiger Flowers. The place offered Monk not only a way to stay reasonably in shape, but a venue in which to partake of the uncanny insights of the raspy-voiced Aesop of West 48th Street.

And maybe, if he didn't anger the Tiger, the older man would tell him one more time a story or two about his adventures in the Army with Monk's late dad, Sergeant

Josiah Monk. After that, swing over to Simply Wholesome on Slauson and chow down on a vegetarian burger or two. If he wasn't going to have the old lady home tonight, well, by God, no sense getting the Cro-Magnon part of his brain hopped up on red meat.

Cradling the library book, Monk went downstairs, hoping he'd be invisible to the suspicious Mr. Gorzynski.

Kodama kissed her mother on her slightly rouged cheek. After forty-some years, Uhiko Be Kodama still wore Arpaige like a high school girl ready for her junior prom. She applied only a tentative amount of the perfume, allowing only a suggestion rather than the fact of the fragrance's existence to be apparent.

"How are you, dear?" Her mother pulled back, her lined face looking up at her daughter's.

"Better," Kodama said honestly.

"Good," her mother said, tugging lightly on Kodama's elbow. "Come on in the kitchen with me while I finish the potato salad."

"Where's Pop?"

"Golfing."

"He changed his days," the judge remarked, following her mother through the tidy, comfortable frame house on Dublin Avenue in Gardena. In the living room, off in the left corner was the Rosewood hand-carved etagere which had been in one corner or another, one abode or another, since before Kodama was born. It was a large, towering thing that was nearly as tall as her mother. Kodama had imagined as a child the stand held some cosmic secrets in its various nooks. Maybe it did. Even as an adult, she continued to have flashes in her dreams of one particular ornately painted wood box her mother or father would take from it and open to remove an unidentified object for some purpose yet to be revealed to her.

That box was still there, on the second shelf from the top. Inside it these days were a couple of hand-painted fans made of rice paper, and some wood blocks with Japanese characters carved into their soft wood.

Over the stand was a painting she'd given her folks on their thirtieth anniversary. It was a rendering of an Asian couple in a room imbued with late afternoon sunlight. The woman, dressed in a red polka dot '50s-era dress and darker red pumps, was standing. The man, clad in work pants and boots and an athletic shirt that contoured his lean muscles, sat on the edge of an unmade bed, fingering a set of pearls. Before them on a round heavy table was a model of a wooden guard tower.

Her mother began to slice the boiled eggs. "Yes," she said with a sigh, "they changed their golf day because Shab Ozumo got sick last month."

"Oh no," Kodama replied, "I didn't know." The Ozumos and the Kodamas had been interned together at Poston in Arizona during World War II. Shab and her father, Mark, had been track stars at L.A. High when they were teenagers. Their goal of college and expanding Shab's father's printing business was bitterly curtailed by the politics of race and opportunism. The distinctions between nisei and native born were no more a concern to the authorities than the intricacies of a Duke Ellington composition to the tone deaf.

At Poston, the Japanese and Japanese-Americans were composed of ultranationalists—some of whom had relatives in the expansionist *Genyosha*, the Dark Ocean Society in Japan—the pro-Americans, the civil libertarians, and the ambivalent. There were terse discussions in the bunkhouses at night, and even people getting jumped or an occasional knifing.

There were also efforts at maintaining aspects of the outside world too. They started a camp newspaper, the *Poston Chronicle*. Kodama's mother wrote articles on proper etiquette for the publication.

"Yes," her mother went on, adding the chopped red onion bits to the firm, parboiled yellow-white chunks of potatoes and mayonnaise. "He had another stroke."

Kodama asked, "Is he mobile at all?"

"Not much," her mother said. She deftly poured two equal amounts of Johnnie Walker Black for them and continued talking as she handed her daughter a glass. "He can barely move his left arm and leg. His mind, thankfully, is still with him and he and Gisele talk—when he's not at his physical therapy sessions."

Her mother began combining the potato salad. "Take the *ingen* out of the icebox, honey."

Kodama got the bowl of string beans out of the refrigerator, nibbling on one. The pungent taste of the sesame paste and miso filled her mouth and nose. "But Dad and his partners changed the day," Kodama repeated. Her father's consistency was something to set the Union of Atomic Scientists' doomsday clock by.

"He said it just happened that way, changing their golf day. But I think they did it to honor Shab." She reached over, placing a piece of egg on her daughter's tongue.

"Leaving Wednesdays open for his return," Kodama said appreciatively.

"And they say only the married ones are wise," her mother teased. She halted her work and tried her scotch. "How's Ivan?"

Kodama clucked her tongue. "Knee-deep in black Muslims, Aztec gods, and gambling dens."

"You know what I mean," her mother retorted. She opened the oven door and removed the top of the roast pan to check on the meat. "You are our only child, Jill." She fetched a long-handled wooden spoon and basted the beef as she spoke.

"It wasn't too long ago you two weren't exactly lighting candles to the ancestors about me going out with Señor Monk. Now you want little dark babies."

"You ain't the first one to cross the street, honey." Her mother straightened. "I can tell you some tales of proper nisei girls who came out of the camps to discover the forbidden taste in Bronzeville." She cackled, half-turning and dipping her body back the way she did when she amused herself. Bronzeville was the name given to Little Tokyo during the war due to the forced excision of the Japanese and the continuing influx of Southern blacks into an area with available, inexpensive housing.

"Bars all along First Street were filled with returning black soldiers feeling like they'd won something for themselves. My folks pooled their ration books with others so our temple could buy food at the Chinese market. Looking for work, but none for the slant-eyes except domestic and gardening." Her mother went back to preparing the salad.

Kodama's mother could go on about incidents of cross-pollination during that mercurial time after the emperor's surrender. But she had to be tight to do so. And it had to be after her father had gone to bed or wasn't around. "Is that right," she wheedled.

"Don't be such a lawyer. Set the table, will you?"

"Okay." She got the plates out of the cupboard. Sure enough, her mother had one more quick bite of the whiskey, then poured the rest down the drain. There had been a time when she'd goad her mother for taking steps into the modern world, yet always allow herself to be shackled by hidebound tradition. But experience had taught her that sometimes the crane is stronger than the bear because the crane, to survive, can't blunder around like its animal brother. Because this gentle bird must observe, it is this creature that becomes the one who understands the vagaries of the river, and the season of the fish. Unlike the bear, it does not merely stand at the banks and dip its snout into the water, blindly hoping for a catch. The crane watches for the right time to strike.

The dining room was decorated with hanging cloth embroidered with ideograms proclaiming harmony and understanding. Intermixed among the hangings were several photographs. There was one of Jill Kodama and California Supreme Court Justice Ming Chin at a charity dinner. Another framed shot was of Mark Kodama at his thirty-year retirement dinner from MacDonnell Douglas, another one with his golfing buddies, and finally a shot of a hoop-skirted young Uhiko. She had her arms spread around the slender shoulders of her stern father and reserved mother. It was evident the elders did not know what to make of their Americanized daughter.

A car door closed, pulling Kodama out of her plunge into her teenaged mother's eyes captured in the photo. "Dad," she said, as he entered.

"Hey, Jill." He kissed her lightly on the cheek after first setting his clubs and bag in the closet. "Good to see you."

"Sorry to hear about Shab, Dad." Involuntarily, she noted his reaction.

"Yes," he said, drawing in breath. "Just let me wash up, okay?" He walked off to the bathroom.

Downright effusive for Pop, Kodama sarcastically noted to herself. She headed back toward the kitchen, passing the *obutsodan*, the shrine to Buddha, on the wall unit. There were fresh flowers in a small vase, and Kodama hovered over the golden figurine on her way to the kitchen. The regulation of her youth always took over when she visited her mother and father. She was not quite a follower, but not quite a heretic either.

The dinner of smothered short ribs, a deep-fried stuffed eggplant called *nasu hasami-age*, the string beans, and the potato salad graced with pepper vinegar, were delicious. Her mother's forte with food had always been the casual way she blended Japanese and American cuisine. The recipe for the salad had originated with Monk's mother, Nona.

Their conversation included her mother reminding Kodama to research cases supporting her position in her upcoming appearance on a radio talk show debating Jamboni. Her father nodded appropriately at this advice as he worked on another helping of salad. Other topics revolved around Kodama's dad stating he was finally going to build the sun room addition her mother had wanted for three years now, and her mother wondering aloud what kind of activity she might get Gisele involved in.

Dessert was *manju*, sweet bean pastries rolled in sticky rice. They were fresh from Fugetsu-Do, a shop that had managed to hold on for more than ninety-four years in Little Tokyo. Kodama poured a few grams of Johnnie Walker for her mother and herself. Mark Kodama was a strict two beers on Friday night man.

"We might take our vacation to the Grand Canyon this year," Uhiko Kodama said, relishing her tiny amount of whiskey.

"You guys haven't been there since—"

"You were twelve," her father finished, plopping a rice ball into his mouth. "But it's not like it's changed in all that time, right?"

"Want to see if your memories match reality, Dad?"

"Going to camp out, drink sake, and write some poems," her mother furnished.

The skin at the edges of Mark Kodama's eyes crinkled slightly as he ate another piece of manju. "I'm going for the water."

Later, they sat around the living room, talking about the African-American and nisei neighbors they used to have when they lived on Field Avenue on the outer edges of the Crenshaw District, Saturday matinees at the Kabuki on the Boulevard, and the barbecue her dad would drive down to get in Compton at least once a month.

"Nobody could smoke chicken like Will Sunday," her father lamented. He sat in his BarcaLounger, reclining, his slippers on.

Kodama snorted. "I remember you taking me down there when I was eight or so. Standing at the front counter with you, I would look around the corner through the open doorway. I could see Mr. Sunday, tall and gaunt with forearms like Popeye's. He was in his bloodstained apron, his gristly hand flipping a chicken onto the cutting board like he was dealing cards."

"One clean movement." Her father chuckled, making a flitting, almost ephemeral movement with his hand.

"The experience didn't turn you into a vegetarian," her mother piped in. "You know his wife was Japanese," she said with mirth in her voice. "Japanese used to go to Compton High in pretty big numbers before the war. The southern end of Watts used to be farmland; Compton had cattle herds and dairies up through the thirties."

"She couldn't wait for the 'special chicken,' she used to call it," her father kidded.

It got on to twenty past eleven, gaps and lags increasing in their conversation. The silence was not due to a lack of things to say, but reflected the pattern of those attuned to each other's moods.

"Well," her mother said, raising her slim frame off the divan. "I'm all played out for tonight." She stood near her daughter, massaging her lower back with one hand. "Don't forget you're speaking before our homeowners' association in two weeks."

"I shall be the upright and uptight jurist before the members Satozo." She bowed slightly.

"Hmm," her mother remarked doubtfully. "Good night, honey."

Kodama also rose and kissed and hugged her mother. "I guess I better get on my way, too."

"Will Ivan be up?"

"If I didn't know better, Mom, I'd say you were trying to slip past a double entendre."

"Oh?" her mother feigned, patting her father on the head on her way to the bedroom.

"Modern women," Mark Kodama mumbled, righting himself in his recliner. He got up, too, stretching and making noise.

Kodama eased into her leather jacket, purposely looking at the ancestors' shrine. Her mother had lit new incense earlier; its silky smell was comforting and honey-sweet.

She kissed her father on the cheek and squeezed his shoulder. "See you soon, Pop."

Mark Kodama used a finger to probe the briar of his seldom lit pipe. He kept the thing in the side pocket of his chair, and he'd clamped it between his lips like a businessman's pacifier.

"I want you to know how I think the world of you, Jill."

She just stood there, unused to her father being so emotive.

"You stand up to these bastards," he said. He kept messing with the pipe, alternately glancing up at her then at his probing digit. "Everybody says Asians are supposed to just take it, be stoic and roll with like it was in our genes." He glanced up again, seemingly focused on a speck in another galaxy. "But you stand on it—don't let them make another Ito out of you. You've always had your own mind, and that hasn't been so bad, has it?" He smiled, tugging on the pipe's stem.

"I love you, Pop."

Mark Kodama put an arm around his daughter, giving her an affectionate squeeze. "I'll see you at the homeowners meeting." He watched her get in her car and turn the engine over before walking, ponderously, back to the house.

As the Saab slowly drove off, she turned her head to see, in sharp silhouette from the light in the open doorway, her old man half-turned, his open palm up and stationary. The smoke, like levitating silver threads, filtered out and up from his pipe.

Fifteen

"The alignment is connected with the various eras this world has been through. As the planets in their centuries of phases have passed through our cosmos, so too has the sojourn of the black man, the travails of the black woman, been part of that panorama. There are 365 days of the year, and there have been 365 years of oppression and subjugation of our people.

"But do not despair, my brethren, for just as the shadow must fall across the sundial's face, so too must our time to shine be upon us. But as we embark these young souls to God's hands, so too we must measure how we're living our lives in the eyes of Allah.

"For this sickness we perpetuate on one another, this disease we infect one another with via injections of mercury-tipped bullets, must stop. And I'm not just talking about black on black, but black on brown and brown on black. Why? Why, when our real climb is a hill constructed from those who practice tricknology daily in our communities.

"Don't you see? We must stop placing stones beneath

the heads of our brothers and sisters, our *raza* and our *rukas*. No amount of blood can wash away the debt owed to the past. All about us Malcolm and Du Bois, Wells-Barnett and Mandela Nkhruma, Zapata and Martí, Chavez and King, Hamer and Nasser and Mother Jones—yes, I said Mother Jones—are watching and waiting. They're asking how long will you waste your strength on recriminations and retributions. How long will you foolishly fight for chunks of sidewalks that don't belong to you, streets with no deed in your name on them? How long, my brethren? How long must this spiral of destruction go on?

"These are horrendous days we face; time is no longer a luxury we can afford to twiddle our thumbs over. Open up your eyes, and see where this crooked road will take you. I'll tell you where it will take you; here, in this fine polished box of pine and metal. If that's what you want, the taste of ash and disappointment in your mouth, then you're welcome to it. I turn my back on you.

"Yes, if you wish to sup from the cup of righteousness and redemption, then I shall hold such a chalice for you. We will make sure all who wish to drink get to drink. For it is filled with the tears of the mothers who've wept for the senseless slaughter of the ones like Antoine Felix and Dubro Morris in these coffins before us.

"But the cup shall hold no bitter taste. For just as the caterpillar sheds its cocoon and becomes the butterfly, a creature of self-worth and peace, thus so can we, my brethren. So can we, my sisters. Stop putting on those . . . those hoochie mama outfits, your butt hanging out all over the place for men named Bergman and Moscowitz to put in videos to sell filthy music. Rap songs that talk about making a joy out of murder and how many women one supposed man can bed down. No responsibility, no self-respect. That is no way to live. Come forward, my fine

African warriors, drape robes over those thong bikinis, cloth all up the crack of your butt, and reclaim your proud heritage, my good African queens.''

Minister Tariq continued his speech that was part eulogy, part admonishment, and part challenge to the gathered at the funeral. Dual semicircles of his devout, and martial arts trained, bodyguards stood at thirty-degree angles to either side of him. The men looked properly intimidating with their blue and black wool suits, close-cropped hair, and thick necks.

Mari Sicorro tapped Monk with the program. ''So which one was this Junior Blue?'' she whispered.

They were standing off to the side in the last rows of the assembled crowd. The sun was beaming, the Muslim leader's speechifying meandering, and Monk's Nunn Bushes felt tight. He remembered his foot falling asleep the other day, and was momentarily terrified he might have phlebitis or some other ailment that would necessitate the amputation of his feet. ''How in the hell should I know,'' he crabbed.

''Well,'' she said, making a face and fanning herself with the program.

''You know anything about circulation and feet?''

''No wonder you don't know which one it is. You can't keep your mind on business.''

''He-yuk.''

A mourner turned to shush Monk. But other eyes had already been on him. Including the steel-piercing bore he received from Antar Absalla when he'd spotted his former employee.

''We can leave any time now, Mari.''

''You said that fifteen minutes ago,'' she said while continuing to make notes on her pad. ''I've got a story going, buzzhead.''

Monk mumbled something and focused on his shoes, looking for swelling. Custom Caprices trimmed in metal flake golds, drop-ended Impalas with Cyclone rims, chopped Blazers with eight-foot speakers dug into their rear compartments, and tricked-out El D's dipped in twelve coats of lacquer choked the narrow lanes running through the Masonic Moor Memorial Park. Adding to the mix were their owners dressed in black shirts or turtlenecks, slacks, and tennis shoes. Almost none of the Scalp Hunter crowd wore a jacket. Conversely, the Ra-Falcons and Muslims were formal in attire and manner.

"You going to try to interview Tariq?"

Vigorously she bobbed her head as she wrote. "This will make double truck in the paper, home base. No other media bothered to make the scene," she said covetedly.

Monk was about to say something when a beat-up Dodge van cruised past the cemetery gates. He was pretty sure it was the one that had taken him to see Maladrone. The vehicle did a U-turn and doubled back on the other side of the street. Monk's alarm broadcast a vibe the savvy Sicorro noticed.

"What's happening, Ivan?"

He said nothing, his mind preparing his hand to reach down and get the Glock strapped to his ankle. The van rolled out of sight.

"What the fuck is going on?" Sicorro looked around as if she could see what he was imagining.

There was the squeal of tires as Maladrone's messengers returned for the third time, not to look, Monk feared, but to do. Tariq seemed to actually be working toward his windup.

"Everything's fine," he said, patting her in the middle of her back.

"My ass," she countered.

"That too."

She arched a thick brow. "Careful, I don't think you could handle two women like me and the judge at once. Although," she joked, batting her eyes, "we might could work out a tag team arrangement."

"Knucklehead." Evidently, the van had moved along.

Sicorro slapped his arm with her pad and sought to position herself closer to the minister. Various people were now stepping forward and taking their turns shoveling a mound of dirt on the now lowered coffins.

Minister Tariq's guards, a seemingly impermeable physical and psychic barrier, stood around him. He clasped his large hands in front of his athletic frame. The minister was wearing red-tinted Gargoyle sunglasses, and his unlined face—Monk recalled he was a grandfather five times—was unbroken by sweat or consternation. Tariq was dressed in a camel-colored sport coat, starched blue shirt, and a dawn-grey bow tie. His burgundy trousers broke just so on the crest of his coffee-with-a-hint-of-cream Stacey Adamses.

Sicorro managed to get the attention of one of the grim *burkandaz*, showing him her press credentials. Monk was drifting along the rear wall, anxious to look up the record of Dubro Morris. He was the twenty-two-year-old identified in the program book as Junior Blue, the cousin of Kelmont "Kid Blue" Reeves.

"You must be trippin' to show up here." Absalla came up and latched onto his arm.

Monk knocked his hand away. "I ain't on your dime, Absalla, and where I show up is my goddamn business." He squared up in front of the Muslim chief. He was acutely aware that he was facing him down in hostile territory.

Absalla's hand did its flexing routine, his eyes alert and transmitting a building rage. "What the fuck do you think you're doing?"

"The thing I'm good at, Absalla."

A sturdy finger bluntly pushed its way close to Monk's down-turned mouth. "You better take your monkey ass out of here before you dip your dick in business where it's likely to get snapped off."

"Trying to get back in solid with the head man, huh?" Monk goaded. "You pay for his ticket out here?"

Absalla charged forward and Monk jammed the heel of his rigid palm into the crux of his sternum. "Better be cool, fool, or the big man will think maybe you ain't got it back together after all." A sliver of what might have been joy tugged his lips to one side. "But it don't unhinge my world if you want to tumble."

There were some people coming over, but none within earshot yet. If they were, Monk was certain Absalla would have had to swing to maintain what he felt to be his manly stature. But the absence of other earwitnesses allowed for room to dance.

"You best be staying out of my way, chump. You might find out I ain't always willing to settle things with talk."

"You mean like Malcolm X found out?"

By then, others were crowding close, including Keith 2X, who was jostling to the front. Monk couldn't take his attention off Absalla, but could feel their presence. He very much wanted to talk with 2X alone.

The growing crowd was parted by the prow of Tariq's berserkers. His decked-out chasseurs then opened at the juncture of their base and the charismatic minister glided into view.

"Mr. Monk, I presume." His voice, even at rest, had the quality of a tempestuous ocean right before a squall.

"He's been fired," Absalla said loud enough for all to hear, " 'cause he's responsible for these two deaths."

Murmurs couldn't drown out Monk's desire to slug the smug Absalla.

"Is that so?" Tariq's head rotated toward Monk.

"That's his opinion," Monk countered. "But I have a different theory." He wanted to look at 2X but resisted the impulse.

"So you're still looking into this? For who?" Tariq inquired.

"My own enlightenment. You're for empowering the black man, aren't you, Minister Tariq?"

"Indeed." Tariq pondered that then said, "I hope matters will remain peaceful with all these goings-on. Don't you, Mr. Monk?"

"Naturally."

His audience over, Tariq returned to the graveside with his brutally efficient entourage. Absalla trailed behind, not deigning to look back at Monk. Keith 2X also followed, but he did look back. Monk winked, and the young man blanched. Sicorro made a menacing face at him and went to try to get her story.

"Why can't I go in, dammit." She kicked at the floorboard.

"Because I don't want to get grandma in there all worked up. She's got to feel comfortable with me asking the questions."

"Yeah, like you're Madeleine Albright. Tell her I'm your assistant. Which is kinda accurate considering the day I've had." Sicorro pouted.

Monk was already half out of the Ford's driver side. "You're getting all this great background for the piece. And you can always come back and talk with the old girl after this is over with."

"That's assuming your sorry ass ain't doing ten to

fifteen in Mule State.'' She tapped his dash. ''How come you don't have a CD player in this ride?''

He was standing and closed the door calmly. ''Whatsa matter, Mari, ain't ya getting it steady?''

''Sexist dog,'' she retorted. ''We all can't be enjoying the priapic life of Ivan Monk, the Sleuth of South Central. Now don't be forever, huh? I'd like to get over to the office and get these notes typed up.''

''On it.'' He marched up the cracked walkway to Constance Smalls's house. She was the maternal grandmother of the Morris clan, and had been at the funeral. Monk recognized her choice 1982 Frank Sinatra Edition Chrysler Imperial in the driveway. If he recalled correctly, fewer than three thousand Imperials had been built that year. The following year was the last go-round for the model. Too bad, he mused, knocking on the security screen, he'd always wanted to see Chrysler do a Sammy Davis edition. Ca-chung, ca-chung.

The inner door opened. ''Yes? . . . You were the one having words with Absalla this morning at Dubro's funeral.'' The screen stayed shut.

''Yes, ma'am, I was. I'm sorry to come calling on a day like this, but I got your name from a bail bondsman I know here in Compton.''

''You some kind of policeman, is that it?''

''Not really. My name's Ivan Monk. I'm a private detective originally hired by Absalla to find out who did the murders over in the Rancho.''

She said nothing and Monk was worried she was going to shut the door. ''This have something to do with my grandson's death?''

''I think so, at least, I want to finish what I started to find out.''

"What Absalla says about you being responsible, is that so?"

"I'd be lying if I told you that was a hundred percent the opposite. I don't think I was followed to the meeting where Dubro was killed. I have been doing this kind of work for some time now. But I'm man enough to come back and tell you if I played a part in it after all this is over."

The screen cracked open. "Come on in. I guess anybody who can get under Absalla's skin can't be all bad."

She was a tall, large, and solidly built woman who couldn't have been over fifty-five. Though not fashion-magazine pretty, there was a compelling allure to her wide brown eyes, flaring nostrils, and well-proportioned full lips. They were African features little diluted by the Middle Passage and centuries of the American journey.

Her short, curly hair was pinned to one side with only wisps of grey sprouting at the roots hinting at her years. She was still wearing the dress she'd worn at the funeral. It was a black, midlength sheath dress. The hemline bordered a strong-looking pair of calves. Her matching pillbox hat with its arching peacock plume rested on a chair in the corner.

"I just got back from my sister's, where we had the get-together. His father managed to drag his pitiful self over there." She shook her head at the surreal pathos of it all. "What do you want from me, Mr. Monk?" Her hand was on her hip. It wasn't from exasperation, but from a life lived too much at the behest of others' dreams delaying her own. The death of her grandson, nothing more than a blip in the annual crime statistics compiled by the state, was just one more chunk taken out of her soul.

"I'd like to know who Dubro's friends were. Are they the same as Kelmont's."

She angled her head again and walked past him to the kitchen. "Come on, I was about to have a cup of tea."

Monk sat patiently as the water boiled and Constance Smalls talked about growing up in Arkansas, and coming out here when she was in her teens. She'd married young, and gave birth in Los Angeles. Her daughter, though attentive to her grades, got tangled up like so many young girls do, and wound up pregnant at sixteen. But unlike her mother, the daughter had no man to at least stick around for the first ten years as Constance's husband had.

If the story hadn't had a human face, it would sound stereotypical, a litany used by the moral values bunch to further browbeat the denizens of the nation's urban core for having no goals beyond Pampers and TANF checks.

"It's crazy, I know. But I swear what with all this Nintendo, and shoot-'em-ups on cable all night, and rap stars killin' and makin' songs about their real lives, then how the hell are our young men supposed to come up right?"

He listened and sipped and leaned back in his chair. Her downcountry accent became more pronounced as she told of her daughter's efforts to raise Dubro, the setbacks, the sometimes father coming around, and her own contributions over the years. Kelmont's mother, Smalls's second cousin, helped when she could, and Smalls of course did what she could for her daughter too. Underneath her words, Monk could hear her disappointments, keen and sharp like the swath of a machete.

"Kelmont got out of the life," he ventured eventually, "but Dubro remained in the Scalps."

"Nature or nurture," she said, holding up her hands. "You would have sworn Kelmont would be the gangster till I die the way he was ripping and running in high school. Dubro was the one in the science club in his freshman year." She looked at a photo on the wall in a round gold frame of a man in overalls, sitting before an ancient tractor in a plowed field. "Who could tell?

"By his junior year, while his friends and even his cousin were getting themselves together, he got it in his head he was going to have big bank, as they say out in them streets. It ain't like he knocked up one of these tight-skirted heifers." She shook her head again at the great imbalance of things.

"I saw you talking with Keith 2X this morning."

She made a dismissive wave. "I've known that boy since before he got the call, when he was just plain Keith Burroughs. Him and Dubro been knowing each other since grade school. Eddie Waters too. He was there today. But don't misunderstand, Ivan, I think Keith's doing good. He's a couple of years older than Dubro, and both him and Kelmont tried with the boy."

"You don't think much of Absalla though."

She chuckled. "It shows, huh." She leaned forward across the table in the breakfast nook. "I got a stepbrother who became a Black Muslim, back in Philadelphia. According to him, word was Absalla was always more about building himself up than working to better the conditions there. I know he's supposed to have cleaned up, and I guess there's something to that. But when it comes to doing the day in and day out work, he was always more interested in finding the nearest camera or microphone to stick his face in.

" 'Sides, Jesus is good enough for me and mine. I wasn't raised up believing in no god who didn't let you eat a little pig. But maybe that's just a weakness, huh? I like them smothered pork chops too much." She guffawed and Monk laughed with her.

She put aside her cup and said, "Listen, it's been nice

unburdening myself, but I've got to get over to Helen's.'' His mystified look brought clarification. ''That's Dubro's mother.'' She got up, shaking into her mantle of responsibility.

''Can you tell me where Keith lives, Constance? It was his information that led me to the house on Trinity, and I think he knows more than he's been willing to tell me.''

''Keith wouldn't do anything wrong,'' she said guardedly.

''I'm not saying he did, at least not knowingly. But I need to see him, away from the Rancho, to talk freely with him. Maybe it will help get those who killed your grandson.'' As he said the words, it occurred to Monk Big Loco was still nowhere to be found.

Constance Smalls evaluated the man before her for several long spaces of time. She shifted her large, firm body and scratched at one side of her shoulder blades. ''If something should happen to Keith because of me, Lord help you.''

''I understand, Constance.''

''Alright,'' she finally agreed, wagging a warning finger at him. She went to a pile of sympathy cards in the living room stacked on a TV tray near the big-screen Panasonic. She rifled through them until she got to the one she was looking for. ''Helen asked me to take care of these.'' She handed Monk the envelope with the handwritten return address of Keith ''2X'' Burroughs.

He copied the address, a number in the 6800 block of Madden Avenue. It was a location too far south to be in the Crenshaw District. Monk guessed 2X's place was in what was called the Hyde Park section, bordering the city of Inglewood. ''I appreciate this, Constance.''

''You better.'' She picked up her hat, more for something to do than seeking to put it on. ''You make sure that whatever's going on, it don't take any more of our black folk from us, Ivan Monk.''

Coming from her, a woman who kept on giving, who didn't stop believing in some hope that transcended the buffeting her daily existence took, it weighed him down with a sense of duty as tangible as stone. "I'll do my best.''

"That's all I can ask.''

Monk went out to his car and got in next to an irritable Mari Sicorro.

"Were you building an addition to the house?''

"Relax, I'll buy you a late lunch before I take you over to the office.''

"Mr. Mellow.''

"Humbled, baby, humbled.''

Sixteen

The two figures made their way around the hedges with missing sections that stood in front of the duplex on Madden. Monk waited a respectful time, then crept toward the residence of Keith 2X—a little frame house behind the duplex.

He'd been watching the place since before sundown. He knew 2X's schedule at the Rancho, that he didn't get off until six-thirty. It was now past nine, but no one had been around until the two had arrived in a dark-colored Isuzu Trooper. He was planted in his Ford when the two had driven past, parked, and exited.

Monk couldn't tell much about them at night, their race nor their intent. Even their body types weren't too revealing as to gender. The phantoms had moved quickly.

Monk wrote down the sport utility vehicle's license number and, as quietly as he could, went along the cement path toward the little house. The front window's blinds were slatted closed, and Monk could perceive no light from within. He debated waiting some more, but not knowing 2X's car he couldn't take the chance the recent arrivals weren't his quarry and a fellow Ra-Falcon.

He pushed the doorbell and heard it buzz inside. He pushed it twice more. He heard no movement. He knocked, and got the same result. Just for the heck of it, he tried the knob on the security screen. It turned.

"Keith, it's Monk, I want to talk with you," he said, gingerly stepping into the house. A single lamp glowed on low wattage from a corner. A premonition tickled his cerebellum nanoseconds before a flash and a crack from a darkened doorway had Monk moving sideways, sending a stereo unit crashing to the floor. "Keith, it's Monk, man," he announced anxiously, working to free his .45.

Another blast from the doorway slammed home to the right, and a few inches above, Monk's head. The doorway was to his left and Monk, crouching and pressed up against the wall partially behind an off-color divan, let go with two of his own into the void. There was a *plop*, and a body fell into the dim light. Big Loco had two dark spots staining the back of his white form-fitting T-shirt. There was no gun in his hand.

Monk assessed all this as he threw an African statue from an end table at the lamp in the corner. He knocked it over, waiting and listening as the room went dark. There was still a second player, and he had to be back through that doorway. Monk crawled out from behind the divan on his stomach. If the second gunman was still in the house, no sense staying in the same spot.

He heard the sound of a spring releasing and something whizzed over his head. What was that? It wasn't a bullet. He stopped, the gun steady before him. He couldn't see his pistol, but its weight let him know it was ready. There was that sound again and Monk rolled reflexively. As he did, he sensed he'd landed his shoulder on something thin and hard.

Suddenly his legs jerked, and bursts of light collided like

meteors on the inside of his eye sockets. He couldn't hold
the automatic, and a large wet ball of phlegm clogged his
throat. He yelped, trying desperately to get to his feet. Hearing footsteps scuffing across the house's funky green shag,
he let loose with two more shots in the general direction
of the doorway to drive the interlopers back.

"Shit, motherfuckah's still dangerous," a voice protested in a high octave.

"I'm gonna one eighty-seven 'em," another promised.

Monk aimed for the source and cranked off another
round. He scrambled across the floor to where he thought
the kitchenette had been. A shot sounded when he stumbled
headfirst into one of the stools at the barlike counter.

"Fuck me," he swore softly, groping to get around the
corner. How many shots had he pulled off? Five? Six? One
or two left? No extra magazine, no backup piece on his
ankle. Damn. Is this the end of the counter? Two more
rounds meant for him sounded like M-80s going off in
buckets in this joint.

Lying on the cold linoleum of the kitchenette, he
squinted to see his attackers but he was having a hard time
getting his vision to clear. The lights were off, right? Forming coherent ideas was work too. He felt as if his head were
in a velvet-lined C-clamp, alternately tightening and loosening on his skull.

The damn thing that jolted him must have been some
kind of stun device like a Taser. The juice made his brain
fluids sizzle. There was a tittering like giant rats on psilo-
cybin and he was sure his intestines were liquefying. But
he was pretty sure he wasn't the one laughing like a nut.

"Hey, motherfuckah, I got something for you to investigate. Come on over here." The inane giggle went up
again.

"Shut up," the more mature voice admonished.

There was movement again and Monk held the .45, the heel of his hand supported by the other. "Come on over and see me," he invited around the saliva pooling in his mouth. He felt drunk, disoriented. Only the potential for immediate death kept enough endorphins going so he didn't pass out.

Nothing happened for several minutes as Monk's heart rate returned to normal. He chanced feeling around for the lamp but could feel only the broken ends of the bulb. He got up and flipped on the light switch in the kitchenette. He immediately crouched down, but it appeared that Big Loco and he were the only occupants.

His sudden movement had made him fuzzy again and he went down on all fours and crawled over to the inert form of the late leader of Los Domingos Trece. He gaped uncomprehendingly at the openings he knew his .45 had made in him. Monk couldn't seem to summon enough energy to walk about the house, so he propped himself against the doorjamb, staring at Big Loco.

"Goddamnit," he managed. He reached over and groped the cooling body. There was no gun, no fucking gun. He got the dead man's wallet out and fumbled through it. Various scraps of paper rained down and one in particular, a bright orange piece, registered in his distorted senses. He tried to bend over and wound up on his back. The horror of dying in his own vomit got his motor going and he turned over, the orange card right on his nose.

The item was a VIP comp ticket from the Airport Casino. He'd seen a few that day he'd tried to get in good with Isaiah Booker. He gathered up the other cards and slips of paper and put them back in Big Loco's wallet. Then he returned the wallet to Loco's back pocket.

Monk righted himself and stuffed the comp ticket in his own wallet. He got over to the phone and called the law.

The pumped and psyched uniforms arrived to the muffled pulse of a helicopter overhead, its strobe lighting up the small frame house. Monk had wisely placed his .45 on the kitchenette's counter, and placed himself in front of the house, arms outstretched.

He was proned out, and cops' feet were shoved into his back and buttocks. Searched, his hands were cuffed behind his back and finally the muzzles of the several 9mms that had been imbedded in his neck and upper back were drawn back. He was hauled up and marched toward a patrol car.

"There's a couple of detectives down at Newton who would like an appointment with you," a sergeant politely told him after he was placed in the vehicle.

"Tell their people to call my people," he slurred.

"Surely," the cop said. He stood up from where he'd been bending down and said, "Get this asshole over to see Zaneski and Fitzhugh."

Monk fell asleep on the way to his interrogation.

Seventeen

"**T**wo shots he admits are from his piece."

"There are other bullet holes in the house which show my client was under attack."

"By a person or persons he conveniently can't identify," Zaneski said sarcastically.

Parren Teague responded. "Your officers on the scene reported forced entry through the bars over the bedroom window."

"But," Fitzhugh piped in, "we don't know it wasn't how Monk got in. There was no sign of forced entry through the front door. Plus, and this be the biggie, Counselor, the preliminary on Big Loco's hands and shirt were negative. He wasn't firing anything." He produced some clippers, and began to clean under his nails with the short file that came with the thing.

"Implying . . . ?" Teague's eyebrow arched.

"That Mr. Monk at the least could be facing manslaughter if not murder two." He worked at the dirt under his thumb.

Teague removed his thin-framed glasses. "He's already

ID'd Ismael Vaccarano, aka Big Loco, as one of the hitters that night of the shoot-out on Trinity. It's not too much of a leap, even for LAPD detectives, to believe he and some of his crew would be lying in wait to ambush my client.''

"Save that shit for the jury," Fitzhugh snarled.

"If need be." The slender man put his glasses back on. "Along with your comments."

Zaneski gave a look to Fitzhugh, who declined a comeback. In an accommodating tone he said, "Where's Keith Burroughs, Monk?"

"I don't know."

"Who were the other hitters?"

"I don't know."

"Why were you watching Burroughs's house?"

"I was in the neighborhood."

Zaneski didn't break a sweat. "In about . . ." he glanced over his shoulder at the wall clock, which read 5:17. "In about another four hours I'm going to give a call up to Sacramento and request the Bureau of Consumer Affairs pull your license. I already made one complaint. Then I'm going to get that permit to carry you got over in Inglewood revoked."

Monk tasted his cold coffee. Once upon a time, the LAPD was adamant about not granting concealed weapon permits. But California law was such that as long as you got a permit in any one municipality, it was good for the whole state. The L.A. cops had gone through a change and were now granting more concealed weapons permits in L.A. City. Hell, since everybody else was doing it, why not get a cut of the action? God bless the NRA lobbyists, and gun nuts everywhere.

"Are you trying to interfere with Mr. Monk maintaining his livelihood?" Teague said icily.

"Oh hell, we're just trying to ensure public safety."

Fitzhugh stretched and groaned and massaged his lower back. " 'Sides, we can throw Monk's ass in the klink on a B&E beef and keep y'all running around for a few days dealing with that."

"You should keep in mind my client has given you the license number of the vehicle he spotted the men who attacked him driving."

Zaneski pointed at Teague. "Yeah, that was kinda oh-so-helpful, wasn't it?"

"Who does the plate belong to?" Monk asked.

"We ain't here to do your work, Monk," Fitzhugh said, leaning in a corner and continuing to work on his nails.

Teague stood up. "I would suggest you allow my client to get some rest and some quiet, or I'll have you all up before a judge before twelve." Teague's voice hadn't once cambered above its usual steady wavelength, but the force of his sincerity was apparent. "He's answered your questions several times since before eleven. This is enough for now."

There was some poking of tongues in jaws and shifting of bulks in their Men's Warehouse coats. "Okay, we'll let Monk cool out in a cell awhile. Maybe later, after a nice nap and a taste of the hearty breakfast sandwich we serve 'round here, he'll be a bit more illuminating."

"I'll be back by ten, Ivan, hopefully with a writ."

"Thanks, Parren. Call Jill, will you, and tell her good luck."

"Yeah, yeah, enough with the slap and tickle. Let's visit the other part of our playground, shall we?" Fitzhugh put a hand on Monk and pulled.

Monk pulled back and the heat in the cold room went up twenty degrees.

Teague said calmly, "He's not handicapped."

Zaneski's chest rose and fell rapidly until Fitzhugh

leaned on the table where Teague and Monk sat side by side. "Let's go, gentlemen."

Teague didn't make it back by ten. Monk did get to sample the breakfast sandwich, a salty piece of ham with fried egg on toasted white bread. The coffee wasn't bad and he did have the tiny cell all to himself. Newton Station, given its proximity to downtown, routinely rotated those awaiting trial down to the pit that was central booking. But his being kept there meant Zaneski and Fitzhugh weren't through with him yet.

Stretched out on his bunk, alternately drifting off and staring at the concrete ceiling, he was glad to see Teague around noon at his cell door.

"Sorry, Ivan, but the chief's jumped in too. He's macromanaging this affair and is insisting you tell everything you know and then maybe they'll see about only charging you with manslaughter."

"There's not much else to add, Parren. I was shot at as I entered. I announced myself and was shot at again, then I returned fire. Obviously, Big Loco was somehow being held and deliberately put in the line of fire."

Teague's bony hand gripped a bar. "Do you think he was being held inside the apartment? I've learned that Keith 2X went disappearing shortly after you saw him at the funeral."

"I think he's on the run, Parren. Whoever told him about that meeting on Trinity must also be the one who hipped Big Loco." Both Monk and Teague were well aware the cells were monitored by camera and sound. Their conversation served partly to bolster Monk's credibility with the detectives.

"Why?"

Monk remembered the van belonging to Maladrone's men cruising the funeral, and Maladrone's talk about instilling discipline and order. He'd intimated in their meeting that Big Loco was getting out of hand. After all, the iron lung gangster had taken shots at members of the Domingos. Presumably for committing the shoot-out.

"Damned if I know, Parren. Have they charged me formally with anything yet?"

Teague rubbed the bridge of his nose between thumb and index finger. "Zaneski has officially requested that your license be suspended."

"Don't they have to give me a hearing?"

"They can suspend pending a hearing to revoke. I'm supposed to hear from them by tomorrow."

"And it looks like they will." Monk made a helpless gesture. "What else?"

"Your permit will more than likely be lifted by the time I bail you out of here. And speaking of bail, do you plan to put the judge's house up for collateral?"

Teague had only intended it as a factual question. But a continual irritant to Monk was the disparity in what Jill made and what he netted in a year. He didn't make half of her base salary, and she pulled in extra income from speaking engagements. "No. I'm hoping the donut shop will do."

"Yes, I forgot about that," Teague said sheepishly. "I'm afraid you'll have to endure another session or two with the Gold Dust Twins before they decide what to charge you with. Until then, the amount of bail can't be determined."

"You're telling me I may not get out of here for another day or two. Or three."

"Unfortunately."

"What about the license number?"

"They're not telling, but I've got a bright intern from Loyola Law School hunting it down."

"I appreciate your help, Parren."

"Anything for one of my favorite sometimes investigators."

Monk lightly knocked the other man's knuckles on the bars with his own. "Peace out, black man."

A bemused look shadowed Teague's perpetually dour face. "I'll be back."

Monk stretched out again, ruminating on the complexities of the case. What if there were some connection between Maladrone and Isaiah Booker? Cash makes no enemies. But is there that much money in hot cars? But maybe not just cars. Drugs? Why not? Pedestrian, but the struggle for cocaine or marijuana profits gets people canceled every day.

Hell, maybe Maladrone and Absalla are the hookup. An Aztec/Muslim combine. That had possibilities. He got up to see what time it was. "Damn," he intoned, "missing my girl."

"Don't you see, Stan, this is the problem we're faced with now at the end of the century. Liberals have taken a beating, and they should get the message. But like termites they've burrowed deep in public offices and still try to impose their values on the majority."

Showing his very white teeth, Kenny Young, black neocon radio talk show host, swung a hand toward Kodama on the other side of the console. "What do you think about what Sally from Rosemead has to say, Judge Jill? You liberals are on the ropes and just don't have enough sense to lie down."

Kodama had lost count of how many times this self-centered asshole had called her "Judge Jill." "I hate to be the one to tell you, Kenny—No, wait, I do want to be the one to tell you, Ken. Liberalism isn't dead, and there's plenty of evidence that supports that proposition. Fair-minded people up and down this state have recently passed bonds for education and have condemned the police for beating striking immigrants. And don't forget, the people of this city in a recent poll said overwhelmingly they felt the county's welfare-to-workfare rules were too restrictive.''

''The will of the people was also expressed in passing three strikes,'' Jamboni mentioned. ''And certainly that was my intention in prosecuting the case the judge saw fit to impose her beliefs on.'' He was sitting at the apex of the console, while Kodama and Young sat opposite. Each had on headphones.

''And a lot of those same people have also said they didn't vote for three strikes to put people in prison for twenty-five years for stealing a slice of pizza or a case of beer. They did it to rid the street of violent felons, not petty criminals as Mr. Wright's history attests to.''

''Don't do the crime if you can't do the time, Jill.'' Young punched another light on the twinkling array of lights on the phone. ''Jolie from Lomita.''

''Kenny, I guess as a black man you've never been stopped by the cops for driving in the wrong neighborhood. I guess they just knew by the suit you say you always wear and the nice car you didn't fit the profile.''

''This isn't about police abuse, Jolie.''

Kodama snarled inwardly. Every time he said a woman's name, he made it sound like Big Daddy talking to Maggie.

''You see, it is, Kenny. It's about do we continue to pump money and resources into the prisons and jails or do we make a decision to put the money into job training and schoolbooks.''

"What's your status, Jolie?" Young asked, not bothering to mask his hubris.

"My what?" the electronic voice crackled.

"You know, are you here legally or did you come across the hills in San Diego?"

"Your mama." The line went off.

"I thought so," Young said smugly.

"I think it's evident from the reaction to Judge Kodama's ruling that she's out-of-step with what the public wants, Kenny," Jamboni theorized. "People want safe streets and the ability to walk into a convenience store and not have to worry that a quart of milk won't be the last thing they ever buy."

"So you feel confident, D.A. Jamboni, that Judge Jill will be recalled in the special election that's been set?"

"Well," he stammered effectively, "it's not for me to comment on that situation, Kenny. I wanted to come on your show to make it clear the D.A.'s office are not a bunch of vindictive, uncaring individuals. We are a concerned, humane group of dedicated prosecutors who represent the interests of law-abiding, hard-working citizens of the city and county."

Young looked at Kodama. "What do judges represent, Jill?"

"Reason and balance, Kenny. Our system of justice, far from perfect, nonetheless has been constructed so that defendants not only have a right to a jury of their peers but an arbiter as well. The jury decides the facts, the judge applies the law. And the law was never meant to be a cudgel, but a method by which the rights of the individual are considered with regard to the desire of the people. Edmund Burke talked about the cold neutrality of an impartial judge.

"Those are powerful words," she continued. "For it

implies that the judge must walk between the sometimes heated passions of a populace that calls for retribution and the fate of the individual brought before the docket.''

Agitated, Jamboni said, ''The law is the law.''

''It is in the application of the law, it is in the intent of the law that the judge has some say. Three strikes seeks to straitjacket the ability of experienced jurists from being able to apply those factors that determine a convicted person's sentence. Is twenty-five years for a stupid robbery going to stop others with the same background as Mr. Wright from committing similar acts? I doubt it, as long as there's few alternatives we can offer such men and women.

''Further,'' Kodama added, taking a swift gulp of water, ''according to a RAND study, three strikes may result in a $5.5 billion annual price tag for the taxpayers. More prisons would have to be built and maintained if this madness isn't curtailed. Drug interdiction programs, conflict resolution services, literacy programs for ex-felons—that's crime prevention.''

''Ulp, there you go again,'' Young jibed. ''Sam, from Indian Wells.''

''Jeez, Kenny, it tries my nerves to sit here and listen to this supposed upholder of the law go on about how it's all society's fault for making the criminal.''

''That's not what I said.'' She knew this voice.

''Why don't you just hang out your shingle and cut out the middleman. If you want to hold these thieves' hands, why not go all the way and become an ambulance chaser?''

''Well, Mr. Yorty,'' Kodama said triumphantly. ''When you first came to office as mayor of Los Angeles you had promised the black constituents of the Democratic Party you would do something to curb the police under Chief Parker. A man who openly recruited crackers from the Deep South.''

"Wha-what's that got to do with this subject?" the former mayor sputtered.

"It has to do with priorities, Mr. Yorty. Elected office is about how sometimes the needs of the minority, needs that may have not been met, have to at times outweigh the desires of the majority. The law is the law, but that doesn't always make it fair and just. What wasn't done then to set things right have a consequence now. The past has a way of determining the future."

"More liberal gobbledygook," he squawked. "You're gonna find, young lady, that you are seriously on the fringe of where the flag and country good people of this city are at."

"So be it," she answered. "But I remind you of what California Supreme Court Chief Justice Ronald George, appointed by a Republican governor, has said in regard to three strikes: 'To the extent we deny judges discretion, we lose a lot. The judge is in the best position, having heard all the evidence, to impose an appropriate punishment.' "

"Thanks for calling, Sam." Young clicked him off and went to another flashing line.

Another forty-five minutes of being broiled on the charcoals of public opinion and Kodama pulled off her headset at twenty-eight after two. Keyed up, she felt like she could go another hour and a half at full throttle. If the voters wanted to turn her out of office, then go down swinging, girl. Fuck that reserved jurist shit. She got up, trying hard not to smile.

"Nice going, Mr. Jamboni." Young shook the prosecutor's hand.

He garbled a "Thanks" while eyeballing the judge. "See you in the voting booth," he said on his way out. He knocked his briefcase against his leg as he walked.

When Kodama went to get her purse, she was surprised

to find Young lounging against the studio door.

"You were much better than I would have thought, Jill." He'd slipped a couple of breath mints in his mouth. He smelled like a eucalyptus tree. "Women like you give liberalism a chance after all."

He all but licked his lips. The Big Bad Right Wing Wolf. "Gee, thanks, Ken." She came up to him. "Open the door."

He bowed slightly and turned the knob. "You know, I hear you dig black men."

Kodama did a movement with her hand. "Well, lookie here, Ken. I happen to find one black man of particular interest right now, and for some time to come."

"But y'all ain't married." He was laying his "black" affectations on.

"We're serious."

"So am I."

"You know, I'm willing to get my first strike if you don't get out of my way."

"Ohh. You promise to tie me up and spank me?"

"What would those matrons in Van Nuys say if they heard you now."

"They might want to join the fun."

Kodama yanked the knob from his grasp and opened the door all the way. "Honey, if I found myself in bed with you, the queasiness I'd feel would be anything but hilarious." She began to walk away.

"I like hard women," he called after her.

"With your charm, maybe you ought to try hard men." Kodama got to the parking lot and dialed Newton Station on her cellular. After some runaround, she got the watch commander and demanded to know Monk's status.

"Just heard you on Young's show, Judge. You gonna come down here hollering about how we be abusing the prisoners and such?'' The heavy voice was like a glacial thaw.

"Let me speak to Zaneski or Fitzhugh.''

"Who?''

Her patience was thinning. "The detectives on the case.''

"Ah, gee, Your Honor. They be nowhere around. But I'll tell them you called.'' He hung up before she could speak.

The phone glinted in the sunglasses on Kodama's face. She punched redial and got a busy signal. Again, and still a busy signal. She wanted to speed over there and give an earful to that asswipe. But she had an appointment to be interviewed at *Rafu Shimpo*, the Japanese-American daily that had been publishing since the early part of the century. It was in Little Tokyo, across town.

She sighed, placing the phone back in her purse. She hated talking while driving, so the call would have to wait. After the newspaper interview, it was back west to the Crenshaw District to a meeting with the heads of the Deltas, the politically connected black sorority, at the Union Bank on Jefferson. A meeting she and Monk's friend council-woman Tina Chalmers had set up.

"Sorry, baby.'' She fired up the Saab. Driving off the lot, a peculiar tickle made her look around. Young was in an upstairs window, waving at her. She clenched her teeth and drove off, north on La Cienega. A mental picture of dragging Young and Jamboni from the Saab's bumper made for a pleasant ride through traffic.

Eighteen

Monk was buttoning his shirt when Seguin came into view outside the open cell. "Marasco." He unbuckled his belt and tucked the tail and front into his pants.

"So they're seeking a charge of manslaughter." Seguin had his hands in his pockets, his angular frame only partially visible in the half-light of the hallway.

Monk rolled the towel around the razor, toothbrush, paste, and the shirt he'd been wearing for the past three days. Teague had brought him the gear. "It's a bullshit beef. It's just something to fuck with me because Zaneski's a lead dick cocksucker."

"Big Loco didn't fire a gun, Ivan. At least not that night."

"That's right, Lieutenant, he didn't." Monk was not in the mood for a debate. "But are you going to stand there and tell me this doesn't seem to you like some kind of setup?"

Seguin didn't answer.

Monk had the towel and its contents held under his arm. He held out a hand, palm up as if knowledge might be dropped on its surface. "All the time you know me you think all of a sudden I'm capable of some cold-blooded shit like this."

"You're always taking advantage, Ivan."

"Of what, the law?"

Again he didn't answer. His face a blank.

"What the hell are you talking about, Marasco?" Although he had an idea.

"I mean you step all over the rules like they were a rug in the bathroom. You think they're for chumps like me." He started to walk off.

Monk followed. He signed out and found the cop lingering in front of the station, dusk settling like soot over the factories the precinct was surounded by.

"I ain't on the city's payroll, man. And sure I hedge, but damned if I don't put in work. I don't exactly have all this wonderful computer-age outfitting and a department at my disposal." He waved his hands at the old station house.

"Neither do I. You try being a brown man in this here Army."

"This some kind of midlife crisis?" Monk said lightly, trying to break the tension.

"I'm carrying my load, Ivan," he solemnly replied.

"You still on this kick that I'll shortchange the investigation because it might implicate blacks in the murders of the Cruzados?"

Seguin dug a cigarette out and stuck it between tight pressed lips. He smoked when he was stressed. He didn't light it. "No, of course not. But you will cut some slack for the brothers if you feel they're backs are up against it."

"If Absalla isn't involved, he isn't involved, Marasco."

"But he wants to impose black power over the Rancho."

"Bullshit." But it didn't sound convincing even to him.

Seguin took the cigarette out of his mouth and pointed with the wet end. "There's no Latino on the Ra-Falcons. And don't say it's 'cause of the Muslim thing. Other cliques in the country actively recruit among *la gente*."

"I can't do everything," he rationalized lamely.

"No one's saying you're supposed to, Ivan. But I've got commanding officers giving me a sigmoidal if they even sniff I might not have gone by the book on some barrio buster and people in the community thinking I'm one step removed from Pancho in the old Cisco Kid show.

"And to add to my joy, I got some pardners in La Ley who think just hanging out with a black dude makes me some kinda *pinche* love-and-kisses faggot."

"Alright, you got it tough, but who don't? I'm sure there're black officers in the Oscar Joel Bryant association who feel the same way about black cops fraternizing with Chicanos. What's that got to do with you and me, Marasco?"

Seguin slapped his thighs with his open palms and twisted his torso back and forth in exasperation. "You ain't getting it, man. Everything's changing, Ivan. Latinos are the largest minority in the state now, not black folks. Even Asians outnumber you."

Monk could almost hear the whisper of Tlaloc, his incendiary breath searing him and other African-Americans into ash on the streets and in the homes of the city. A city that had once belonged to Mexico. "But we helped found it too," he finished his daydreaming aloud. "And Latinos come in all colors and cultures. There's even Mexicans mixed with black blood along the coast down there, Guerro and Chiapas, right?"

"True. But this Rancho business is one more example of the wheelbarrow of bricks I got to push uphill as a Chicano cop. I want the guilty to pay and so do a lot of those folks down there. I don't give a fuck what the brass down at Parker Center want.''

"All of a sudden they don't want the same thing? And don't you forget,'' Monk added, pointing, ''those decent people down there include a lot of blacks.''

Seguin looked off. ''I'm not saying Mejicanos have got the monopoly on morality. Everybody plays racial politics in this city, Ivan. But even these days good and evil can stand stark naked before us, and you can choose which one you'll embrace.''

"I realize you pay bigger for the consequences of your actions, Marasco, given the bureaucracy and egos you have to deal with. But that don't mean I skate along either. I have to answer in the 'hood.''

Seguin threw the unused cigarette into the gutter. ''But you can walk away, Ivan. Absalla, Los Domingos, all of 'em. But the next immigrant that gets knocked in the head, the next kid shot for his bike, and it's me that gets the call. If not in the Rancho, then somewhere else in the city. I'm trying to keep the blacks and browns from tearing each other's hearts out, and still find time to go after the perp.''

"I don't have an answer for you.''

"No shit.'' He put his hands back in his pockets and went in the opposite direction.

Monk hailed a taxi. Several Bell and Yellow Cabs scurried about the precinct, their drivers used to the newly released having no means of transportation. Waiting for a bus this time of the evening in this part of town you'd have better luck seeing the next appearance of Halley's Comet.

He rode absorbed in his own thoughts over to the house on Madden, running over and over the rant from Seguin. It had been disjointed but there was a kind of sense to it. His friend, if he could still use that word, had been expressing an anger with a core of desperation.

But the more he tried to understand, the more it seemed to grate on him too. Seguin was acting like it was only he bearing the weight of these murders. Hell, Monk was the one facing a trial and a possible prison term if he couldn't find some shooters. He said it was a tough row to hoe being a Chicano cop—try being a black private eye who's everybody's favorite kick toy, Monk reasoned.

He wanted a cigar, a shot of rum, and then would like to drape his body all over Jill's hot, muscular form. He'd called, but she was out. Anyway, he needed to do this other thing.

The small back house was of course padlocked and plastered in plain sight with police yellow tape with the usual written warnings about tampering. But the front house, belonging to the landlord, had the porch light on.

After the usual introduction, which always ended with him showing his license and handing over a business card, Monk was pleasantly surprised he didn't have to also hand over any cash to solicit a little conversation. It helped that the two occupants had been out the night of the shoot-out, so they weren't all hyped-up about Monk's reappearance.

"Oh, no, Mr. Monk. I haven't seen young Burroughs since, oh, four days ago. The day he left for that funeral." Mrs. Freeman was in her seventies. Her son, a bookish man in slippers and a paisley print satin robe, was in his forties and lived with his mother, the talkative Mrs. Freeman had informed Monk to the son's visible consternation.

The mother was a retired timekeeper who'd worked for some thirty years at the now no longer existant Arden Dairy processing plant that had been on Slauson near Vermont. At that time, there had been a Sears just east of Vermont on Slauson that Monk's mom and dad would take him and his sister to on their birthdays to pick out new bicycles. He still dreamed of how he and his friends, Herman, Carl, and

Dimitri, used to pop wheelies, flying off a raised rectangle of plywood, on their Stingrays with the tuck-'n'-roll banana seats and chrome sissy bars.

The older woman made references to the son, Hinton, working on the periphery of the record industry—at what exactly wasn't made clear. On a built-in sideboard, several liqueurs were arrayed, including Drambuie, Prunella, and a long, slender bottle of Midori.

"Have either of you seen anybody around here? I mean except for that same night of the shoot-out?" He savored the rich coffee she'd insisted on brewing and serving in the delft china cup and saucer.

"Except for the police lingering around." The son sat opposite Monk, legs crossed, casually dangling the biography of Paul Robeson he'd been reading over the arm of the club chair.

"Yes, that's what I meant. The night I was here the men I spotted drove up in a black Isuzu Trooper." Both the son and the mother gave him an unknowing stare. "You know"—he made a boxlike pantomime with his hands—"a sport utility truck, sits up high. This one had silver trim."

"No, we haven't seen anything like that," the son said curtly. He'd been annoyed at the first sight of Monk. Maybe he didn't like having his reading interrupted.

"Wait," the mother offered, looking at the old Oriental carpet as if a replay were pooling in its designs. "I did see that black, oh, I don't know what you called it, truck, jeep . . . something."

"When was this, Mrs. Freeman?"

"The day before all the excitement." The son gave her a look but she pretended not to see it. "It was parked out front for a while, then drove off. I was going to call the law but it seemed like the two in it were just talking, so I didn't want to start no trouble for just that. Anyway they drove off and that was that. At least then.''

"And this truck doesn't belong to Keith 2X, ah, Burroughs?''

"Not as far as I know. He drives some small car or another.'' She looked questioningly over at her son.

"Some kind of Toyota, I think. I don't know much about cars,'' he said disdainfully. He placed the book in his lap, but Monk wasn't heeding the cue.

"Could you see the people in the truck?''

She pushed out her bottom lip. "Not really. I made a thing of going out front like I was checking on my flower bed, but I couldn't really tell. 'Cept—'' She halted herself.

"What?'' Monk prodded gently.

"Well, now, I ain't saying it was so, but I think the one at the passenger window, he's the one I could see better. I think he was a Mexican fella. That's what made me remember him.''

A sour look curled Hinton's lips. Could be his unctuous mother was another burden like not being able to read when he wanted to.

"Don't misunderstand me, I think it's fine to have all kinds of friends. Lord knows they're moving in all over the place, even 'round here.'' She broke off again, straining her sight past the walls.

"You tell the police this?'' Monk wanted to know.

"No. Nobody asked me about the black . . . Izod, you called it?''

"Maybe we should call them and let them know.'' Hinton sniffed loudly. "That Detective Fitzhugh left his card too.''

"As a good citizen you should.'' Monk put down his

cup and saucer. "I appreciate your time, Mrs. Freeman, Mr. Freeman."

An anemic "Alright" escaped the son's tight lips and he didn't bother getting up as Mrs. Freeman opened the door for Monk. Outside, he walked west along Hyde Park Boulevard to Crenshaw Boulevard and found an intact pay phone. The device was next to a closed furniture store specializing in red velour and free layaway.

Monk had asked Curtis Armstrong, proprietor of the Alton Brothers Automotive Repair and Service, whose business shared a lot with the donut shop, to fetch the Ford. The car was tucked away there but getting back to it this evening was a tertiary concern.

"Hey, jailbird." Kodama said breathlessly.

"Just getting back in?"

"Yeah, debated the president of the Lydia Homeowners Association over at Temple Leo Beck. I kicked his ass, if I might be so humble."

"Right on. Can you come get me?" Two male teens in pants big enough to clothe rhinos slowed up as they neared him. One leaned into the other and whispered something. They walked a little farther and lingered on the sidewalk. Monk feigned ignoring them, and finished talking to Kodama.

"Wanta blunt?" One lisped as Monk started to walk past.

"I look like I got time for weed?"

"You got all the time to talk to us," the larger one rasped, stepping close.

Monk also stepped closer; negotiations were over. He tossed the towel he'd wrapped his belongings in to the ground. He'd left it outside in the bushes while talking with Mrs. Freeman. "Well, young fellow, what's it going to be tonight? Maybe your friend has a roscoe, and maybe you do too. But I'm going to be on you 'fore you can draw yours and I can assure you I ain't been around this long because the baddest thing I do is drink tea at three. I got business to take care of, and you're in my face for no good reason.''

The one he was talking to just stared, openmouthed and sullen. "Let's hat," he said to his friend after a stretch. Horniness had a way of giving you a certain something extra, Monk reflected on his way to the corner to wait for Kodama.

She leaned on the chair, Monk pulling her dress up over the wonderful mound of her thighs. The black lace panties were a heady contrast to her tan skin. His throat constricted with passion. Monk reached his hand between the part of her legs to rub his woman.

He stepped closer, pulling her sheer undergarments down across her rear. Kodama reached back, taking hold of him while she gyrated. "If only the good burghers of the Valley could see you now," he said, delirious.

"It might get me a few more votes," she whispered.

"Uh," he grunted.

They made love with her bent over the chair, he entering her from behind. They had rented a room at the Snooty Fox on Western near King, not far from the LAPD's Southwest Division. The motel was a tastefully appointed two-story business with clean rugs and airy rooms, an upscale "hot sheet" rendezvous. But a quickie was not what the parted lovers had planned for tonight.

Later, Kodama stood naked before the sink counter, pouring liberal amounts of VSOP into two plastic cups. Monk, also nude, the crevice between his pectorals slick, walked up to her and put an arm around her waist. He pulled her close and licked her ear. She watched him in the mirror.

"I guess this isn't a good time to talk about the charges against you." She had some brandy.

"Sure, then maybe we can talk about whether there will ever be permanent peace in Rwanda." He pinched her butt, and lifted his measure of the booze to his mouth.

"This is serious, Ivan." But she had turned, wrapping one leg around him.

"Is this what they mean by gafflin' ya?"

"Uh," she grunted, taking him in her hand, working her grip up and down on his stiffening penis.

They eventually got into the bathroom and Kodama shoved Monk against the tiles in the shower, warm water pelting them from the shower head. She bit his shoulder, near the area where a ricocheting bullet had caused a chip along his collarbone. She worked her way down, her tongue and mouth eventually working between his legs.

"Good goobyldywook," Monk managed between pangs of pleasure.

Kodama started to giggle. She put a hand against his thigh to steady herself. "Wait, didn't Grady on *Sanford and Son* used to say that?"

"I believe I understand how he invented the phrase."

After some time she stood, and latched her leg around him again. He got his hands up under her and hoisted her aloft. They made love again: in the shower, against the bathroom door, the Home Depot wood paneling, and finally wound up entangled, sitting on the floor, Monk's back against the bed. The couple lay exhausted and entranced with the rhythm of each other's bodies.

"I got rug burns," he complained on the way back home. He reached over and caressed the inside of her leg.

"God, how would you be if you were away for a year?"
She stopped at a light and kissed him.

"Crazy, baby, crazy." The Saab pulled into the
driveway. He was looking back, down the slope from the
house. In the night, Silverlake Reservoir shimmered like
hope just out of reach.

"I think too much sex must addle your mind."

"Who said I had enough yet?" His hands went under
her dress and tugged on the lacy material.

"Damn, honey," she murmured. She helped get them
off. Monk kissed her, his finger buried beneath the dress.
Deftly, he reached across her and unlatched the seat so it
reclined flat out. He put the gear shift in fourth position to
give him room and, her legs spread apart, bent his head
toward her moist patch.

Coming closer, the musky smell of her vagina filled his
senses like a ripe fruit of hypnotic properties he couldn't
wait to taste. He was engulfed, gloriously lost in an
experience one part of him wished he would never find his
way back from.

She sighed, thrusting her pelvis into his face. His hand
worked along the underside of her rear, he kissed and
nibbled on her inner thighs.

In the world outside the car, beyond the calm black skein
of the Reservoir, the hard boys were waiting. Bad night
was falling, and the other part of him, the part that needed
more than this woman, the part that wanted discernable
patterns and an accounting for murder, was hungry to
confront the lurkers.

Let it come, some distant train's whistle cajoled him
from a track spanning the cosmos. The leather of Kodama's
heels rubbed along his upper back and he worked his

tongue in slower and slower motions. She shuddered, her fist pounding the side of the seat.

Let it come, let them all come. He wanted to taste the sweat and fear, for it would destroy him or he it.

Nineteen

"**Q**uite an assortment of artifacts," Fletcher Wilkenson commented. He stood, hands in his rear pockets, looking at the various objects tacked about Monk's office from his travels as a merchant marine. At the moment, he was touching a Maori figure on top of the filing cabinet.

"Thanks," Monk replied. The older gent had left several messages for him while he was in jail. He'd forgotten to tell Teague to call him. When he'd gotten in this morning he'd called him to ask him to come over. Monk was still deciding how much Wilkenson really knew about his former boxing disciple, Jokay Maladrone.

"Sit down, will you, Fletcher." He sounded stern, like his mother.

"Okay." He sat before the Colonial desk, enjoying more of his coffee.

"When you gave me the 'City of Promise' manuscript, did you know I knew Grant?"

Surprise lighted the pleasant face as he held his cup midway to his mouth. "No. In fact, had I known, I might have been less forthcoming. Why are you telling me now?"

Monk told him of his relationship with the ex-cop, and the blowout he'd had with him. He found the retelling uncomfortable. Afterward, he said, "But I'm in this to finish, despite the ghosts this case might upset."

"And of course to beat the manslaughter rap," Wilkenson illuminated.

"Sure, there's that," Monk agreed, laughing heartily.

Wilkenson's smile disappeared quickly. "But you can't always let your pride or principle drive you too hard, Ivan. Sometimes the friendships you brush aside in the process don't get replaced." A haunted cast shaded his watery blues.

"Don't you want to pay Dexter back?" The question had several layers of meaning for Monk.

Wilkenson played with his cup. "I'd be lying if I didn't admit I wanted the ones who torpedoed the Rancho's dream. If the goals had been realized, it could have been a model for the whole city. So yes, I guess I want the real manipulators to suffer a painful retribution in Teutonic hell. But frankly, Grant and Jakes are low on that list. They were messenger boys. If they didn't do it, some other kind of delivery would have been made."

He rubbed a hand through his short mane. "After I was forced out for helping my friend with her . . . problem, my marriage went bust. Not that it wasn't rocky by then anyway."

"Your wife wasn't in the movement?"

"No, no, she was dedicated, Ivan. She was a staunch member of the Civil Rights Congress. She knew the deal. She herself had been pressured to sign a loyalty oath because she was a social worker for the county."

"What happened?" Monk had a weird premonition like he was hearing a future past version of what could happen to him and Kodama.

Wilkenson rubbed his hands on his lower thighs. "After I was bounced out, there was an article denouncing me in the *Times*. I'm pretty sure that was Parker's doing. Our house got shot into, we got obscene phone calls at all hours." He shrugged. "That didn't scare Rena, she could take it." Wilkenson brought the cup to his mouth then set it back down.

"She'd met another man. A man who would listen to her rather than rush off to the next meeting, or arrange a back alley abortion, or whatever else was more important than paying attention to his marriage . . . to my wife. So the new man was as fiery about the revolution as he was about her."

Wilkenson's body went slack. "So do I want revenge? My research backs up the claim your judge friend told you. Grant did encourage DeKovan to go ahead with the job training center."

"To try and balance his sins," Monk commented.

"Sure," Wilkenson said quietly. "Of course the center was designed to fail without the infrastructure we'd worked hard to put in place. Besides, Jakes was the one who really enjoyed sticking it to a red."

"Dexter still did it."

"He had a family, Ivan. Better a man with half a conscience than one with a blowtorch and a dead soul."

Monk made noise in his swivel. "You still wind up dead in a ditch. No matter how painful it was for the one found pulling the trigger."

"Friends ratted on boyhood pals at HUAC. Men and woman hid or burned their Unemployed Council pamphlets and publicly denounced comrades they'd bled together with on strike lines, to keep their teaching jobs." Wilkenson leaned forward, his hands clasped before him. "Who can say what any one of us will do to protect the ones we love?''

''You didn't roll over, Fletcher.''

Wilkenson leaned back, an exasperated air huffing from his lungs. Involuntarily, he quickly glanced over his shoulder. ''I was a contact for what the Communist Party used to call a closed or unavailable but operative member, you understand?''

''Not exactly,'' Monk admitted.

Wilkenson adjusted his rangy frame in the chair. ''I get into this in the preface of the book I'm writing now. In 1951 the U.S. Supreme Court upheld the Foley Square convictions. This was a move begun by Truman, Hoover, and their ilk to railroad Communist Party leaders under the Smith Act. You know what that is?''

Monk did a motion with his hand. ''Treason, plotting to overthrow the United States. Wasn't there talk of slamming that against Jane Fonda when she went to North Vietnam during the war?''

''Right. The Foley Square case, so-called because the trial took place at the Foley Square Courthouse in New York, began in 1949 when the Party's General Secretary Eugene Dennis, Ben Davis, an African-American, Gil Green, and other leaders were convicted essentially for teaching Marxism and Leninism. Keep in mind none of these individuals were proven to have instigated or committed physical violence. But the power of their words was enough to get them sentenced for their ideas.''

''You must have just been a teenager then, Fletcher.''

''Yes, I was. But my folks took their Lutheran duty to heart. They'd come out from Milwaukee before the war like a lot of Midwesterners. We had a tradition of being neighborly and helping those less fortunate. I know it sounds like the missionary complex, but for my parents it translated into standing up to the bigotry against blacks and Mexicans that they saw perpetrated here in Los Angeles.''

''So your folks were members of the Party?''

Wilkenson laughed like he was sucking in air. ''Mom flirted with the notion, but she believed too much in the here and after. That was one contradiction she couldn't overlook. But they worked in social justice organizations, some with Party members, who were doing their good Communist work.

''And of course there were other organizations that were fronts, constructs of the Party that gave the appearance of grassroots organizations, but which actually were headed by cadre members.''

''So you came up in all this?''

''Yeah. I remember people like Dorothy Healey, once called the Red Queen of Los Angeles, coming over to our house. She smoked like the devil, but she would always ask me how I liked school, and recommend books for me to read. We lived on Manhattan Place just off Adams. Ben Dobbs, another Dorothy—Doyle, I think her married name was—hell, even the old reprobate Gus Hall were over several times.''

''The last true Communist,'' Monk remarked. He recalled seeing the obstreperous octogenarian Hall in an A&E documentary still extolling Communist Party, U.S.A. rigidness post the fall of the Wall and breakup of the Soviet Union.

Wilkenson said, ''You got to give him something for consistency. Anyway, after the sentences were upheld, the Party took the position that fascism was fast approaching. They operated on the premise that it was five minutes to midnight. This was the same mind-set of the resistance movements during Nazi-occupied Europe. So the Party sent specific members to other cities—with new names, the whole bit.

"It sounds like Looney Toons today, maybe, but you gotta recognize the times."

"That isn't so crazy, Fletcher," Monk said soberly. "Those times may yet be back again."

"How true," the other man agreed. "So my folks helped with some of this ferrying people about, securing new identities for them and so on. It was quite an adventure for me and my brother," he said fondly.

"A lot of people went underground in L.A.?"

"Not like in the cities back East, no. In Healey's memoirs, she pretty much chalks it up to Keystone Kops antics. But she too had the value of decades of hindsight. Like you said, if you think you're in the gun sights, then you damn sure do something not to be a target."

"You hungry?"

"I could stand to dirty a plate," Wilkenson enthused.

"Let's get a bite downstairs." He also wanted to see if Gorzy had calmed down any about his wife and the supposed missing money.

At one of the grey Formica tables in the Cafe 77, Monk asked, "Skipping a few years, I gather some of the people you knew in and out of the Party worked in local government." Monk quickly put a hand up like he was warding off a blow. "I'm not saying it was a conspiracy. It just makes sense that if you want change, you go where change is made."

Wilkenson chewed his egg salad on wheat. "Sure, that's where the goddamn Merchants and Manufacturers Consortium and the Golden State Realtors had us. That sumabitch Parker could've given Hoover lessons on information gathering. When I first got in the Housing Authority in fifty-seven, I got word from those fat cats that if I named names, I could continue in the department.''

''Since you didn't, how come the big boys didn't come after you then?'' Monk looked around for Gorzy, but only the waitress and the cook seemed to be around.

''Remember what I said about closed and so on? When some of the others, Dorothy Millhouse, Chuck Mosley— you know he was a bodyguard for Paul Robeson when he came to town? Anyway, when they got bounced, they'd done a disinformation campaign of their own. The Party made it seem that me and a few who were left were really just a bunch of college kids who didn't know anything. That we'd been their flunkies. To prove they were telling the truth, they gave up a couple of closed members in the Planning Department.''

Monk's brow went down. ''What?''

Wilkenson dabbed a napkin on his lips. ''It was part of a larger plan to ensure at least some of us would survive. As the political climate changed, it was hoped we could bring to fruition some of the things so many had sacrificed so long to see realized.'' He ate more of his sandwich.

''The closed members who were given up went along with this willingly?'' The concept was a strain for him to grasp.

''Not much choice. You see, Ivan,'' he rolled the name around with a touch of irony, ''you see, there had already been a series of discussions, like the ones a man named McReynolds of the Socialist Party in L.A. had organized. And there were the American Forum discussions that took place in fifty-seven. These were all part of the dialogues that took place among many on the Left who heretofore hadn't had much to do with one another. This was an historic occurrence, you see what I mean?''

"Necessity being the mother," Monk noted, "because of McCarthyism and whatnot."

"Yes. And Stalin was gone too—died in fifty-three. Inside the Soviet Union there was also beginning to be a thaw, an opening up if only by degrees. So by the time we're talking about, late fifty-eight, this first *glasnost*, combined with what the comrades had gone through here in the States, created fertile ground for a new crop of ideas.

"And then the real bomb was dropped." He ate some of his coleslaw. "Party leaders finally 'fessed up to the murderous outrages committed by Stalin." A tenseness had crept into his voice. "So, really, what choice did these closed members have? There were splits among the Party members over the Stalin revelations, and again friend turned against friend."

"But there was still hope," Monk ventured.

Wilkenson said nothing, but the creases at the corners of his eyes deepened as if a gravitational force pushed in on him. "Good, strong men and strong women who knew the good fight was not won in a single battle. Or even a hundred. By sixty-one, the wall had gone up in Berlin. . . . Still, there was that period of great flux, of possibilities. That's what we held out for, Ivan."

"A fight that continues."

Mrs. Gorzynski had entered, easily carrying a cardboard box full of honeydew melons. She put the produce down on the counter, and went in back to the office. Monk's feeble plan consisted of merely confronting the woman with what Gorzy had said. That approach really had little appeal, as he might cause a problem when he really didn't think one existed. Anyway, he had his own concerns, what with zealots dancing around the Rancho, gunmen in the night, and a possible trial.

"Do you trust Maladrone?" he blurted out.

Wilkenson stalled. "How does one answer that? Do I think he's sincere in attempting to do what he says he is. Well, yes, I do."

"Yeah," Monk said impatiently, "he's not the first gangster with a warped sense of honor. Meyer Lansky attended Temple and died devoutly in Israel."

Wilkenson smiled. "Certain friends of mine ascribe to the theory of progressive gangsterism, that the iron hand must be applied when discipline is absent. If the enemy is using ruthlessness, then maybe strong-arm methods are needed to counterbalance such machinations."

"Aztlán by way of the AK."

"Sounds awfully harsh when you say it like that," Wilkenson retorted. "Jokay is nobody's saint, but I think his illness has forced him to see beyond mere illicit profits."

Monk's eyes got wide. "If the two names he gave me are real, he might be orchestrating one big setup so he can use me to get the Ra-Falcons out of the way."

Wilkenson held his hands up. "But why? I don't think there's gold buried under the land."

Monk moved his empty Miller bottle around like a glass chess piece. Mrs. Gorzynski was still in the back. "When will your book be finished?"

"In about another month or so, I'm hoping. The publisher is a university press," Wilkenson said. "Basically now I'm fact checking, and following up on where those who were active then are these days. At least the ones still alive. H. H. DeKovan is particularly interesting in that he's become a recluse in the last few years. Yet he continues to buy and develop sports stadiums and shopping malls, has his hand in gambling ventures, and is reported to still have connections in politics."

Monk stopped playing with the bottle. "What are the other gaming interests he has?"

"He's a partner in that combination casino and amusement park in Vegas laid out like a Turkish bazaar. You know the one *Newsweek* had on a cover last year?"

"You don't think DeKovan wants the land the Rancho's on to build one big supercasino, hotel, and indoor mall?" Monk imagined wildly.

"So he could ship new Chinese capitalists in to fleece 'em?" Wilkenson seemed to take joy in the idea.

"How many acres is the Rancho, Fletcher?"

"You have to take into account there's that field behind where the hulk of the job training site sits. That part was intended for a shopping center. So all together it's around 230 acres I would guess."

"Good-sized piece of land," Monk fantasized about the possibilities.

Wilkenson remained silent, not sure where their conversation had gone. Finally he said, "What are you suggesting?"

"Maybe your old pal DeKovan wants to build an Aztec-Muslim playland. Where the rides include flying fatted calves, the sun sacrifice roller coaster, and the fast food is lamb-on-a-stick with salsa."

"Crickets."

"Huh?"

"Ancient Mejicano food included crickets," Wilkenson said.

"Oh, my bad."

They both laughed.

Twenty

Monk spent the next three days chasing down all manner of leads and rumors concerning H. H. DeKovan. He salvaged information from on-line and at the refurbished, and swank, downtown L.A. library—which had a section on the DeKovan family due to an endowment from his maternal grandmother, Genera Smith Berringer. And he read and reread the research material Wilkenson had accumulated on the odd multimillionaire.

Photos of DeKovan from the late sixties up through the seventies showed a dark-complected, athletically built man, jackknife deadly in Botany 500 and Saville Row suits. In several of the shots he had the obligatory starlet-on-the-rise on his arm, and invariably the women had busts protruding like the prow of a destroyer and hemlines only a gynecologist could have designed.

DeKovan, in bell-bottoms and puff sleeve shirt, at the opening of *Hair* at the Aquarius; buying drinks for the house at Perinos; escorting the merry widow Jacqueline Kennedy to the opening of *The Fantastiks* at the Dorothy Chandler Pavilion; watching his horses run at Santa Anita with a dour-faced Stanley Kubrick; hosting a private party at the Griffith Park Observatory where the Doors were performing live, driving an Ingot stock car at Daytona; holding a shovel like a rifle, standing in a field announcing his role in the acquisition of land that would become the Magic Mountain amusement park; clasping a cigarette holder while groping Mamie Van Doren at the Playboy Mansion; looking aloof at the ground-breaking for the Century Freeway. Portraits of H. H. DeKovan, the hip capitalist, as he squired and accumulated women and money over the years.

Taking several of the photocopies he'd made from the photos on microfiche, Monk put them in chronological order. Along with the knowledge he'd gained from Wilkenson and the other source material, a rudimentary psycho-history of DeKovan was laid before him in the reproductions. In the early shots DeKovan had a genial, almost mischievous quality to his facial expressions and poses. But as time progressed, there seemed to be more of a strained quality in the flashes of caps, the worried set of his eyes not in sync with his forced grins.

Even his physical posture indicated the internal change. There was a picture taken in 1979 on Melrose in front of the place that had been the Ash Grove, a famous folk and blues landmark where musicians like Bob Dylan and John Lee Hooker had played. He was pointing at the building, standing in a knot of people that included then–Secretary of State Jess Unruh, and several Sacramento types.

DeKovan's body was doing a swinger's imitation of Nixon. His cheeks were blue with whiskers, and his suit didn't have that pristine, just-out-of-the-cleaner's look of the early days. His shoulders were hunched forward and one of his hands was grabbing his own leg midthigh. He was facing Unruh, but his orbs were drifting away from him, a deviant glare evident on his face.

According to a November 1984 piece in Wilkenson's
file, an article reprinted from *Esquire*, the writer had set out
to find the once outgoing, gregarious DeKovan. Somewhere
around 1980, DeKovan had taken to holing up in one of
his estates. It was the one in L.A. above Temescal Canyon
Fire Road. He'd quit certain boards he had been on because
they required him to attend meetings. The writer had interviewed business partners, former girlfriends, and politicos
who knew him, but he couldn't pinpoint a specific incident
that might have brought on the need for DeKovan to secret
himself away from public view.

The writer speculated that maybe it was an illness or a
disfigurement he'd gotten from an accident skiing or sky-
diving. The rakish millionaire was adept at both sports, but
there was no empirical evidence to support the writer's pre-
sumptions.

Monk looked at the clock, it was past eleven-thirty, and
he was not going to have a third cup of coffee at this hour
of the night. Kodama padded into the breakfast nook in her
bare feet and terry cloth robe. She had that morning's *Daily
Journal* under one arm.

"What it be like on the trail of the Pink Panther?" She
kissed him on the cheek and sat next to him, rubbing his
back.

"I do feel like Clouseau," he groused.

"I was just playing, honey." She kissed him again.

He shoved the table and its load of material away from
him. "I think I've pissed away three days I ain't got to be
fooling with. DeKovan may be living in a reconverted nu-
clear testing bunker in the Nevada desert growing orchids,
or holed up in a suite at some hotel he owns in Amster-
dam," Monk said, exasperated. "Well-endowed nurses in
uniforms riding up their heavy thighs giving him enemas
and bee pollen shots on the regular."

"I know that's how you want to wind up." Idly, she sifted through his papers. She came upon a shot of De-Kovan touring the *Herald Examiner* newsroom with a bleary and bloated Elvis. "Quite the player," she mused.

"He was. But he might as well be the man who invented the water engine as far as trying to find this strange bastard." He backhanded some of the papers, revealing several more beneath.

Kodama looked through more of the stuff, stopping at a listing of the names of various enterprises. "These are the companies he owns?"

"Or at least has significant interest in." Monk yawned.

"Business parks, stadiums, casinos—and what are these?" She pointed at names like Eridanus Enterprises, Trentex, and White Hall.

Monk jabbed his thumb at the companies she was looking at. "That first one builds water recycling units, the second one some kind of software concern, and the third is a line of premium cigars."

"Well," she drawled, "have you ever had one of his?"

"Every once in a while. But generally, White Halls are too rich for my blood." Suddenly, he hit the table with his fist. "It was a recycling concern that bought the Randolph Center."

"What was the name?" Kodama studied the list.

"I'll have to ask Henry Cady again." Monk also glanced at the list. "Look"—he pointed to a name further down—"he even has something to do with the Dancing Dinosaur chain."

Kodama scrunched her features. "What? The children's playland with those loud kill-the-slobbering-alien video games, singing dinosaur waiters and waitresses, comic book panels for wallpaper, and jumping pits full of sticky, gummy rubber balls?" The mention of the facility, with the attendant carousing children, seemed to bring her up short.

"You forgot the wholesome menu of chili-cheese potato skins, popcorn-fried chicken, triple-cheese pizza, and pirate flagons of strawberry soda and root beer." Monk rubbed his stomach.

"The name Trentex was in the news recently," Kodama said, jabbing the paper.

"You remember why?" Monk asked excitedly.

Kodama got up. "We might still have it." She went to search through the previous week's newspapers in the yellow recycling tub in the back end of the kitchen. Presently she returned with the folded Business section from the *L.A. Times*.

"There you go, champ."

Monk read through a story about Trentex, a boutique software designer located in Burbank. The high-tech firm had produced three of the most popular CD-ROMs currently on the market. One of them was called L.A.'s Hidden History. "I bet DeKovan included a section on Wilkenson just for laughs."

"The arrogance of the rich and untouchable," Kodama lamented, stretching. "Let's go to bed. You need some rest. We'll get through this."

Monk wanted to continue his forays into the paper wilderness in an attempt to find DeKovan. But he also knew he would only get to know the man from secondhand accounts: photos, rumors, conjectures. DeKovan was like the fairy tales his grandmother used to tell him when he was young. He didn't remember details about them, only the impression that her bedtime stories were of a different timbre than Mother Goose. The people and situations she talked about were more in line with the nihilism of the Brothers Grimm.

Not much later, he lay awake, spooned with Kodama's

body, his arm around her bare middle. "When I was a kid, Grandma Riles, my mother's mother, used to tell me about Anansi," he whispered softly in her ear.

A drowsy "That's nice" issued from her.

"He was the Spider-god of the Ashanti, I learned much later. Although I don't think Grandma knew that, or actually, she probably didn't remember it. This was a story her folks had passed down to her."

"Huh."

He kissed and bit her back. "DeKovan's like this character, tricky, a manipulator, but he's got magical powers, see? He makes things happen, conforming the world to his will, he bends human lives. While he hides in the corner, spinning his web."

"Japanese got spider gods too, baby." She patted his leg. "Now go to sleep."

Reluctantly he ceased talking and gently withdrew his arm as slumber overcame her. He rolled the other way and turned the radio on low volume. Bobby "Blue" Bland was singing "Sad Street," and Monk stayed awake past two in the morning listening to the blues, his mind overworked, his body tired. Outside their bedroom windows, he felt certain, the city contained figments of scattered memories, disconnected and disconsolate, swirling in and out of this dimension. Somewhere inside those memories were the answers he sought, frustratingly just beyond his reach.

Twenty-one

"**F**uck," Monk swore into the receiver.

"Sorry, Ivan," Parren Teague said from his car phone. "The D.A. wants to show that the boyfriend of a judge doesn't get any special attention."

"That's 'cause the motherfuckah was embarrassed when he got busted by the press for giving undue consideration to the relatives of some of his contributors."

Teague's voice was lost momentarily in electronic fuzz. ". . . upcoming election, and Jamboni has announced he intends to run for the job. The D.A.'s going to go out of his way to show he's not soft."

Monk clamped down on one side of his mouth. "You and me ain't got no argument, Parren. What's the date for the hearing again?" Monk had his appointment book open.

"Three days."

"If they indict me, I can still be out on bail, right?" he asked anxiously.

"There's more than that."

"What?"

"Your buddy Zaneski is making noise; they may try to

compound the charge with obstruction and breaking and entering.''

''Hey, just make it three strikes and save all the time and effort,'' he said, defeated.

Car noise filtered across. ''We'll prevail.''

''If you say so. Did your eager intern find anything on that plate number of the Isuzu Trooper?'' Monk could have routinely looked the number up via a service he'd used in the past, but he might as well have his lawyer work hard for his as-yet unrealized money.

Teague hesitated. ''You're making this my morning of sorries. It turned out to be a stolen plate. I believe she faxed a copy of the police report over to you. She's going to be another Gloria Alred someday.''

''You mean that as a compliment?''

''Don't make fun of your lawyer. Talk to you.''

''Later.''

Monk pawed through a short stack of letters and papers on the left side of his desk. Two of them turned out to be the fax from Teague's office. The intern related that a receptionist at a company located on West Olive Avenue had reported to the Glendale DMV office that someone had stolen her license plates a week before Monk spotted them on the Isuzu.

Another dead lead. Disgusted, he balled up the fax and tossed it away. He fetched a dark-bodied Santa Rosa cigar from his desk and contemplated spending the rest of the useless day smoking and scratching his crotch. At least he'd have accomplished something.

He'd like to believe he was going to plow ahead with his investigation into the Cruzado murders, but what was the point? The fucking LAPD was on his jock, he was disappointed with Dexter, Seguin was pissed at him, and

Keith 2X Burroughs was either hiding out, or dead by other hands.

It mattered to Monk he'd assured Connie Smalls he'd see to it nothing would happen to Burroughs, though he hadn't given the words much thought as he had said them to her. His turn of a phrase was an art he'd worked at over the years talking to people involved in his pursuits. The words were easy to use in order to gain information from a woman who wanted to know some good might come from all her travails. And he had been too willing to play the protector. But what had he set into motion? And could he really do anything to ensure Burroughs's safety?

Conversely, Jill was batting a thousand. But now that she was finally into fighting for her career, her time and attention were obviously concentrated on winning. He lit the cigar and smoked with reserve. He could only have so much credit with Teague, and the bill on the other end was just one more worry.

What did Teague say, a morning of sorries? Sorry, little Marisa, sorry for your pops and grandma too, honey. But Ivan Monk's got his own shit to swim through, and the bastards have got concrete blocks chained to my ankles. I guess you don't get no relief either, no answers for your cruel deaths.

Delilah came in while he stood at the window smoking. "I'm going to lunch, want to come along?"

"You go ahead, D."

"Ivan," she started, stepping into the room, trying to ignore the choking aroma. "You know if there's anything . . ."

"I appreciate that, Delilah. I really do."

She kissed him on the cheek and went away, closing the door quietly.

Monk sat on the couch, chewing the stump of the Santa

Rosa to keep busy. After some time, he got up and by rote went through the material he'd accumulated on DeKovan again. A destitute prospector digging one more time for the mother lode he knows just has to be there. It had to be, because it was all he had left to keep him going.

He shunted aside papers with barely a notice until he came to the list of his companies. The address for Trentex clicked. He read it again and then went to retrieve the fax he'd thrown away. The addresses were the same.

"That's the kind of sugar Daddy likes," he said, quoting an elated Bogart upon finding his vein of gold in *The Treasure of the Sierra Madre*. "Careful," he warned himself, continuing to talk aloud, "you'll wind up like him at the end of the movie."

He put his finger under each address and reread the two. Yes, they were the same. Then his happiness faded like newsprint in a summer rain. This and the comp tickets to both Isaiah Booker and Big Loco certainly seemed to confirm DeKovan's involvement in this mess, but neither piece of information got him closer to the elusive millionaire. He was still a fictive being, known only to Monk as black type on paper, and halftones with terse captions.

"Shit." He tossed the butt onto the pile. He put his head down, interlacing his fingers behind his head. He reared back, staying like that for several moments. He knew he had to do it. He consoled himself that he'd have found DeKovan with enough time, but he was on too short a leash.

He got in the Ford, and drove to Lake Elsinore.

"So I'm supposed to be the great big wonderful white-haired old codger who couldn't wait for his old saddle pal to return? California Carlson who would forgive Hoppy for his damning him?" Grant plodded through his living room like he'd only recently moved in: bumping into furniture, colliding against lamps. "But now you come whining and sniveling back 'cause you need me. The Gunga Din, lowlife motherfucker you thought was no better than dog shit tracked in from the yard."

"Dex—"

"No, don't talk, I'm not through." His cheeks were blowing in and out and he was clutching a standing lamp. His gnarled hand was shaking. "You may be short on humility, Mr. Monk, but you damn sure have got some giant brass balls."

"I'm in trouble, Dexter." Saying it like this, to him, even now, the significance of the words washed over him like brackish oil—thick and heavy with a presence he could feel but not identify.

"You fucking right you are, Sonny Jim."

"Jill told you."

Grant rubbed a hand over his lower jaw, grinning. "How the hell would you tie your shoes in the morning if you didn't have her?" He glanced out the front window. "She's very . . . concerned." He leaned against a wall, drawing in on himself. "I wish I—So you've been talking to Wilkenson?"

Monk, who'd been sitting on the arm of an overstuffed chair, shifted his weight. "He has a lot of history."

Grant huffed, straightening off the wall. "How come your boy wonder can't put you on to DeKovan?"

"He's not the focus of his book, Dex." He knew what he wanted to hear. "Let's face it, he's not going to have your connects." Monk hoped he was satisfied with that much ass kissing.

"But you still take his side on what happened when I was on the force?"

"Dex, do you think what you did was right?"

"What am I, a child? You gonna use that kind of tone with me?"

Astonishment iced Monk's words. "Dex, we can go 'round and 'round on this all you want, it doesn't change the past, nor what you did—for whatever reasons. It also doesn't change what I think of you, deep down. Yes," he conceded, getting up, "I'll admit it sticks with me, but you can't honestly believe I'd be any other way about this."

"If it was the other way around, what would you think of me?"

"Maybe you would've been man enough not to go along with the program." The fury dissipated from Grant, and he leaned against the back of the couch.

Monk walked toward him. "I don't know that and neither do you. I haven't had a family to worry about."

"That's what I tell myself, Ivan. Sometimes I even half believe it."

Monk fixed him with a look. "I know you're the one who told DeKovan about Wilkenson's idea for the job training center."

Grant snorted. "That wasn't exactly heroic. But it did let me sleep a little better." His light greys were wet.

"DeKovan," Monk said.

Grant punched him lightly on the shoulder. "Okay, boss. But I haven't heard much about the son of a bitch for some ten years now myself."

A hole opened up in his chest. "Nothing?"

"I said *not much*, not *nothing*," Grant replied. "Since we're being on the up-and-up, Perry Jakes was doing work for DeKovan when he left the force."

Jakes had died over a year ago. "What kind of work?"

Grant made a gesture as though he were describing a globe to a blind man. "Security. In the old days it meant setting up the banging parlors for the starlets and debutantes he was bedding." For the first time since Monk had arrived, Grant finally loosened up.

"That was then," Monk prodded.

Grant shook his head up and down. "Right. I saw Jakes every once in a while after we retired. He never told me directly what his odd jobs were for DeKovan. He always liked to be more obtuse than necessary. Make himself into a big man, you know? But the work was mostly bullshit, I gathered."

He made for the kitchen and Monk followed him. There he opened the battered Frigidaire with its pull spring handle. He produced two Millers and handed one to Monk.

"How do you mean?"

"DeKovan had nutted up, or at least seemed to. He'd gotten into going to these conspiracy meetings, UFO clubs out in the Nevada desert, even had a flirtation with those Heaven's Gate yahoos for a few months."

"Lovely," Monk said sarcastically.

"And he got wrapped up in divining secret Masonic ceremonies, studying Illuminati writings, all kinds of weird shit."

"What brought it on? Drugs, booze? Some bimbette squeeze his head too tight between her thighs one night?"

Grant grinned, holding the bottle of beer to his mouth. "I haven't the foggiest. Perry did say one time he was in a poker game with DeKovan, Yorty—this is after Bradley beats him, see?—and a couple of the businessmen from the old days. Now mind you, this cat was still making money, and for the rest of them their day on the mountaintop had passed.

"Anyway, here sits DeKovan, his hair is damned near to his shoulders, the nails on both little fingers grown out and pointed."

"Did he act strange?"

"No, Perry said. His hair was combed, he didn't stink. He was dressed casual-like. But they're talking and so forth—Jakes said Yorty even made fun of DeKovan's appearance and he seemed to take it just fine. So they're playing and carrying on, and they get to talking about why didn't DeKovan ever marry."

"And . . . ?"

"Perry, for one of the few times while I knew him, gets serious when he's telling me this. He says DeKovan stopped laughing and suddenly got all choked and maudlin. He started lamenting the death of a woman named Irene. But as he's telling them this, Jakes realizes he's describing the movie *Laura*. He's changed this "Irene" woman's death from a murder to a car accident, but it's the plot of the goddamn movie."

"The one with Dana Andrews?"

"Yeah. Now, Jakes never lets on and the others, as far as he can tell, believe this story to be true. So what do you make of that, Bulldog Drummond?"

"What? A confirmation that DeKovan's a fuckin' loon?"

"Or doing the biggest performance of his life." Grant said. "Later, out of earshot of the others, DeKovan nudges Jakes and asks him how did he do? Jakes told me this, right. Well, there was a little something I told him. Something only I knew 'cause one night I had to fetch one of DeKovan's B-picture maidens from a laudanum and brandy party up in the hills." Grant's eyes shone brightly.

"She's whacked out and rambling on and mentions when DeKovan was in college, he'd studied at the Pasadena Playhouse. Pretty good student too. A natural, she said."

Monk unscrewed his top. "He is crazy, and he's pretending like he ain't."

Grant held up a finger. "He was making all kinds of

smart money deals, Ivan. This is the period in which his holdings grew.''

Monk took a swig. ''I don't care if this chump believes the alignment of Pluto and the starship *Enterprise* over the Washington Monument will bring back vaudeville. The supposed stolen license turns up on the vehicle of the two looking to send me to Jesus. Big Loco had a comp ticket to the Airport Casino, a place where an OG of the Scalp Hunters was also getting the house treatment.'' Monk produced the pass he'd retrieved from the gang leader's wallet and waved the card.

''Fascinating,'' Grant said with a smirk.

''Fascinating my ass,'' Monk retorted. ''Fletcher has a Xerox of a shot from the *Herald Examiner* showing Maladrone and DeKovan together at the opening of the job training center.''

''That goddamn job training center.'' Grant slowly rubbed the bottle of beer between his hands. ''What do you want me to do, Ivan?''

''How tough will it be to get me a meet?''

Conflicting thoughts contorted Grant's seasoned face. ''It means I'll have to see Jakes's widow.''

Thinking he was understanding his tone, Monk asked, ''You two didn't get along?''

''She's the third wife. Ex-stripper and silicone for brains.'' He shook his head in private amazement. ''No, that's not fair. Actually, Khristi is alright. Bad breaks and shitty husbands. She really made an effort at, ah, self-enlightenment I'd guess you'd call it.''

''She's read *The Celestine Prophecy* twice?''

''Some of us aren't gifted with your raw insight.''

''Oh,'' Monk drawled, Grant's previous expression finally making sense. ''She hot for teacher?'' he jibed him.

''Don't start,'' he snarled.

"Her name again?"

"Khristi," he said, and spelled it for him.

"If he only married this Khristi for her body, would Jakes have told her anything worthwhile about DeKovan?"

"You'd be surprised what a man will tell a woman after he's rubbed the ol' fire pole between breasts the size of casabas."

Monk considered Grant's sagacity. "Master Po may have something there."

Beer in hand, he made a call on the wall phone in the kitchen. "Khristi? This is Dexter. . . . Uh-huh, yeah, I know, I meant to call sooner. Well . . ." Grant listened and drank. "Listen, I was wondering if me and a friend might come on over. No, no, don't get a date for him, this is kind of a business and social call." He had more Miller while she talked on the other end. "Khristi, Khristi, I don't mean it like that. It's just that my friend—His name? It's Ivan. No, he's not Russian. Anyway, he's on a case and I need to talk with you about Perry's work with DeKovan." He was quiet again.

"Yeah"—he laughed, ingratiating himself—"he was a fucking maniac. Calling Perry at all hours and everything. . . . Oh yeah? He sent him to get that once? Oh, more than once." He winked at Monk.

The conversation went on another ten minutes and then the two drove out to Khristi's in their respective cars. She lived in San Dimas, in the San Gabriel Valley. The journey took serious navigation of the several freeways laced about the grid of the Southland: the 15 north into San Bernardino County, to the 10 west into Los Angeles County, then a quick swing north again along the 210.

Heading there they got hung up by a jackknifed tanker, which fortunately had left one lane open so their delay was only an extra forty minutes. To fight agitation, Monk tried to calculate how many millions of tons of concrete it had taken to lay out a freeway system that had begun with the building of the curvy Pasadena, first called the Arroyo Seco Parkway, in the late '30s. Southern California now had more than fifteen hundred miles of freeways, and others were either being considered or under construction. Maybe, Monk fantasized, he ought to see about erecting an elevated Continental Donuts at a busy freeway exchange to service gridlocked commuters.

The day was hot and the smog was fierce. By the time they got to Khristi Jakes's house, it was past four, and the back of Monk's shirt was soaked. "We better get something out of this," he complained to Grant.

"Relax." Monk had the sense that Grant was anticipating something, and it made him even more irritable.

Her house was a modest frame job with a covered redbrick porch and colorful flowers lining each side of the matching brick walkway. A pewter boar's head with a massive ring in its snout was centered in the peeling, pale blue door. Grant rapped gently.

Presently the door was opened by a tallish, slightly heavy but solid-looking woman. She was wearing white espadrilles, black peddle pushers, and a worn-out man's single-stitch oxford. The shirt's color nearly matched that of the door's. Her brunette hair was pulled back, strands of gray untouched in its masses. There was a touch of rouge on her cheeks and she'd applied a deep terra cotta–colored lipstick, the kind Monk had seen young Latina *rukas* use. She was either in her late forties or early fifties. Time had been on her side.

"Doll face." She reached up and bestowed a wet kiss on a willing Grant.

"This is Ivan," he said, looking at her, his arms still around her waist.

"Hi," she said, still staring at Grant.

Jesus Christ, Dex, you lascivious bastard. "We sure appreciate your time, ma'am."

"You bet." She finally managed to unwrap herself. "Come on in, sports fans."

Monk had expected the woman to have gaudy taste, given her background. The home was done in somber but warm hues with dashes of pastel. The furnishing was neat, the knickknacks at a minimum. Late afternoon light gave the living room an airy, springtime feel, and it helped to ease the tension he'd built up on the long drive.

Khristi Jakes was holding Grant's hand and guided him to an oxblood-colored leather couch. Monk found a perch in a similarly styled chair. Grant and the woman made small talk and Monk crossed his legs, taking in the room.

"Here, let me get you fellas something to drink." She got up with a bounce. "I hope fresh orange juice is okay. I don't drink the hard stuff anymore."

Monk was amused by the disappointment on Grant's face. "Sure Khris, that's fine," he fibbed.

She left and the older man went out of his way not to look at Monk. She returned with their drinks.

"Thanks," Monk said.

The two got involved in stories about mutual friends while Monk sipped and sipped. He was able to stand it for another fifteen minutes, then he said, "If you don't mind, I am about to be indicted, Dex. That is, if I don't get capped first."

"Right you are, old son." He shifted on the couch to look directly at the woman. "I need to find DeKovan."

She laughed briefly, touching his arm. "After you called, I went through what I have left of Perry's stuff. You can look at it. Mostly it's his morgue books and funny little items he collected over the years." Morgue books were cops' personal Polaroids of crime scenes and gruesome deaths. Grant's included dead and bloated bodies that had imploded in rooms where the deceased had lain for several days in still air, until discovered when someone opened a door.

"That'd be fine, dear." He nodded knowingly at Monk.

"While you two do that, I'll fix us something to eat." She touched his arm again.

Monk had the impression he was included reluctantly in the dinner invitation.

Out in the attached garage, amidst now-unused fishing equipment, Monk looked over several file boxes of the ghoulish photo albums; notes on a book Jakes had planned to write; a TV pilot script he'd consulted on; and his assortment of remains from various cases—a gold tooth with a diamond lightning bolt embedded in it, a bra with an interior pocket for a derringer which Grant pointed out, a stuffed Aardvark whose base Monk took apart to reveal a circuit board, a lead model of the Capital Records building which Grant pulled apart to reveal a serrated knife, and other such matters. The material was an exhibition on the archeology of crime.

"But no goddamn clue to DeKovan—as you figured," Monk summed up.

Grant had been going through the other things in the garage. A broken wicker chair, the tackle box, lamps, and so on. He was on his knees, crawling around on an area of the concrete.

"Dex—"

"Hand me a screwdriver, Ivan." He was probing the edges of a portion of the sectioned concrete with his blunt fingers. "Perry was a Cadillac man. He'd lease a new one every two years or so.'' Monk handed him a screwdriver from a shelf of tools. He stood nearby.

"Big on leather seats," Grant added. "He used to park his car in this part of the garage. The head would be that way," he explained, pointing toward the back, "the tail end hanging over this part of the floor. It would have to be like that so he could get to it by lying flat on that piece of carpet." Grant pointed toward a stack of boxes and paint cans along the wall. Looking behind it, Monk saw a rolled-up section of a rug used by shade tree mechanics.

Grant worked around several edges of the concrete. The floor pattern was grooved in lines that formed squares as if it had been put together with individual tiles. Grant found what he'd been scratching around for—there was in fact a square of concrete that actually came up. He got it free and lifted it with the blade of the screwdriver.

"Perry had a brother-in-law who worked construction," he said offhandedly. "I knew Perry helped him put in this floor." Beneath the concrete tile was a small chamber, which contained a black leather-bound book and a set of keys.

"I'd have never found that," Monk said admiringly.

"You partner with a guy for so long, you get to thinking in the same sneaky way. I knew his mind better than my two wives'."

The book was a Bible. Thumbing through it, they didn't see any passages underlined or highlighted.

"Find anything?" Khristi Jakes asked from the doorway into the house.

Grant said, "The keys to the kingdom." He jingled the ones they'd found.

"Well, come on, I've made eggplant, spinach vinaigrette, and carrot curry."

"No meat?" Grant asked, perplexed.

"I think you're supposed to supply that," Monk said under his breath.

"You think these keys lead to something?" She asked, examining them as the two followed her back into the house.

"None of them look familiar?" Monk sounded forlorn.

She stopped in the light. "This long one seems like I should know, but I'm sorry, I can't remember."

"You mind if I hold onto them?" Grant reached out.

She hesitated, then handed them over. "This ain't gonna bring down some heavy shit on me, is it, Dexter?"

"I'll see that it doesn't." He looked at Monk, making him part of the pact. "How about this Bible?" They reached the kitchen.

She laughed vigorously, leaning into him. "Oh good Christ, Dexter, why in hell would Perry Jakes have a Bible? Much less under the floor of the garage! What— was he hoping to fool God into forgetting his own ten commandments, each of 'em Perry probably broke more than once, if he hid the rule book when his time came?" She laughed again and got wineglasses out.

After the tasty meal it was sundown, and Monk said his pleasantries and started out of the house to go back into L.A. Grant and the widow of his ex-partner said good-bye from the backlit doorway. "Bye, kids," he called, waving back.

Two days later Monk was summoned to a Dancing Dinosaur on the top floor of the Westside Pavilion, a massive upscale shopping mall that stretched over the intersections of Westwood and Pico. The joint was jumping with children as old as fourteen and as young as three tearing through the aisles, careening off one another, begging quarters to buy Dino Credits to play the video slash-and-burn and exploding-groins games, and in general letting out enough caterwauling to bring down the Walls of Jericho.

Monk spotted Grant and Khristi Jakes on an upper tier sitting at a table with a pitcher of soda between them. Walking up the stairs, an employee in a green and blue happy T-Rex ,suit passed him saying, "It's hotter than a motherfucker in this thing."

"In my day, I took my kids to Hoppyland," Grant shouted when he got close.

"What the hell was that," Monk asked, sitting down and pouring himself what turned out to be root beer.

"You remember William Boyd, played Hopalong Cassidy on the radio and in the movies? Black hat, ivory-handled six-shooters, and a horse named Topper." Grant watched a youth make faces behind a harried employee in a stegosaurus suit with a look of condemnation.

"I've heard some of the adventure shows rebroadcast on the KNX Old Radio Hour from time to time," Monk said.

"Uh. Well out in the Ballona swamp—what you city slickers call Marina del Rey now—Big Bill and some investors built theyselves an amusement park off of Washington Boulevard. The place had a baseball diamond, picnic grounds, rides, and a pony cart. Man, my daughters really went for that." He stopped talking, surveying the youngsters with new, kind eyes. "It only lasted three or four years though."

"Are you going to jail?" Jakes blurted.

"The hearing is tomorrow," Monk tipped his glass toward her.

"I'm sorry, I didn't mean to be so rude. But Dexter speaks well of you, and how important it is to get you cleared."

Monk smiled at his mentor, who was purposely looking

in another direction. "The great one supposed to make an appearance?" he finally asked.

"Not exactly," Grant hedged.

"What then, an emissary?"

"Hold on, you'll see," Grant answered.

Soon a walking pterodactyl with pizza sauce on its fluffy chest came over to their table. "Would you three follow me," the cotton and fabric beastie directed.

They did and found themselves in a windowless turquoise-walled back room devoid of everything except three folding chairs facing a metal table. A TV monitor with a built-in video camera was on top of the table.

"Video conferencing unit," Jakes said.

Monk stared at her.

"I read *Popular Science*." She sat down with panache.

"You sit in the middle." Grant pulled the chair back for Monk. He also sat down, glaring at the sleek, flat, large squarish screen.

Grant clicked the device on and sat next to Monk. The picture instantly snapped into clarity, displaying a plain industrial metal folding chair like the ones they were sitting on. Behind it Monk could make out a peach-colored room with Roman-style drapes on one side. A painting was in the background, but he couldn't tell what it was. The transmission imparted an ethereal, inchoate quality to the art. He thought this might possibly be an omen for the experience he was about to have.

Suddenly a body filled the screen, moving like a drawn figure in a flip book that teaches one how to animate characters.

"It's not full motion because of the regular telephone input," Jakes explained. "You'd need some ISDN or T-1 lines to get real-time quality."

"Hello," the man onscreen said pleasantly. His hand gestured in a herky-jerky motion and his head seemed to go in and out of focus. He was shown from midchest up, in a plaid short-sleeved shirt. DeKovan's once keen features were now slack, his square jaw undefined, and his eyes were hard to perceive given the folds of skin around them.

His hair was grey, unkempt but of moderate length. It lay about his still-high, lightly lined forehead. He seemed at ease.

"H.H.," Grant said. "You remember me?"

The face in the monitor didn't move while wispy words floated from the thing's speakers. "You've held up well, Dexter Grant." The hand moved and suddenly the image onscreen became merely a finger pointing out into the world. "Isn't this one the one who used to be in the Pharaohs down at the Rancho?"

"No, I'm Ivan Monk, the one investigating the recent murders that happened there. How are you?" The Pharaohs, along with such social organizations as the Slausons, the Business Men and the Bartenders, had been black gangs in the fifties and sixties.

"You were fired, weren't you?" The finger was again raised in his direction.

"How'd you know that?" Monk wanted to know.

DeKovan ignored the question. "I heard Perry Jakes passed away not too long ago."

"Yeah, Father Time don't play favorites," Grant said. "This is Khristi, his widow." He indicated the woman.

"I believe we talked once or twice, did we not?"

"Yes sir, that's right."

Son of a bitch was going to have it his fucking way, but he'd try. "Mr. DeKovan, do you know Isaiah Booker or an Ismael Vaccarano, better known as Big Loco?"

Grant sucked on his bottom lip but remained quiet.

"Their names both begin with *I*'s; how interesting," the elliptical man responded.

Monk grimaced at Grant, who subtly signaled with his hand for him to go slow. "H.H., I hear you spend some time in Mexico now and then. Monterrey, Zacatecas, Mexico City, right?"

"Oh." The stop motion head moved and halted again. "I like the jungles they have down there."

"And the pyramids?" Monk ventured.

The head didn't move and Monk got the feeling DeKovan had inserted a still picture of himself. Eventually, "Why yes, I have a fondness for the Mayas' architecture."

"The Mayas were superseded by the Aztecs," Monk said.

"Precisely."

"And what of the ancient ways?" Monk inquired.

"The first sun was created by Tezcatlipoca, the god of Earth." He pronounced the deity's name flawlessly.

"But he made a mistake: he made men as giants, and made only half a sun." Monk recollected the tale from his reading. "The inadequate sun could not grow the right food to sustain their huge bodies."

"The jaguars swallowed that sun, and as darkness descended, they also swallowed the giants, too big and too malnourished to save themselves. And after three more suns, there would come Nanahuatl, who would throw himself into the Divine Fire." The head had tilted up, the image coming several seconds behind the last of the words. He looked off at something only he could see or imagine.

"And is that how the last sun is born?" Khristi Jakes asked.

Monk grinned at her. "You also read Aztec mythology in your spare time?"

She grinned like a porcelain harlequin. "A mind is a terrible thing to waste."

"But that would mean blood, and the awful redness like before," DeKovan said.

"Like before, H.H.?" Grant probed.

"The red tide," the recluse went on. "The Soviets are no more. The Vietnamese are doing business with us. Do you know I have two bottling plants and a circuit board operation there now? The only Communists left are the Chinese. But really, they want to hide their capitalism with phrases from Mao." He'd turned his head again, this time at an angle like a child bewildered by the antics of adults.

Monk asked, "Are there still Communists at the Rancho?" Maybe to DeKovan's way of thinking anybody who squawked like Efraín Cruzado was a Communist.

"Ross Perot was a friend of Deng Xiaoping. How do you think the Chinese were always able to copy our electronic devices so facilely?"

Soothingly, Grant put in, "Is that so, H.H.?"

"You don't think I'm telling the truth," the sharp voice said from the immobile face. "I thought you believed in me, Dexter. In our crusade."

"It's not that, H.H. But Ivan here has to be convinced you know the score."

It was like dealing with a moody nine-year-old. Between that, the stilted picture, and the stress of his upcoming hearing Monday, Monk was getting a serious headache. He wanted results. "Like the Cruzados, they too believed. You can tell by their name."

"Is that why they were sacrificed?" The face of stone retorted guilelessly.

"Did you—"

Grant cut Monk off with the flat of his hand pressed against the younger man's chest. "Is the jaguar on the loose, H.H.?"

"Margins of profits," the TV man said.

"What kind of profits?" Monk said, ignoring Grant's facial injunctives.

The image again jerked and twitched and suddenly DeKovan was staring at his hands. "Sifting about, dodging Mictlanteuctli, but he can't be ducked. The price is too great."

Monk was about to go off.

Noticing his body language, Khristi Jakes patted his arm with her silver-nailed hand. "Who sets the terms for this price, Mr. DeKovan?" she purred.

"The Randlords, of course."

"What the hell," Monk admonished sotto voce.

"Let's stay with it," Grant whispered back. "They were the rich mine owners in South Africa, right H.H.?"

"Exactly."

His first direct answer. Monk made a face at Grant but remained quiet.

"Have they set loose the jaguar?" Grant leaned forward.

The head again went through its slow-motion gyrations. It was apparent that DeKovan was moving about in his seat as if a comfortable position were impossible to attain. "So much has changed since Fletcher Wilkenson's time. I guess it was wrong to make him leave." The TV man became motionless again. "Do you sleep good at night, Dexter?"

"Most of them."

Rhetorically, Monk said, "How would the Rancho be different if Fletcher had stayed, H.H.?"

"Jokay would always have been Jokay," DeKovan mused.

"He would still be working with you?" Monk also leaned forward.

"I'm not Ralph Bunche. I can't make everybody happy."

"Who's Ralph Bunche?" Jakes asked quietly.

"He grew up off of Central Avenue, not too far from where the Rancho stands now," Monk replied. "He brokered a peace accord in the Mideast for the U.N., and won the Nobel Prize."

Grant said earnestly, "Who's at war, H.H.?"

DeKovan's image flickered and Monk half rose from his seat, fearful the man had severed the connection. It snapped back to clarity and he sat down. The headache was worse.

"Everybody, Dexter, everybody's got it in for each other."

"But who at the Rancho is behind the fighting?" Monk blared, his tolerance way past breached.

The head on the box did several shakes and it finally occurred to them DeKovan was laughing. Over the crisp speakers his high cackle only made Monk feel like strangling him.

"Come on, H.H.," Grant cajoled. "You were the one who wanted compromise, right? You were the one who bankrolled the job training center, put money into drug rehab programs up and down Watts and Boyle Heights. Even gave money to the Panthers and the Black Muslims when they were on Broadway."

Monk gaped at Grant.

The head was at rest again. "Is there still time for fairness?"

"You can make it so, H.H.," Grant said.

His head cocked. "I've tried. Ask Absalla. That's why I hired him to see about my other places."

"What places?" Monk asked.

"Oh," the voice ahead of the image crackled. "Hawaiian Gardens, Cerritos. Electronics assembly plant, bushings manufacturing . . . I like to diversify, you see."

"Absalla sees to your security at these places?" For once, the headache seemed secondary.

"Yes he does." Another amazing direct answer. There was more stillness, then, "Maybe I'll bring back Hoppyland." With that, the delayed image reached a jumpy hand forward and the screen went black.

"God, what a mind fuck," Jakes said, throwing back her head and laughing.

"More like root canal of the brain." Monk rubbed his forehead with the heal of his hand. "How in hell did you find him, Dex?"

"Perry's keys. We set to thinking and talking about them some more, Perry's habits and so forth, and I guessed one of them led to a locker down in Vernon. It's in a meatpacking facility that belongs to the brother of his first wife."

"We, huh?" Monk glanced at Khristi Jakes.

She added, "In the locker Dex found a book, a diary really. Perry had been keeping a record of what he'd done for Mr. DeKovan and where."

"Blackmail?" Monk wanted a nap.

"That's not clear, since he never hinted anything like that to me," she said.

"You or I'd have done the same. Just to be thorough," Grant indicated to Monk. "Anyway, there's some phone numbers listed in it and we start calling around. A voice eventually calls back and tells us to be here."

The pterodactyl opened the door and said, "I've brought some root beer." The Dancing Dinosaur employee came in with a tray containing an ice bucket, three plastic cups stenciled with the firm's logo, and a liter bottle of the soda. The tray was set down and the two-legged bird man stalked out. Its wing accidentally brushed against Monk's face.

Grant made their drinks.

"Well, what do you guys think—" Jakes began. She halted when both men held up an open hand.

"I sure like root beer," Grant said.

"Me too," Monk piped in.

Jakes popped eyes at them and Grant handed her a glass. "Have some, Khristi."

She sipped as the two of them gulped theirs down.

The two men finished and Monk lightly touched Jakes's elbow. The three left the room and made their way past a throng of kids screaming for Lord Raydon to pluck the pulsing heart from Lu Kang's heaving chest on a large display of the Mortal Kombat video game.

Outside, the trio walked along the third-floor tier to loiter in front of a sports equipment store.

"What was the deal with the root beer?" Jakes asked excitedly.

"Maybe he wanted us to feel relaxed and loose enough to talk in there." Grant was sizing up a pair of Shaquille O'Neal–signature high tops through the window. "Do you think it was just coincidence he mentioned Hoppyland?"

"Ah." She nodded her head. "The Dancing Dinosaur might have been bugged. But how the hell could any one voice be picked out with all that noise?"

Grant worked a toothpick he'd produced from his shirt pocket. "I read *Popular Science* too. You can hide a camera and audio pickup in anything these days."

Monk was leaning on the rail, looking out at the westside Saturday buyers swinging their brand name shopping bags stuffed with Polo this and Bijon that. "You wouldn't know there was any other way of life," he observed icily. He turned around. "What did we learn from this excursion, Ancient One?"

"Humble student must see beyond the words and recognize the intent," Grant teased.

"He's a fucking nut, Dex. And if he ain't, then he gets off putting on this act."

"Maybe it's a little of both," Jakes interjected.

Dexter came close. "You did learn something, Ivan. I know this isn't a good situation you're in, but you've got to remain objective, clearheaded."

He felt like arguing but didn't have the emotional strength. Intellectually, he recognized the value of Grant's point. "Okay, I have maybe Absalla gets work from DeKovan."

"And that he knew you'd been fired," Jakes contributed.

Grant flicked the toothpick into the air. "He had to know who you were from the get-go."

"He talked about wanting peace," Jakes said. "He sounded very sincere to me."

Monk regarded the cop's widow and former stripper. "You got a lot going on there, Khristi. But I get the feeling Mr. DeKovan's notion of peace is right along with Stalin's and Kissinger's. Kill 'em all, then hand the survivors the terms of surrender."

"Kissinger has a Nobel Peace Prize on his shelf." Grant hitched his pants around the waist.

"Big goddamn deal," Monk snorted. "DeKovan seemed pretty hep on the Aztec lore. Which may mean he's the conductor orchestrating Maladrone and whatever the hell it is he thinks he's bringing about."

Grant made a gesture with his large hand. "That's all just so much blue smoke."

"Absalla," Grant repeated. "Get on him about his connection to DeKovan. Like you said, it means something the supposedly stolen license came from one of H.H.'s factories. Maybe brother Absalla's security people are at that one in Burbank also."

"Smells like team spirit to me," Monk quipped.

"Now who's being cryptic?" Jakes said.

Monk held out his hand. "Thanks, ol' pardner."

"I didn't do anything yet." He shook the younger man's hand. "I've still got a couple of leads to run down concerning DeKovan's activities."

"If he is behind all this, he won't let the burden of the past stop him from moving against you," Monk warned.

"Nor you," Grant shot back.

Jakes looked perplexed. "You two seem to take the prospect of painful death a little light, don't you?"

"It's not that," Grant began, staring at Monk. "Anybody tells you they don't get scared is either a psychopath or a goddamn moron."

"Then what does that make you two?"

"Late." Monk laughed. "I'll call you in a couple, Dex." He trotted off.

Walking arm in arm in the parking structure, Jakes looked at Dexter. "You really care for him, don't you?"

"Men don't admit such things." He kissed her quickly.

"What do men admit?" She encircled his waist with her strong arms.

"Their mistakes, sometimes." They walked to his car then drove to a revival moviehouse to catch a showing of *Three Hours to Kill* and *Johnny Apollo*.

Two Tylenols and a snooze in the Saab had Monk feeling fairly spry by the time Kodama pulled to a stop at the motel cabin in the town of Joshua Tree in Little San Bernardino. Stars poked through the early evening sky and the air smelled of smoke trees and piñon pines. The Grey Granite Lodge was a testament to a bygone era of roadside onomatopoetic architecture. The mini lodges looked like slanting, dark grey granite slabs, the doors and windows constructed off center.

"I'll get the cooler." Monk stretched on his tiptoes as he stood up.

"I got the door," Kodama said.

The Joshua Tree National Monument was several miles to the south, back down below the Riverside County line. Kodama enjoyed camping, and the brief getaway was her idea, but he got his way insofar as the fact that they were staying in a room and not a tent. The absence of the reassuring comfort of hot running water and the swellness of TV was more than Monk would let slide.

"Man," he groaned, falling into the bed covered with a Navajo-pattern spread.

Kodama shoved the cooler out of the way with her foot and closed the door. "How do you feel?"

"A slight ache, but much better than this afternoon." He stared at the ceiling with its pretend crossbeams, trying not to think about Monday.

She sat on the edge of the bed. "What's going to happen should you get convicted?"

"A little late to be worried about your reputation, baby." He rolled over to look at her.

"I'm worried for you." She held his face and he kissed her scented palm.

"I know you are, Jill." He left it unsaid that he was more concerned about getting shot than he was about the trial or doing time. Though the idea of doing eight to ten wasn't all that thrilling either. "We'll make it through."

He also didn't go on about how conflicted he felt about not actively looking for Keith 2X. Kodama had pointed out that should he do so, the gunners hunting for him would be operating in the same spheres of existence, and would no doubt tag him.

"If this teleconference with DeKovan was a bust, what's next?"

"Jam Absalla up about his connection to the crazy *gavacho*."

She regarded him and his words for several moments. "If he's carrying water again for Tariq, neither of them will appreciate you meddling in Black Muslim business."

"As far as I'm concerned, both these cats give Islam a bad name."

"But you're a heathen."

"There you go."

"And it doesn't mean there aren't some folks who take what they do quite seriously," she said pointedly.

He sat up. "What do you really want to say, Jill?"

"Maybe you should concentrate on your defense, and let the rest of this thing go. For now at least. You back off and could be they, whoever 'they' are, will too."

"We just go on with our lives," he said doubtfully.

"I'm not asking you to quit, Ivan, but be realistic about your priorities. You've got a serious charge to deal with, so why antagonize others needlessly?"

"Absalla may well be involved in this."

"Agreed." She got off the bed. "But you can't take another run at him if you have to be in court every day. You're a hell of a detective, but you can't be so divided. Your demeanor, your posture, everything you do while sitting in that seat the jury picks up on, Ivan. After two O.J. trials and the Menendez brothers, everybody's hypersensitive and everybody's a goddamn expert.

"If you look tired, or distracted, sitting next to Parren, that can be misinterpreted as arrogance or aloofness. The jury will think you look like somebody who thinks they got it in the bag, somebody the jury will want to punish."

Monk considered her admonishment. "I understand what you're saying, Jill. But it's also in my best interest to find out who shot at me. Because it is tied to the Cruzados' murders.''

''I want you safe, Ivan.'' She knelt down in front of him and they hugged for a long time.

''We'll beat them, Jill.'' He hoped he sounded more confident than he was. He had to hold on to the belief that the luck he'd been making for himself all these years wasn't all used up and he just didn't know it. That his bad night wasn't on him yet.

Kodama leaned over him, pushing him back on the bed. They kissed and nibbled and made love, the warm desert air a balm against their wet bodies.

Later, he sat outside the room in his robe smoking a fat Padron Churchill. The cigar's grey smoke twisted this way and that on the currents as it rose. Monk wondered if his fate was also so easily shuttled about. He smoked and listened to the sounds of the night. The door opened behind him and Jill stuck her head out.

''You going to come out here buck naked and give the grizzlies a thrill?'' he asked.

''You talked to the woman?''

''Who?''

''Rosanna I think you said her name was.''

''No. I tried to find where she'd gone, but if you recall, I never exactly made headway among the Latino tenants. She and her surviving daughters may have gone back to Mexico for all I know.''

''You should ask again.''

''What will that get me?''

''You're not working for Absalla. In fact, you two had a falling out. And people in the Rancho know you did Big Loco. As perverse as it sounds, some may think of you as a hero. Including the Latino tenants he also terrorized.'' She bowed slightly. ''Good night.'' She quietly shut the door.

Monk looked at the door and then at the evenly burning ash. He took another puff. ''Damn smart woman.''

Twenty-two

Monk was indicted on a second-degree manslaughter charge and bound over for trial. He made bail by putting up his donut shop for the bond via a procedure worked out in advance by Teague. By one-thirty he was at the window of his lawyer's fifteenth-floor office looking west at a giant Marlboro Man billboard—the cowpoke flinty with testosterone—perpendicular to the Sunset Strip's Chateau Marmont hotel.

The funky digs were infamous as the place where John Belushi fatally OD'd on speedballs, and where Boris Karloff kept residence for years. Monk turned from the window and his guidebook-reminiscing. "It's a funny feeling, Parren. Being able to walk around, but also knowing the hammer has got to drop. It's kinda unreal, man."

"The first round is coming up, Ivan." Teague leaned his thin frame back in his imposing banker's chair. Its black leather and brass studs gleamed with an unreality like a computer-generated picture. "The LAPD's case is weak."

"But to a jury's mind, they ain't throwing the book at me." He began to move about in front of the window in small circles. "I did kill an unarmed man, and what's five or seven years for that?" He threw his hand up and brought it down forcefully against the pant leg of his suit.

"I know I don't have to say this, but you're not thinking about running, are you?" Teague continued to lean back casually, fingering one of his Mont Blanc pens. "You've been to many ports in your travels in the merchants."

"You worried I'm gonna skip on your fee, Counselor?"

"Hardly." He rocked forward and put down the pen.

"New Zealand is nice and hot."

"You had to surrender your passport."

"Pshaw." Monk grinned. "Dex's got certain friends who can hook me up."

Teague pointed with the pen. "What you better do, pardner, is get your ass out there and dig up something for me to use."

Monk rubbed the underside of his goatee. "Yeah, well, I can always write my autobiography if I go to the big house. Something like 'Me and the Judge.' "

"That sucks."

Monk took a slip of paper out of his coat, which he flung onto the couch. He punched in a number on the phone and waited. On the sixth ring the receiver on the mobile was picked up on the other end.

"Andrade? This is Monk."

Distantly he said, "I heard you were in jail."

"Not yet. You ready to go to work?"

"I was going to Hollywood Park today."

His voice sounded thick, but not slurry. Monk'd noticed that when Andrade was working the racing form, he might be hung over, but not in the bottle. "This is important," he enunciated.

A silence crawled by. Then, "Alright."

Don't get too overwrought there, champ. "I'm going to

come over and pick you up in about forty minutes."

"I'll meet you at the shop."

Before he could reply, the receiver was disconnected. The odd sometimes accountant and his secrets. "I'm on it." He flopped onto the couch.

"What's happening?" Teague uncapped the Mont Blanc, and poised it like a targeted Katusha over a legal pad.

"Called a Mrs. Limón back at the Rancho yesterday. Jill's idea, I'm not too proud to admit. Anyway, the old girl's suddenly got a soft spot for me since she heard I cussed out Absalla, and reduced some of the criminal element. So I tell her I still want to find the murderers of the Cruzados."

"And now she's a little more sympathetic?" Teague asked.

"Indeed. 'Course, there seemed to be something else going on with her, but whatever. She actually seemed nice. I tell her I want to talk with the wife if that's possible. Even if it's only over the phone so I don't spook her." He winked broadly at Teague.

"This guy you just called . . . ?"

"My translator. I understand Mrs. Cruzado's English isn't the best. Better than my Spanish I'm sure, but still. . . ."

"That's why you need the box and had me switch the service over." He made his notes.

"Yes, sir, conference call over at my office." He got up holding his coat and headed for the door. "Don't worry, Parren, I'll put this all down on paper. But right now I gotta jet."

"Keep me in the loop." He toyed with the pen again.

"Would I have it any other way?"

*   *   *

Andrade sat erect and still in one of the Eastlakes next to the desk. He was attired in a serviceable checked sport coat, grey slacks, and a shirt with fraying cuffs. He looked neither at Monk nor at the floor. Rather, he seemed like some sort of space-age soldier who between battle engagements simply revved down to conserve energy.

Monk watched him and plucked up the handset on its first ring. He glanced at the Seth Thomas clock on the wall. It had been in his quarters on the last ship he'd been a merchant on, *The Achilles*. A minute past the time Mrs. Limón said they would call. Pretty good.

"I'm here, and so is my associate, Mr. Andrade," he told the tenant's association leader.

"I want you to know this is very painful for Rosanna," Limón replied.

Monk took the opportunity to kiss her ass. "I appreciate your intervening on my behalf, Mrs. Limón. And please tell Mrs. Cruzado I wouldn't have bothered her if it wasn't important."

Limón told her in Spanish but there was no reply. "She is on the other line?" Monk fretted.

A new voice spoke in Spanish. Rosanna Cruzado was speaking softly, but steadily. She stopped, and Andrade, who'd picked up the other line, listened.

Monk made a motion at the sometimes accountant which he only blankly acknowledged. He put his hand over the receiver. "You have to talk, that's why you're here," he scolded.

A few clipped words in Spanish issued forth from the man. The effort seemed to require great expenditure on his part.

"Is that man ill?" Mrs. Limón demanded hastily.

"He's just tired, Mrs. Limón. Mr. Andrade works hard."

If the other man picked up on the sarcasm, his unchanging expression of cosmic ennui didn't show it. "Can we go on, please?" He knew this was Limón's show and that he'd better temper any impatience he might have with her and act like he had some good sense, as his mother would have advised.

Limón had questioned why it was Monk wanted Andrade present, as she could translate for him. The real reason was that he didn't want her filtering or altering his words and wanted another ear there for Mrs. Cruzado's answers. Of course he couldn't tell her that. So he'd lied and told her Andrade was eager to become a detective and had been assisting Monk on this case.

"Very well." She translated her English for the other woman.

"Mrs. Cruzado, I know the police have talked with you," Monk began, allowing a space for Andrade to jump in. This time, unprompted, he did so. "What were you able to tell them, if I might ask?"

In that same quiet, but methodical voice the woman replied. Mrs. Limón said at an interval, "She said she told the two detectives it was her opinion that some of the black gang members had done the murders. She told them about how her husband had several confrontations with the drug sellers."

Rosanna Cruzado slipped in something.

"What, something about Big Loco?" Monk questioned Andrade.

"The drug selling wasn't just among the blacks," Andrade amplified. "She herself saw Big Loco and other members of Los Domingos Trece also selling the small plastic bags of crack."

"Yes, we know it's a problem," Mrs. Limón harped defensively.

Monk held back a comment about enough sin to go around, and kept on course. "Did you see anything the morning of the fire as you came out of the apartment?"

He got a "No" after the translation.

"Then why do you think it was some of the Scalp Hunters?" he continued.

"They were the ones threatening her husband," Limón interjected.

"I'd like to give Mrs. Cruzado a chance to answer." He tried to moderate his tone.

"Ah," Limón growled.

The other woman laughed quietly and quickly, then made a comment.

"She wanted Mrs. Limón to take it easy," Andrade explained. After she spoke again, the accountant went on. "She told the cops Efraín had mentioned to her he'd been confronted by a couple of Scalp Hunters for speaking out too much at resident meetings, putting up flyers, and trying to organize some of the immigrant tenants."

Monk picked up on that. "Did your husband get involved in those kinds of activities back home?"

"*Sí*," Mrs. Cruzado said after Mrs. Limón repeated the question to her.

"Back in Zacatecas, on the north side, her husband had run for the local council seat," Andrade translated.

Monk asked what happened.

"He'd run on a . . . change, a reform platform, you understand. After the elections where the PRI's power was finally challenged successfully, there was of course a new spirit among people that actual democracy was possible. Unfortunately his side lost. Too much influence, too much money being spread around by the local gangsters. The old ways didn't change overnight.'' Monk was sure the last sentence was Andrade's contribution.

"La Pandilla Zacatecas?" Monk said.

"*Sí,*" Mrs. Cruzado confirmed.

"After they lost, one of the candidates was shot to death outside a bar. Another was beat so bad he lost an eye. It was time to leave." For the first time, inflection had crept into Andrade's voice.

Monk was assembling the data. "Do you know a Jokay Maladrone?"

"No," came her reply after Mrs. Limón relayed his question.

"But really," Andrade said in English as she spoke, "Karla would know some of that business. She was the manager of his campaign. The both of them liked to be in politics. Me, I think it was a waste of time."

"The sister," Monk announced. "Is she with you now?"

Something was mumbled. "She can't say," came Mrs. Limón's terse rejoinder.

"This is important," Monk emphasized.

"I can't speak for her" was Andrade's version of Cruzado's words.

"I think that's enough," Mrs. Limón cut in.

"No, it's not." Monk's footing on the precipice was loosening. "There's death and money and the rot of old fixes dancing around the Rancho, lady. Somebody's gotta tell what they know."

"And the Lord appointed you his archangel?" she seethed back.

"What are you worrying about, Mrs. Limón? 'Fraid I might stumble on more criminals than just some black gangbangers and dope slangers?"

"Go fuck yourself." She severed the call.

Andrade replaced the handset like a man setting a gem. He sat and waited.

Monk wanted to try out some theories on him, but the absolute immobility of his features ruled such an exercise ludicrous. He pulled the caller ID machine he'd borrowed from Teague closer and wrote down the phone number Mrs. Limón had called from. "Well, at least they didn't have the line blocked," he said to himself. He'd had Teague transfer the caller ID service he received to the phone in his office.

Andrade folded his hands in his lap.

"Where do you want me to drop you?" Monk felt steamed at the man. He was displeased with him for being so goddamn complacent about everything like he was some kind of goddamn Scientologist on Prozac, and angry at him for being able to speak bilingually. But his tongue was not exotic or quaint or out-of-the-ordinary. It was the language of the waiter, the bank executive, the nanny, the newscaster, the teacher.

The xenophobes had tried to brand Spanish as somehow subterranean, yet it had always flowed through this land. For it had belonged to the founders of the pueblo nestled in the Valley of Smokes. Those forty-some pioneers who were Spanish, mestizo, black, Indian, dark and light.

Despite what the Pat Buchanans and Pete Wilsons of the world would have the anxious masses believe, the past, and the burden of truth, remained. California had belonged to Mexico, the land had been taken by force and sanctified by the pen strokes of crooked lawyers and land grabbers.

And so the inevitable weight of time's gravity was swinging the pendulum back, and the state would once again become an extension of Mexico. The Latinization of the city he'd grown up in was happening every day, and no amount of right-wing jingoism or regressive initiatives was going to stop that. You could make all the English-only laws you wanted, but culture had a way of seeping into your pores and the canals of your brain. Short of sanctioning the language police, busting women cautioning their daughters as they crossed the street or men joking in a bar, neither Spanish nor the people who spoke it were going to disappear from California. Maybe Maladrone was going to realize his version of Aztlán sooner than he thought.

"I'll catch the bus, you're busy."

The anger had dissipated with the certainty of the inevitable future. "Come on, I'll buy you a coffee at the best donut shop I know."

Andrade touched the phone as if it were sculpture. "Okay."

Driving over to his shop, Monk considered his next steps. He hadn't confronted Absalla on what he'd found out about his extracurricular security work. Was the information a decent hole card anyway? It could well be an indication of a closer link between the Muslim leader and DeKovan. But where did players like Booker and Maladrone fit in? And why the hell did the Cruzados have to die?

Was it all just for control of the drug trade in and around the Rancho? Highly unlikely. Unless the Rancho was seen as some sort of cocaine way station. As he came to a stop at a red light at the corner of Rimpau he found himself liking the various facets of that idea.

Or, he mused as he gunned the accelerator, the missus had intimated the sister may know more, so he'd take a run at her next. He knew the phone number wasn't Mrs. Limón's, and was hoping they'd called from where the Cruzados were now staying. The suffix of the number indicated it was in the Boyle Heights/East L.A. area. The same part of town where Maladrone had had his men pick him up. The reverse phone directory he had on CD-ROM should provide the address.

Monk coasted into the parking lot as the black Isuzu Trooper zoomed out from around the corner of Curtis Armstrong's garage and two-pump gas station. He didn't wait for introductions as his right foot sank and the tuned-up 352—Curtis and he had, five months ago, replaced the rebuilt stock 289—V-8 responded. He cranked the big, rectangular car forward, twisting the wheel savagely to the left as he did so.

"Down," Monk screamed at Andrade as the rear side window dissolved into hurtling fragments and puffs of cotton popped out of the back seat. The Galaxie fishtailed, the rear panel slamming against the side of the donut shop. Monk hurtled the machinery past the doorway and caught movement on the driver's side as he went past.

Twin rachets of gunfire filled the air and Monk saw the Trooper skid and circle on the 11th Avenue side of the lot. The utility vehicle righted itself and Monk, already unlatching the driver's door, grabbed Andrade's arm and the two went out through the opening.

"Don't move," he ordered, pushing the alcoholic accountant down against the side of the car. The Ford was at an angle to Continental's front door, the Trooper coming in straight like a swordfish on attack.

"Chief!" Elrod yelled, tossing him the automatic Remington shotgun he'd used to blast at the vehicle. Monk caught the weapon as the big man was spinning away, diving back into the shop. Monk got it up and over the lip of the trunk as incoming rounds tattooed the rear of the car.

There was a torso leaning out the passenger side of the Isuzu, its semiauto whatever prattling away. Pieces of sizzling metal torn from the trunk ripped skin away from

Monk's face as he crouched as low as possible to get his shot. He clacked off three rounds, the rubber-cushioned stock recoiling with unfamiliarity into the nexus of his shoulder and chest.

The third rapidly dispersed load did something to distort that leaning torso behind a crimson haze. The Trooper veered abruptly to its right, rocketing out onto Vernon. The driver took it screaming east.

"Aren't you going to chase them?" Andrade asked, wide-eyed.

Monk laughed nervously at the image of tearing up city and private property. The resulting suits would have his grandchildren in debt. His heart was beating so fast he was afraid he was having a stroke. He sagged against the car, his knees watery.

Elrod reappeared, brandishing the .357 Magnum Monk kept in his file room. "Sweet baby Jesus rocking his cradle," he exclaimed.

Monk put a shaking hand up to wipe the sweat from his forehead. "You ain't never lied."

"I hope you trigger-happy niggaz realize this kind of shit tends to decrease my walk-in trade." Curtis Armstrong's tinny voice seared from his large, round head. He was carrying the dusty little Beretta he kept taped to the bottom of his drawer under his office desk. He pointed at the ground. "Hey, Wild Bill, I think you got yourself another buffalo."

On the ground near Armstrong was, after some discussion among the four, what they determined to be segments of an ear and skin. A dull white chunk shone from among the blood and bits, and Monk was sure it was a bit of bone. A peerless gold hoop was attached to the lobe.

By the time the cops arrived from Southwest Division, Monk was arguing with Armstrong and Elrod that determining the DNA of the ear would be of no value to him. Andrade sat at his counter spot, kneading his hands in a pensive mood.

"About time," the accountant complained as the officers swarmed about like ants over a honey-covered hill.

Several hours later, Monk was released on OR. That it was an obvious self-defense situation seemed only to aggravate the D.A.'s office. They were grumbling that they might seek to tack on an endangerment charge to the manslaughter one, but it all seemed so anticlimactic. Monk was tired and scared of being too close to jumping in the big box. More importantly, he was worried these jokers would settle for killing Jill or his mother just to be evil. Just to get him to stop.

There had to be an end to it.

After being released, Elrod picked Monk up in the '68 Barracuda he was restoring. The manager drove Monk back to the donut shop at his request. "Jill called for you," he said.

"You didn't tell her, did you?"

Elrod stole a glance at the passing blurs and lights in the night traffic. "Naw, man, I did like you said. Said you was out on a clue an' all. But ain't she gonna notice you ain't pilotin' your wheels?"

Monk didn't have an answer and he wasn't too interested in coming up with one. His mind was on the task before him. Back at the donut shop, Monk got the reverse directory CD going and found an address to go along with the phone number from where Mrs. Limón had called this afternoon.

He was also trying to determine if it was just an unusual coincidence that the bad boys came a-blazing so conveniently after his conversation with her. But, he allowed, his usual subfrequency of paranoia was notched higher than usual given the personalities involved in this matter. And given their involvement, he was compelled to tell Jill what had gone down. If they should come at her . . .

"No, what I want is you to get the high sheriff on the phone and have some deputies over there."

"Only if you come home first, Ivan."

"Jill, I—"

"My ass. I'm coming to get you then."

There goes the momentum. She brought takeout from the Peruvian Thai restaurant on Hyperion and a bottle of J & B, "for calming purposes," she said. At their joint insistence, Elrod stayed to eat with them. Sitting in one of the booths, Monk tried out several scenarios on Elrod and Kodama while they enjoyed their food. A steady wind beat at the panes.

A teetotaler, Elrod excused himself when the drinks were poured in paper cups. "You be careful going home." Monk pressed the Magnum into his baseball glove of a hand.

"Always." He kissed Kodama on the cheek and the couple watched him as he drove off.

Afterward, she dialed a number and talked for several minutes then hung up. "Deputies deployed, sarge."

Monk was looking at the bottom of his cup. "I know this isn't how it should be, Jill."

"Nobody knows how anything should be, Ivan. L.A.'s ready to rock twenty-four seven and you can't stand still 'less we get swallowed up."

"You been listening too much to them homies you got rolling through your court."

"Shut up."

Kodama dropped him off at a rental agency near the

airport, the only such places open this time of the night. The air was dense with moisture.

"You sure you don't want that efficient little Ultrastar?" Monk was on his haunches, talking to Kodama on her side of the Saab. He didn't like making a point of it, but it was gnawing at him that the Trooper was out there.

"You gonna have everybody you know run around strapped?"

His brows bunched. "Seems to be getting that way. Plenty of judges pack, Jill."

She touched his face. "If we start on this, then I'm afraid we'll get into what you do, and why you do it."

"Maybe I need to be doing something else." He surprised himself with his words.

Kodama leaned up and nuzzled his cheek and bit his neck. "Don't kid yourself. Wake me when you get home."

Monk took the compact silver-blue Suburu east on the 105 to 110 north through the downtown exchange. Making the loop past the Convention Center, he noticed a large sign stretched taut along its side announcing a coming conference and trade show of new technologies. Seeing the announcement, a rueful look altered the bottom half of Monk's face.

His knowledge of computers began and ended with whatever his nephew Coleman deigned to inform him about. Learning arcane codes to troubleshoot his hard drive when the screen invariably flashed FILE ERROR, as it often did, or knowing the difference between RAM and gigabytes stretched his learning curve.

In one form or another—working for Dexter, being a bounty hunter, getting burned out before thirty and going off to the merchants, returning and working for Dexter, then as a PI on his own—he'd been running after people and problems for damn near fifteen years. What in hell else was he going to do? Sit in his chair getting a fat ass while he did personal research on the Net? Even car mechanics now demanded a more than serviceable knowledge of electronics, and of the apparatuses for analysis, what with igniters, chip-metered fuel injectors, and whatnot.

Donut magnate did have its possibilities. People always needed, er, wanted, donuts, even in body-conscious Southern California. 'Course he'd have to diversify and start including a fat-free line. Yeah, he concluded, taking the 5 south coming out of the exchanges, he could get started on that right away. Introduce some low-cal cinnamon rolls and devil's food cake. Even use soybean flour. Get some leggy former Raiderettes to pose with a trayful for publicity shots. Maybe open an outlet with the name Krishna Donut or something equally spiritual.

"Shit."

He got off on Indiana Street then went north to Whittier, then east again, winding past the huge Calvary Cemetery until he got to Ferris in East Los Angeles. He missed the street at first and got as far as Atlantic before realizing he'd gone too far. Doubling back, Monk crept along the street trying to discern the address that went along with the phone number Mrs. Limón had called from. It was dark, and not every house number was painted on the curb.

Eventually he had to park and walk, straining to read house numbers until he got to the right one. The clapboard was set back from the street, partially obscured by an untrimmed lemon tree and an overgrown row of Birds of Paradise. What was left of the lawn had given way to dirt, and a Radio Flyer wagon sat on its side in the yard. A nearby streetlight provided weak illumination. He was sorry he hadn't brought a flashlight.

From not too far away, Monk could hear the sounds of chickens. He took a look around and found a coop on the side of the house. It reminded him of Maladrone's estate, but he shook the idea loose. He knocked.

"What is it?" a male voice demanded with the wariness born of city living.

He told him who he was, and that he'd like to speak to Rosanna or Karla Cruzado.

No light came on and Monk worried that everybody had fled out the back. Presently, the door opened on a Chicano about Monk's height, but several years younger. He was wearing a white T-shirt and grey Wrangler jeans. His hair was starting to thin, and it made his angular face seem as if it were carved from one solid piece of walnut. Three children, two girls and one boy, in pajamas sat transfixed, watching TV.

"She doesn't want to be bothered, eh?"

"She wants an end to this, doesn't she?" He didn't know which of the women he meant, but this was not the time to get into minutiae.

"She wants you to go," he said with finality. Turning his head he said, "You three get to bed."

"Aw, man," the boy complained.

"Now," he repeated. "You got school tomorrow. Brush those teeth."

The three managed to make getting off the couch seem as arduous a task as slugging through sargasso.

"I'll only bother her this once," Monk pledged. "I want to do something about finding the ones who killed her family."

The boy and girls had come over to eye the stranger. The girls clung close to the man, the boy smiled tentatively at Monk.

"What's your name?" Monk asked the boy.

"Tomás, go," the man ordered.

The three went away and the man set baleful eyes on

the private detective. "You ain't working for nobody these days, homes."

"That don't mean I don't know anything," he said casually, folding his hands before him.

"Hmm," the man murmured, pushing the door in, but not quite closed.

With nothing else to do, and no leads left, Monk waited. The chickens clucked and the air smelled pleasant from the aroma of the lemons. The warm evening triggered a physical memory in Monk of a stopover he'd once made in Salvador, a town in the state of Bahia, in Brazil, when he was a merchant seaman. The port was awash with the savory odors of plantains and empanadas cooking in *dengee*, palm oil. These smells blended with the Portuguese-Spanish-French polyglot cadence of the marketplace, where slaves used to be sold. The bazaar sprawled out from the docks like tendrils from a beached kraken.

The door opened again, and a Latina stood there in a loose shirt and tight jeans.

"Karla Cruzado?" Monk guessed. From his talk with Cady, he knew she was the one who spoke English.

"Why do you want to keep bothering us?"

"Can I come in?"

Reluctantly, she allowed him inside. She stood with arms crossed. The man stood beside a woman Monk took to be Rosanna Cruzado in the dining room area.

"My name's Ruzón, from my husband," she corrected him.

Monk assumed the man who answered the door wasn't the husband, not proprietary enough. And asking the whereabouts of the mister wouldn't have been prudent at this juncture, as ex-president Bush was wont to say. "Who killed your mother, your brother, and your niece, Mrs.

Ruzón? Do you believe it was Scalp Hunters?'' It came out so soft, he wasn't sure she heard him.

She put a hand to her mouth, the enormity of his questions overwhelming her. He felt like he'd socked her in the gut as she sat heavily on the couch. She must have had to keep going after the incident, it would have been the only way she could deal with such a horror. She no doubt kept busy helping her sister-in-law and surviving nieces get settled into their new life. By allowing herself to be consumed with trying to rebuild a semblance of life, she probably hoped that she could stop herself from becoming bogged in the quicksand of loss and self-doubt.

"Who killed your brother?' he repeated.

"Understand,'' she started slowly, "I can't prove this, and I won't say this in any court. Here or in Mexico.''

He didn't think it was going to be any other way, that would make it too much like right. "So be it.''

"In Villanueva, a city in the foothills of the Sierra Madre Occidental, Efraín ran for the city council. For as long as we could remember, our family had been pree supporters. You know about the Partidad Revolutionario Institutionale, ¿qué no?'' she asked with an ironic tone in her voice.

"A little,'' Monk admitted. "Some of the PRI's hold has started to slip after all these years. The third party, the PRD, their candidate Cuauhtemoc Cardenas.'' Monk stumbled through his pronounciation. "Is that how you say his name?''

"Close enough,'' she said.

Monk went on, "So Cardenas, a leftist, won over the PRI's boy for the mayor's seat in Mexico City, which is a big thing considering its size and influence. And what with all the Zapatistas stuff, and the Salinas brothers implicated in the assassination of that opposition presidential candidate awhile back—"

"His name was Colosio, but he wasn't a member of the PAN, which is the second biggest party in Mexico. No, Colosio was a member of the pree, the PRI, the ruling party. Colosio was the leading candidate on his way to capture the nomination. He was pushing too fast and too . . . deep for many.

"You see, President Salinas de Gortari promised a more democratic Mexico when he won. A hollow promise as so many had done before him. Yet despite his best efforts to not do so, world conditions deemed otherwise." She laughed to herself.

"But your brother ran as an opposition candidate?"

Patiently she answered him. "Again, you must not see Mexican politics like they are here. My brother ran as a member of the PRI, but as a reformer. You see the difference? Not as one who just wanted the office to do the same as the others before him."

Monk gave a slight nod of understanding.

"My brother worked in a metal . . . ah *horno de fusión.* Oh I don't know the word in English." She gestured while she talked. "You know when you take one kind of metal out of what you dig from the mountains? Ore, is the word I want to say."

"A smelting plant," Monk supplied.

"Yes." She pointed as if he gotten a game show question right. "Smelting plant. The owner's brother was longtime friends with our family. The brother had started one of these plants, right? In Zacatecas, the city that's also in the state of Zacatecas. The rock, the ore came from the mountains."

"And they had one in this city, Villanueva?"

"Correct," she said, "a second one. Efraín was a

supervisor there and I worked on a small newspaper called *El Tímpano*."

"*The Drum*."

"Yes, you know some Spanish?"

"Just enough to keep me in trouble."

"Very good. Sit down, please." She indicated a lounge chair near the couch.

He did as requested. "Both of you had an interest in politics?"

She hunched her shoulders. "Since college. We did work for candidates, walk and talk in neighborhoods, phone calls, all that you see? Finally, it seemed only logical we would want to directly do something.

"On the paper we tried to tell the truth about the political situation as it affected Villanueva. Of course we were not fools. Some truth is more important than others."

"If the mayor got a little *mordida*, as long as he made sure the schools got books . . ." He looked to heaven.

"Yes. But some things you couldn't say in print were the price of business. Newspeople get killed fairly often in Mexico, Mr. Monk. I'm sure you've heard about the assasination of reporters in Tijuana."

"Yes," he agreed, "like the ones who worked for the newspaper *Zeta*, doing investigative work on the border drug lords and their buying off local politicians." And that their greedy reach had worked its way north, he added to himself.

"We decided Efraín should run to . . . you know"—she made motions like she was holding something and moving it back and forth—"to clean."

"To sweep out the old guard," Monk articulated. "And that's what got the gangsters on you, your brother and the others."

She touched her bosom. "First the Party, the bosses, say

ya basta. Then the ones they are partners with, the gangsters also say stop. Only they have more final ways of getting you to stop.''

''On orders from Jokay Maladrone?'' Monk looked over at the other two, the man interpreting for Rosanna.

Her sister-in-law shifted in her seat as if invoking his name brought discomfort. ''Maladrone is a boss on this side of the border, you understand? He is Chicano, not Mejicano, but his mother is from Zacatecas. The heart of the Pandilla Zacatecas remains among those who came from there. But Maladrone does have much say, his thinking is greatly respected. He has made money and of course that means he has their ears.''

''Money in drugs?'' Monk asked.

''Not just the *drogas.* The gangsters have always had the drugs, the *putas,* the gambling. But with Maladrone, they are now involved with *oro.*''

''Gold?'' Monk said.

''*Oro,*'' she confirmed, fingering a thin necklace around her neck.

Monk flashed on the fact that one of DeKovan's companies was called Ingot Limited. ''Is this who you believe murdered your family members?''

She took him in before speaking. ''I'm scared not for me. I'm scared for Rosanna.'' She bent her head toward her. ''She's only been a wife, you understand? Even more, I worry for my nieces. Their deaths cannot be because of me. It cannot.''

''I know, Karla. Nobody knows I'm here, and nobody here will see me again.''

''You found us,'' she stressed. Her implication was clear.

''Then help me to stop them.''

''You can't. They are too big.''

Her accurate analysis cut down the tall horse Monk was trying to ride. "You're right," he admitted. "But the ones who set the fire can pay."

She regarded him again. Through the walls, the soothing clucking of the chickens could be heard. As far as those birds knew, all was right with their world. But Sunday and dinnertime would eventually come around, and a skillet popping with hot oil might be one or more of the flock's destination. "What I know is Efraín and I thought it best we come north after the killings of some of our comrades when the elections in Villanueva were over."

"How'd you wind up in the Rancho?"

"We had to bring our mother, and she couldn't get a green card. The government has really made it hard, more regulations, especially for someone her age. But we couldn't live in a . . . a . . ."—she searched for the word—"*garaje*, where you put the cars."

"Garage."

"Exactly. We could not live like that. A cousin in Mexico City knew Reyisa, Mrs. Limón. She got us a place, but this too made problems."

"You went ahead of black families on the waiting list."

She bowed her head. "We were in fear from the criminals in Zacatecas, and then we came here and got ourselves in more problems."

"Didn't Mrs. Limón try to explain things to the black tenants?" He couldn't call her Reyisa.

"She tried. Mr. Cady tried too. But if people keep not getting what they're supposed to get, then sometimes the reasons sound like excuses. In this country, I know Afro-Americans hear those excuses too often." She sank into the couch. "I'm still not sure who set fire to our home.

"Efraín and I saw the conditions at the Rancho Tajuata.

I found out the Zacatecas were using Los Domingos fighting with the *mayate*—oh, I'm sorry.''

"Go ahead," Monk said neutrally.

"Using the Scalp Hunters and Los Domingos to kill each other, make a lot of blood. That way, La Pandilla Zacatecas could step in and bring order. Be the peacemakers.''

"How did you find this out?''

She started to cry. Monk felt impotent and looked over at the other two. Rosanna Cruzado came over to comfort her sister-in-law. Karla Ruzón wiped her tears away. "I've been doing some freelance, you call it here, writing for *La Opinión*. One of the editors with contacts in Zacatecas was doing a story about them gaining power in Los Angeles.

"What I told you is not a secret, really. It's just that some of the other immigrants who also know this, or suspect it, have no means of acting on it.'' She ran out of energy like a steam-burning locomotive going too long between stations.

"Or some figure so what? At least it would stop the random violence and too much blood.'' Monk also felt a weakness pour over him. Muscles stretched too taut, his mind too hyper to know any state but full throttle. "Karla, have you heard the name DeKovan?''

Her hands were clasped together, her head down. "Once, yes. Efraín had been meeting with some of the nationals, the immigrants. They listened to him because some had heard the news about him from relatives back in Mexico.''

"And one of them had heard about DeKovan?''

"Of course not," she upbraided him gently. "Because he was trying to bring these people to join together, Efraín discovered he was becoming involved in something else.

One time he told me he'd been confronted by Big Loco. That he was on drugs, you understand?''

''High.''

''Yes. Loco was saying how he had something to fight the Zacatecas. He knew what they were trying to do. He said he had a rich *gavacho* who was his friend.''

''A white man named DeKovan.''

''She's tired,'' the man said, getting up from the dining room table. ''You have to go now. You have to not come back.''

Monk got up, sluggish and directionless. He'd made some notes, but the will to decipher them was spent. He wanted to keep going and he wanted to lie down. He wanted to get Harwick Henri DeKovan in the back room of the Satellite Bar and shake him until he stopped acting goofy. He sleepwalked over to where Karla Ruzón and Rosanna Cruzado sat.

''Don't be so rough on yourself, Karla. You didn't set the fire. When Maladrone learned about you and your brother's activities, he was going to do something.'' He touched her shoulder tentatively.

Lightly, she touched his hand. ''Why do you do this for Mejicanos, Ivan Monk? People you don't know. People who a lot of them don't have anything to do with blacks?''

''If I had an answer, I'd give it to you.''

She smiled. ''You have one, you just don't tell anyone.''

Stepping back outside, a light drizzle had begun. Monk glided back into downtown L.A. behind the wheel of the rental. He moved along the quiet freeways, the wipers going at half speed. He slipped off the 110 at the Wilshire exit, and took the boulevard east toward Flower—Figueroa was one-way here, running north, and he wanted to go south.

To the west, Wilshire ran nearly sixteen miles to the

ocean in Santa Monica. The street was named for H. Gaylord Wilshire, a socialist publisher who at one point controlled a monopoly of billboards in L.A. His one-time Wilshire tract had been more orange groves than roadway, but the colorful developer had envisioned the street becoming a fashionable concourse and driveway.

Gaylord had got his wish, sort of. Nowadays, on either side of Wilshire Boulevard were Central American enclaves, yet along its length were Korean-owned businesses from bridal shops to photocopier stores. The wide thoroughfare then went on to touch the edges of working- and lower-middle-class black neighborhoods. It then cut through the mid-Wilshire district, the Miracle Mile of car dealerships, Middle Eastern restaurants, and office supply outlets.

Above that the street got more gussied up to properly represent Beverly Hills and then continued into Westwood and the area with upscale furniture and electronic equipment shops situated west of Sepulveda.

But Monk had a more immediate location to get to. He turned right onto Flower until he came to Olympic whereupon he made another right and right again, doubling back north onto Figueroa. He got to the left on the one-way street and parked at the curb near Ninth.

The Original Pantry sat unimpressive but sturdy on the northeast corner of Ninth and Figueroa. The eatery had reposed for more than seventy years in this spot; it was where his father used to take his mother when they were dating. The Pantry was one of the few places downtown in those days of restrictive housing covenants that didn't slow-service black patrons.

The diner's fare was simple and varied little from week to week. Breakfasts were hubcap-sized pancakes, thick rashers of bacon, and eggs yellowy bright. Lunch and dinners were steaks, chops, rib tips, roasted chicken, sometimes hamburger loaf, fried fish about every three weeks, or, incongruously, lamb curry. The potatoes were either mashed or cubed and fried in a kind of chunky hash brown style. The vegetables were overcooked but the coffee and Pepsi always flowed. It wasn't four-star, but it damned sure filled a hole.

"Hey," he said, his call connecting on a pay phone outside of the place. Several club goers and college types mixed with the truck drivers and security guards on break going in and out of the diner.

"Ivan," Jill said on the other end, "Mitchell told me something you should know."

"Oh I bet he did."

"Don't even go there." Her voice quickly got serious again. "Mitchell said sheriff's deputies found Keith 2X on the banks of the L.A. River down below the Fourth Street bridge. He'd been trussed up and tortured, but was still alive. They left him to gag on his own blood, Ivan."

Momentarily, Monk took the phone away from his ear then brought it back up. "Goddamnit, Jill." The too-constant urban refrain of grabbing the opportunity to waste life, this time a young black man who seemed to be trying so hard, took something out of him. Constance Smalls was at his shoulder, damning him, and he had no words to say in his defense.

Kodama spoke. "The sheriffs have turned this back over to LAPD since this seems to lead right back to Absalla."

Monk found that too obvious. But then again, maybe the Muslim leader was just arrogant enough to believe Allah would protect him. "Have they arrested him?"

"Yes." She halted, her speech jumbling up before she ordered her thoughts. "Fletcher Wilkenson called for you."

"And?" Two woman in skirts shorter than his shirttail

and tighter than conga skins brushed past him. They were laughing loudly and the one in orange heels threw back her head and let out with a horse whinny. They sauntered into the Pantry.

"He said," Kodama went on, "that he got a visit from Jokay Maladrone."

"Great." He imagined Maladrone somehow metamorphosing out of his iron lung into a jaguar and descending onto Wilkenson's porch in his animal guise.

Kodama explained. "Mr. Wilkenson said Maladrone was being transported in a medically rigged trailer truck of some sort. He'd had his men take him to Wilkenson's house in Mount Washington to give him a warning: stay away from you, and don't publish his book."

"They do anything to him?" Monk's hand was wet from the light rain, and he feared if he let the receiver drop, he'd drift out beyond the limits of reason.

"Just scare him." She let the rest go unsaid.

"But he still called," Monk noted. "I'm going to get something to eat, Jill, then maybe swing over to Newton Division and see if I can get a word with Absalla." He wasn't discussing his plan, simply announcing what his intentions were.

"They won't hardly let you see him."

"So I'll follow him or I'll go right over to the Rancho and talk to the Ra-Falcons."

"You have to rest, Ivan." She said it for formality's sake. She knew he was on a gambler's roll, too much in to the house to quit, but not so beat that he didn't believe the golden pot was one throw of the dice away. Whatever, he had to stay in the game, had to be near the tables of chance.

He was tired and wired, and ready to jump whichever way he could force, cajole, or charm an answer out of someone. "I'm alright."

"You have to come back to me." Her voice cracked.

Soft rain began to pelt him. Figueroa was a wasteland, its cars multihued alloyed bugs meandering along not to seek the dark wetness, but heading for the light as if it held safety. But in fact the stalkers could sight you better that way. "Ain't no thing, baby."

He ate his meal and downed three cups of coffee. He got over to the donut shop and caught four hours of sleep. Kodama was right, it would have been an errand of futility to have gone over to Newton Station.

Early morning hadn't yet broken, and Monk had rumbled loose from the comfort of his quilt and futon. It was false security anyway. He washed his face in the sink, and shaved meticulously. Afterward he got the Ultrastar and strapped it to his ankle. His old man's .45 was slipped into a right side belt rig that allowed the muzzle to stick out facing down, the grip up and flat against his side.

"From the Château Thierry to Con Thien," Monk said admirably, snugging the weapon. He put on thick socks, then got his feet into the pair of scuffed work boots he kept in the file room. Over his top he put on a loose sweatshirt, and on his head a baseball cap with the insignia of the old Negro League Monarch Grays on the crown. He went up front and brewed some coffee. It was still early, but he wanted to talk with Wilkenson.

"Sorry to bother you 'fore the cows got up, Fletcher," he said after the older man answered.

"I expected to hear from you," he said, recognizing Monk's voice. "I guess you heard about Jokay coming to see me."

Monk told him about his electronic encounter with DeKovan at his Dancing Dinosaur. "Maybe our nutty millionaire doesn't believe in the First Amendment."

"Assuming he's behind this. There's nothing linking him directly."

Monk couldn't tell if he was disappointed or relieved. "Then why the hell would Jokay care? And more to the point, why should DeKovan care now? He must have known you were working on the book."

"Not necessarily. Most of my background research is either from my own notes from the past, or facts and information I've looked up. I purposely avoided interviewing anybody who DeKovan might pressure not to talk."

"He didn't get it from me." It seemed to him Dexter Grant was somewhere out there, poking at the edges of DeKovan's carefully constructed shell. But Grant wasn't an amateur, and he didn't think he all of a sudden had gotten Alzheimer's. "In all this time you never mentioned you were working on the book to anyone, Fletcher?"

"We-ell," the sixty-plus radical sputtered, "I of course did talk with some of the old-timers at the Rancho. But if your supposition is correct, then that would mean DeKovan's got a spy in there."

"Somebody who probably kept watch on you in the old days too."

"That's not much of a reward, being allowed to keep living at the Rancho Tajuata."

"You got me on that one," Monk admitted. "But he had to find out some kind of way. Some of the Domingos saw you around, right?" A thunder clap made Monk spin around excitedly. A storm had moved in, and rain pelted a heavy staccato on the roof.

"Yes, and some of the Scalp Hunters as well. I even got an interview with Isaiah Booker. He's—"

"I know who he is," Monk burst out. "He was also being comped at DeKovan's Airport Casino."

"Interesting," Fletcher Wilkenson mouthed quietly.

"I'm going over to the Rancho now. One of the Ra-Falcons has been worked over, and the same crew's out gunning for me. There's no place left to go."

"You be careful in that den, Daniel," Wilkenson warned him.

Monk laughed hollowly and said good-bye. He got into his thick, water-repellent Cumberland jacket that Kodama had brought over for him the night before. He looked out, and spotting nothing untoward, left the shop. Monk walked the two blocks to where he'd left the rental so as not to tip off the boys in the Isuzu in case they'd been cruising by the shop.

He was waiting on the couch for Sergeant LaToyce Blaine when she came walking up the stairs to the Ra-Falcons' second-floor office. Her long braids had been pulled back, she was wearing a long, green Army trenchcoat, and she carried the morning newspaper in plastic. She made a point of stopping in front of Monk.

"What in the holy hell are you doing here?"

"You heard about what happened to Keith?"

"N-no," she stammered. "What are you talking about, man?"

"Where you been all night?" He assumed Absalla must have tried to call her or his other sergeant, Eddie Waters.

"With a friend, like it's your business," she snapped.

Monk looked at one of the late-shift personnel getting ready to leave. "Why don't you tell her?"

The security guard, a corporal, older and heavier than most of the Ra-Falcons he'd seen, spoke. "They found Keith damn near dead, LaToyce. Absalla was arrested. And we tried getting ahold of Eddie, but he wasn't around last night either."

Blaine threw the paper on the couch, and sat down on it also. "Shit, shit, shit."

"Who owns a black Isuzu Trooper? This year's model." Monk crossed his legs.

The silence was telling.

"What if I said I did," Blaine growled.

"I saw you drive up in an Acura," Monk leveled.

The corporal was about to say something but Blaine stopped him with slitted eyes. "I think it's best we wait until I've talked with Antar."

"You do that, Sarge." Monk got up. "I'm not going anywhere. You get down to Newton or get the magnificent one on the phone. And when you do, tell him I know the Ra-Falcons, under different names, supply security to some of the businesses owned by H. H. DeKovan."

She fixed Monk with a hard look. The corporal stared at both of them. "Who's that?"

"Ask her." Monk walked out and down the stairs.

With no particular place to go, he meandered through the complex, nearing the abandoned job center across the unused tracks. Monk stared at the series of slabs, focusing east toward Alameda, on the open field that lay beyond the buildings. He was about to go over to the center when he realized if one of the Domingos should see him, and happen to catch him out in the open like that, he'd wind up the skewered morning special on a plate. That fact and the worsening weather finally got him over to see the only one who'd let him in at such an hour of the morning. He rang the buzzer at Henry Cady's door. He heard two locks being undone beyond the security screen.

"Monk?"

"Sorry about the milkman hours, Henry. Mind if I come in and sit a spell?" The heat of confronting Blaine had worn off, and the cold was fast seeping into him.

"Aaaalright" stretched out like bent time behind the doors. The screen was unlatched and Cady, clad in red-striped pajamas, peered out. "You making your rounds kinda early, ain't you, marshal?" He looked past him into the sky.

Monk put a hand against the wall. "What you trying to hide there, Henry?"

His head seesawed. "Company, you know?"

"Oh," Monk was chagrined. "I'm sorry, man. Listen, I've just got two quick questions, okay? What did you tell me was the name of the company that owns the A. Philip Randolph Center?"

"Trentex. We"—involuntarily his head jerked toward the bedroom—"were discussing that earlier."

Monk's eyes crinkled. "Who among the Ra-Falcons drives a new black Isuzu Trooper?"

Cady gave it some thought, still wedging his body between the door and its jamb. "I can't say for sure. But"—he made an exasperated sound and pushed the door wider—"why don't you come on in."

He couldn't deny his curiosity, but tried to look circumspect as he entered the retired janitor's abode, letting the door stand partially ajar. The room was like a cave, the shades still down, a low light going in the corner. Listening, Monk could hear a Barry White cut playing low on the stereo. "Take off that brassiere, my dear," White's enticing baritone requested.

"Who drives a Trooper?" Cady called into the bedroom.

Reyisa Limón walked out in a silk kimono, pink chrysanthemums like kudzo climbing all over the material.

Monk blinked.

She put a hand on her large hip. "You're really something, you know that?"

"Aw, gee, kids."

Cady twittered.

The window next to the door imploded, fragments of glass pirouetted through the air and tumbled across the carpet. Vertical trails of plaster dust erupted from the far walls, the lamp in the corner busting apart like overripe fruit. Barry got cut off in midmoan. Save for the sound of these items coming apart, there wasn't any other indication that automatic fire was invading the apartment.

Monk had Cady by the waist and was shoving him down to the ground. "Hit the fucking floor," he yelled at Limón.

"Henry!" she screamed, crawling toward her bewildered-looking lover.

"Try and call the cops," Monk yelled, crabbing around on the floor in the direction of the door. "It's me they want." He got over to the door on his stomach. He peered out the partial opening. Rain was now driving into the buildings and soaking the ground outside. Visibility was poor and Monk could only hear the sound of the water running off the end of the roof's drainpipe. Incongruously, he could hear music, an old blues number. Charlie Patton?

There was no movement, no figures darting in and out of doorways. But the posse was out there. Somebody had called them. He knew he wasn't followed. One of the Ra-Falcons had to have done the deed. So what? Maybe I should hang around and try to identify that Patton tune. Get your ass moving.

Monk got up in a crouching position, daring to stick his head out into the rain. As he'd guessed, he couldn't see anybody. Time was on their side. Why shoot up the apartment and maybe call attention to themselves? Even if they did have suppressed weapons. Like a bull goaded and blinded with his own blood, the muscles cut in his neck so he couldn't lift his head to charge, Monk was being herded for the killing.

He eased out into the courtyard, the Ultrastar in his hand.

"The phone's out, Ivan," Cady yelled behind him.

Monk slammed the door and ran around the corner of Cady's townhouse. He heard a car's engine and spun to his right, and went down behind a weight bench and barbells held in place overhead. He wasn't sure, but he seemed to remember the lane running behind Cady's emptied onto a parking lot.

The running engine seemed to place it parallel to where he was. Quite suddenly there was a squelch of tires, then the automatic fire muffled by silencers. The sound was like the low trilling of a horde of bees hurtling against a thick metal wall. One of the gunmen was shooting at the car.

Monk came out and around the cinder block apartments onto a narrow walking court. Just ahead, blocked by the building's corner, he could hear the car slamming to a halt. He ran up and could see a dark-colored Crown Victoria being punched with ragged holes as if by phantom fingers. He looked up and, against the darkened sky, he could see a figure on the roof. He cranked off two shots from the Ultrastar, driving the figure back.

Monk ran low and dove around the far side of the car. The passenger door was open, and he could see a man running deftly toward a causeway between two buildings over to the left.

"Marasco," Monk yelled into the storm. "It's me, Monk." Bullets lit into the hulk of the car, Monk covering his head as glass screamed about.

More hushed shooting, and Monk chanced a maneuver around the rear of the auto. Right arm extended, supported by the left . . . take a breath, sight down the **V**, and squeeze. The hunched mass on the roof reared back, the weapon clattering to the ground. Monk was already running toward the crevice.

"They tagged me before I could use the radio," Seguin said, sucking in air. He was dressed in jeans and a light windbreaker, unusual attire for the fashion conspicuous cop.

"But you came to round up some Ra-Falcons, didn't you?" Monk looked over at the apartment house, but couldn't tell what had happened to the sniper.

"Actually, Absalla was OR'd around six-thirty this morning. But Keith 2X was found, badly beaten, by a couple of kids racing their go-kart along the concrete banks of the L.A. River. So I wanted to talk with his fellow workers."

Monk twisted his mouth. "Where the hell're Zaneski and Fitzhugh?"

"When we was kids and we used to ride our bikes down there . . ." Seguin reminisced.

"Ah, Hoss?" Monk said with genuine concern.

Seguin brought himself back to the present. "Those two are talking to the Cruzado sister; they found her living at the home of a member of the immigrant rights group, CHIRLA. The organization had set her and the family up temporarily."

"We've got to move," Monk said.

"We got to try and not endanger anyone," Seguin said unnecessarily.

"They want us over there, anyway." Monk looked east, past the parking lot, and the open space. His gaze was locked on the once-upon-a-time Southern Pacific tracks. "Make it nice and clean. That's how their boss likes it," he said with gallows finality.

Seguin was already moving. "Who would that be?"

"H.-I'm-a-twisted-fuck-H. DeKovan."

Seguin looked at him but didn't respond. "We go back this way"—he was pointing down further between the buildings—"then juke to our right, at least we cut down on the open space we have to cover."

"I'm with you."

Jogging, Seguin remarked contemptuously, "That all the firepower you got? Some goddamn plastic swap meet special?"

"It saved your slow, no-aimin' ass."

They reached the end of the building. Lightning briefly lit up the towers of downtown. It might as well have been Afghanistan.

"How many slugs in that thing?" Seguin pointed the barrel of his eighteen-shot 9mm at the Ultrastar's polymer casing.

"Nine, but I just used two—wait, three. No replacements."

"Six," Seguin said, calculating.

"Don't forget Ol' Betsy." Monk tapped his side.

"Yeah, but you still use the original magazine setup in that thing. So that's only another seven rounds. This is a hell of a time for you to be following the dictates of the Crime Bill."

"Kvetch, kvetch. I thought after the shoot-out in North Hollywood where y'all were outgunned by Matasareanu and that clown Phillips you could now pack any pistol you wanted to."

"I like the way a nine feels," Seguin cracked defensively. "Anyway, the forty-five has the stopping power."

"At seventy feet, and the AK can do—"

"Two hundred yards," Seguin finished. "Hardly seems fair, does it?"

Monk took off across an empty basketball court, expecting to slip and be cut down any second. Seguin sprinted by him with seemingly little effort. Out beyond the Rancho's fencing, which was topped by curved spike bars pointing inward, Monk could see one of those billboards advertising the Baron of Beepers service. The photo layout included a brickhouse in a tiger skin–pattern bikini dry-humping a giant beeper while the Baron hoisted a scepter crackling with electricity.

The two reached a structure that hummed. It was the generator room. Monk tried the door, but it was locked.

"We'd just be fish on the counter in there anyway," Seguin concluded.

The men were crouched down in unrelenting rain. The building's overhang afforded them shadow and some relief from the weather. "You hear that?" Seguin asked.

"Not a goddamn thing," Monk said. "What?"

"Look."

Cutting across the field was a Datsun 510 with fat tires.

"Some of your Domingos buddies are coming to say hi, I think." Seguin smiled wickedly at Monk. "They couldn't possibly be part of this hit. Not being that obvious."

"Morons," Monk said softly.

They waited, the car came to a halt. Norteña music blared from the thing, as it sat there, windows down.

"Now what?" Monk said, exasperated. "Waste what little firepower we got on these chuckleheads?"

"Maybe they are working with the silenced boys," Seguin amended.

"I doubt it. This seems more of a payback visit for Big Loco." Monk got up. "I'm going to step out, you try to get around them."

"They might just cap you, you know."

"Let's hope they want to make me squirm first."

Monk walked out, accordion and horns beating back the sound of the drenching rain. He'd tucked the Ultrastar away. The driver and passenger doors creaked open. The lanky kid with the bad teeth, and another *vato* he didn't know were now out of the Datsun. As he got closer, he spotted a crumpled paper bag on the dash in front of the driver's wheel.

" 'Sup, *moreno*?" the skinny one said, snickering. He was high, swaying slightly as if only he could hear the secret rhythm of the downpour as it mixed with the music on his Blaupunkt.

"You the one," Monk said. Absently, he wondered if it was paint or glue in the sack.

The other one was more in control. "Sumpthin's ain't cool, homes."

"Goddamn straight it ain't," Seguin called from behind. "Don't turn and don't move."

Monk felt their presence seconds before he heard the grinding of the black Isuzu's clutch torque into gear. The vehicle raced toward them fast from the Washington Boulevard side of the Rancho. He snatched the Ultrastar loose.

He bowled past the skinny one and got behind the wheel.

"Say, motherfuckah!" he screamed, advancing and pulling out the revolver he had under his oversized jacket.

Seguin put a bullet in the ground before him. "Put it down, asshole," he barked.

Monk wasn't waiting to see if there was compliance. He got the car around and Seguin piled in. They tore off toward the shell of the A. Philip Randolph Advancement and Placement Center. The Isuzu did a wicked right, and started to angle in after them.

Rain thundered on the Datsun's thin roof, and neither man could tell if the silenced weapons were clattering as they retreated—until the back window spiderwebbed and the side mirror flew off.

"*¡Dále gas, Ivan, Dále gas!*" Seguin bellowed.

The Datsun bounced savagely over the tracks and Monk plowed it through the already sagging chain link fence. Something snapped under the frame, and the car's front end lurched down on the left side. The tire was ground down, unable to revolve unfettered in the tire well. The tire gave, and as it blew, the car vibrated widely. The 510 continued to shimmy and Monk fought the wheel to aim it toward the door on the far end of the main building. The same door he couldn't get into before.

''Somebody's been doing some home improvement,'' Seguin declared. There was new eight-foot iron fencing, spiked at the top, bracketing two sides of the center where dilapidated chain link had stood just a few days earlier.

Just as the cop finished his sentence, the banged-up car whacked against the wall, and the two men leapt out of the thing on the run. Seguin shot the door handle twice and they tumbled inside. ''It's darker than hell in here,'' the cop observed.

''You don't suppose our buddies out there have night vision goggles, do you?'' Monk wasn't kidding.

''I imagine they'll let us know soon enough.''

Monk grabbed Seguin's arm. ''Come on, if I remember right, there are rooms farther back this way.'' They started, their eyes adjusting to the gloom. The grey light of the day provided weak halos around the upper window frames that ran the length of the large room. Cold air settled in where the glass had once been. The lower windows on the far side of the building were opaque with grime and rain.

''Jesus,'' Seguin hissed. The sound of his foot striking something brought both of them to a halt.

Monk peered down. ''It's a mattress, I think.''

''Maybe I'll shoot it just to make sure.''

They both laughed nervously, their breath forming small clouds of condensation.

The door they'd come in through banged against the wall. The figure of a man could be discerned in stark silhouette. He began to lay down fire, his rounds making their vip-vip sound as he rotated the weapon back and forth. Calm and methodical, like a man hosing down his parched lawn.

Monk and Seguin had spread out and each unloaded two shots into the backlit figure. He went over backwards like a cardboard cutout.

"I guess that answers the question about the goggles." Seguin was moving toward the other rooms.

Monk hesitated; he was considering going after the dead man's piece.

Seguin could read his mind. "Forget it, Ivan. That's a sucker's play."

"You're right." They went off. Rounding a corner, Monk collided with something heavy and solid. It took a few moments to recognize the machinery in the half light. "Drill press."

"We can do the tour later," Seguin advised, pulling Monk along. The two wound through several twists and turns until they encountered a stairwell.

"Let me see something. Watch my back." Monk ascended.

Seguin reared back against the wall of the stairwell, his eyes wide in the near dark, his ears seeking to differentiate the thrashing of the rain from the footsteps of predators. There was a brief something in the air his instincts told him wasn't Mother Nature talking, but he stayed put. He'd wait, and watch and sweat.

Presently Monk came back down, breathless. "Let's hat," he gulped. He talked while they moved about. "There's windows up on the second floor in this big classroom. The Isuzu is parked in back, and there's one dude out in the rain, on guard duty.''

Thinking about the noise he couldn't place, Seguin asked, "Did he spot you?"

"I took a shot at him and he returned fire. Maybe they'll check upstairs first, give us more time."

"The question, Ivan, is for what."

"Details, my son, details."

After several more hallways and turns and through a couple of rooms, the two reached a passageway; weak light crept its length. "Could be a dead fucking end," Seguin choked.

"Let's go down the rabbit hole, Alice. At least cinder block is good for something besides proletarian architecture."

"It does slow down them high-velocity projectiles," Seguin agreed.

Their feelers tingling, the two eased along, one on either side of the corridor. "There's a door here," Monk announced. A wind had kicked up outside, shoving even more rain inside through the busted-out windows. The rain swirled and howled overhead like an entity searching for a host.

Monk forced the wooden door open and the two went inside.

Seguin shut the door, listening at it for several seconds.

There was more light from the horizontal windows high up and parallel to the ceiling line. "Okay, six strokes at best, given the seating capacity of the Isuzu. And that would mean one of them riding in the cargo part too."

Seguin tugged on his mustache. "We for sure dropped the doorman. But what about the one on the roof?"

"Let's assume he's still frisky, and may have recovered his AK. Or whatever the hell it is they're shooting." Monk shifted about, wishing in vain that he could hear something above the rain and wind. The sizeable room they were in contained three rows of long, built-in lab style tables and drawers. There was a clump of stuff in the corner, and Monk walked over to investigate the mass.

"Filing cabinets and desks upended, shoved together." He stared at the pile as if it were a paean to office decorating. "Some rolling chairs too."

"That junk ain't gonna provide much cover, Ivan," Seguin said, scanning the room.

Monk halted. Oddly, he could hear a guitar strain coming to him over the sound of the beating rain. It was an old blues refrain, and it teased him, hovering beyond recognition. The tune was the one he'd heard diving out of Cady's apartment. Who in hell was it? Son House? Elmore James? No, it must be Charlie Patton, he was sure of it now. And where was it coming from?

"It's not that, Marasco." Monk forced himself to focus. "This stuff is new, like that fence outside. It has to do with whatever it is DeKovan and his cohorts are up to."

Seguin walked past the furnishings and touched the wall nearby. "Look at this."

Monk joined him. "What the hell . . . ?" He knocked his knuckles against the part of the wall that was recessed. "A metal door."

"A thick-like-lard door, like a friggin' vault, man." Seguin looked the slab up and down, feeling its surface with his fingertips. "Rolled steel, homie."

Rain whooped and Monk pivoted toward the front of the room. "They must be inside by now," he whispered.

Seguin's 9mm was also pointing at the front entrance. "We can make a pretty good stand in here. The doorway's narrow, and even if they come in blasting, those damned filing cabinets are good at least for . . ." He trailed off as both men holstered their pistols and went to work.

Moving as quickly and silently as possible, the two lifted the file cabinets and placed them in front of the door—giant rooks in the game they were trapped in. They knew the office furniture wouldn't serve as effective barriers, but were useful as alarms should they fall.

"Two Bogart through the door," Seguin began, verbalizing the scenario running through his mind. "Get tripped up on the cabinets."

"We send those two to the happy hunting grounds with us," Monk added. He unsheathed the .45, shifting the Ultrastar to his left hand. The private eye held up the two automatics. "I always wanted to go out with my guns blazing, there, Tex."

"The others swoop in, letting loose with their big bad guns. Left to right, up to down." Seguin put his gun under his armpit, in order to rub his slick hands against the legs of his jeans.

"Then we get on either side of the door," Monk assessed. "If they shoot through the door, they'll have to wonder about what they've hit when they hear the noise of their bullets striking the cabinets. They've got to get the door open, and we run up, and pop out from around the cabinets."

"Maybe drop two more that way also," Seguin theorized. "But if we're too close, ricocheting fire might get us," Seguin advised.

"Standing back here is useless," Monk insisted. "Their eyes are used to this light by now also."

"Too bad we can't get inside that room." Seguin jerked his head in the direction of the massive door.

"You got an extra magazine?" Monk asked, his voice low, his senses stretched.

Seguin shook his head. "I keep it in the glove compartment, 'cause it chafes against my side when I'm sitting down,'' he said with chagrin.

Monk was near him, a thin smile on his face. ''I might have lost count, but I think I've got three left in the Ultrastar and still a full seven in the forty-five.''

Seguin looked off, then directly into Monk's grim features. ''Then that's what we got, Ivan, twenty-three shots—''

''Twenty-three tries,'' Monk interpreted.

There were noises in the corridor. The duo sprinted into position. One on either side of the doorway, each man readied himself at least twenty feet from the entrance. Monk had propped up one of the desks for minimal protection. Seguin was crouched behind a legal-sized filing cabinet. The activity beyond the door was becoming more pronounced.

''Ivan,'' Seguin began, barely audible, ''whatever happens, whatever goes down, you know you and me was always straight.''

''Absolutely, bro'.''

The door splintered into ziggurats of wood as their attackers unleashed random firepower. The office furniture piled in front of the entrance lit up as if struck by ball lightning. One of the cabinets fell over and several metallic clangs reverberated in the room. Then the smell of gas filled their nostrils.

''Assholes,'' Monk swore. One of the open gas cans had landed near him, the odor sinister in its intent.

A volley of more bullets was followed by beer bottles being tossed into the room. The bottles were filled with gas and their wicks were lit. As they shattered, coagulating pools of gas erupted into climbing pyres of yellow-white incandescence, casting freakish gelatinous chiaroscuro forms into the pockets of the room. The storm was unyielding outside, the beat it meted out forming a rhythm that seemed to announce their imminent death.

"Motherfucker," Monk announced at their cruelty. It wasn't enough to rush in and blast them to pieces—after all, that might put a couple of their shooters at jeopardy. Better to burn them out, put the victims to the torch, as they had done to the Cruzados.

There were more shots and Monk saw Seguin diving forward, starkly illuminated by a river of flaming gas, and pumping three at an arm trying to throw its payload. The arm jerked, dropping the Molotov in the hallway. There was a commotion, and fire was now dancing out in the corridor too.

"Aw, shit, man," a familiar voice screamed.

"I'm hit," another voice hollered.

"You more than that, you silly bitch. You just keep fucking up like you was taking a class in it." There was a burst of gunfire.

Monk was tired of waiting to die. He tore the cuff and part of his sleeve off, and ignited the cloth in the fire. Then he stepped from around the desk, heat and panic making his face slick with sweat. It was as if he were caught up in some druidic ceremony that only Los Angeles tumbling pell-mell into the twenty-first century could dream up. He and Seguin were the sorry replacements for the unsullied sacrificial maidens.

His friend was pressed up close against the door, submerged in one of the few remaining areas of darkness. Monk had held onto the gas can that had landed close to him, his flaming cuff wrapped around the lip. He flung the can at two men who'd pressed into the room.

The container bounced off the chest of one of the men, and a trail of burning liquid leapt from his torso down to his crotch. Reflexively he swung his gun onto Monk as

Seguin opened fire from the side. The man dived into another patch of shadows on the same side of the room as the LAPD detective.

The other shooter was firing and Monk was moving, shoving the pile of office furniture at him. *Put your shoulder into it, Monk. Drive, drive,* he could hear his old high school coach Jim Young exhorting him as he hit the tackling sled. His body upset the tall filing cabinets as Monk climbed and scampered onto the metal dominoes, his momentum carrying him out into the hallway. Underneath the pile of cabinets, the gunman squirmed, seeking to free himself and his weapon.

Monk was rocked back and forth like he was riding a bronco, and he popped four rounds in rapid succession among the crevices between the toppled items. The bucking ceased, and a cabinet slid over.

The light from the fire in the hall revealed Isaiah Booker's white bodyguard. He was dressed in slacks, sport coat, and a white, banded-collar silk shirt. The shirt was now splotchy with carmine stains. The thin strand of his ponytail lapped over his face like a giant dead worm. A weighty gold ring with a marbled jade setting was on a finger of the killer's hand, which still gripped his warm MK-9. The Raptor suppressor clamped on the end of the gun's barrel was a mat black in contrast to the shiny finish of the wicked war toy.

Images registered in miniseconds as Monk attempted to right himself. Behind him, he heard the truculent echoing of the other attacker's silenced weapon. "Marasco!" he bellowed, his feet and legs tangled in the Staples detritus. He was trying to get oriented, but it seemed like everything was happening in accelerated time, and he was stuck in slow gear.

"Shit yes."

An assault gun clacked sibilantly, and pain racked Monk's leg.

"Put the gun down, chump." It was B.B., the dyed blond with the maroon wedge. His other hoop earring twinkled, catching the fire's light. The other side of his head had a bandage where his other ear used to be. His piece was centered unwaveringly on Monk.

Desolate, he tossed the .45 onto the floor. He'd never reach the MK. His lower leg, where Blondie had shot him, bled freely. But it seemed as if his mind were detaching itself from his body, and that soon all his pain would be a sensation without a home. Was that the "Dead Letter Blues" blowing in below the howl? *Put my baby on the coolin' board.* Would Jill and his mother lay him out?

"I'm going to dot you like you did me." Blondie swaggered closer, giving Monk a better look at the gauze and tape plastered on the side of his head. "Take off half your motherfuckin' face 'fore I shoot you in the dick, then really start on you."

A subconscious clarity took hold of Monk. By the undulating jonquil light, he recognized the man's weapon as an Uzi 41 A.E., with the .40 Smith & Wesson aluminum magazine, adaptor, and suppressor. Very efficient, very professional. Not a gun sold to gangbangers out of the trunks of Chevys like the assembly-line Norinco Chinese model AK.

"What are DeKovan and Maladrone up to?" He was tired, and he let his head thud against the wall. He wanted it to be over. His knee throbbed, and his lower leg was losing feeling. The fire was spreading. Fuck it, let it come. I love you guys. But goddamnit, he wanted to know. "What's in the room back there? The one with that door on it."

Blondie roared and got closer still. He was breathing like

a dynamo whose breakers had shorted. He stood triumphantly over Monk. "I ain't even gonna give you the satisfaction, man." Fleetingly, an emotion that might have been respect nuanced his look, then disappeared. "It bees this way." The gun came up and Blondie blinked, his shots going right and wide of his mark.

Like a man coming up one last time for air, Monk's incentive returned and he reached out with both hands, grabbing and yanking on the other man's legs. Blondie re-aimed the Uzi at Monk's head. Instinctively, futilely, Monk latched a hand around the suppressor screwed onto the gun's barrel. Blondie gurgled and drooled. His face lit from within with purpose as he struggled to free the gun. Yet his strength left him and he fell forward, sprawled across Monk and the filing cabinets. There was a neat hole up high, a little off center, in his upper back.

"Thanks, Marasco."

Seguin slumped down against the doorway, his face sallow. "My pleasure."

"We gotta get out of here," Monk said with growing concern. The fires were congealing together and their growth was imminent. He tried to get up but couldn't put weight on his leg. Monk fell back. "Marasco," he started. Glancing over at the doorway, he could see his friend had gone slack, his chin lolling against his chest.

"Marasco," Monk repeated. He forced himself back up, his wound tearing his eyes. The fire ate away at the insides of the room they'd been in. Monk limped over to Seguin, passing the gunner Blondie had shot in a pique. It was Eddie Waters.

Monk got to his friend as the fire in the hallway whooshed onto one of the walls, consuming an aged poster announcing a Sugar Ray Robinson fight at the Olympic.

"Come on." Monk couldn't handle Seguin's weight on

his bad leg, so he held him by his upper body and dragged him along. Monk got to the far end of the hall, the flames gyrating boldly along the corridor. Monk continued his task, getting some feet down another corridor. But the encroaching brightness told him he wasn't moving fast enough.

"Now would be a good time to wake up, Marasco." He didn't comply. Monk kept moving, coming upon the stairs he'd been up earlier. Sweat soaked his clothes and his arms were numb hubs. He tried to weigh his options rationally, but he knew ultimately he had only luck and intuition left.

"Come on, Slick." Monk started up the stairs, resting at each second landing. Somewhere around midway, as he'd hoped, the bumping aroused Seguin.

"We're still in the building?"

Monk didn't have enough strength to laugh. "Can you stand?"

On the third try Seguin got up, supporting himself on the railing. They put arms around each other and managed to get to the top, collapsing there.

"You hear that?" Seguin eked out.

"Yeah, the rain's let up."

"You're hilarious."

Sirens. "Henry must have gotten to a phone," Monk surmised.

Seguin had passed out again.

Monk propped himself against the wall at the top of the stairs, sweat stinging his eyes. Heat and flame were gobbling up rooms and hallways. Soon it would embrace the two. He was drifting in and out of consciousness when a figure with a face enclosed in an oxygen mask and bearing a hatchet shook him awake.

"We got more than roast on the menu today," the fire

fighter quipped to other squad members who were clambering up the stairs.

"He's a cop," Monk lifted a listless arm, then dropped it. He'd forgotten how to make his fingers work.

"Let's get some stretchers up here," the joker ordered.

"Eddie Waters was a Ra-Falcon, and an old friend of Keith 2X." Monk lay in the ambulance riding over to USC County General. "Keith must have found out from Waters about the meeting on Trinity, and told me."

Seguin, who'd stirred again, was laid out across from him. "When they were pulling us out, I saw some uniforms taking the shooter you'd wounded down from the roof. It was one of the Domingos."

"You two should take it easy," the woman paramedic advised.

"Big Loco knew he was getting squeezed out. But from what Karla Ruzón told me, it seems he was still getting comped at the Airport Casino. Maybe he figured that meant he was cool with DeKovan."

"Probably just part of how they were suckering him," Seguin offered. "Judging from who the regulators were who came after us, it seems Maladrone and Booker were in this together."

"And who says black and brown can't unite," Monk commented sarcastically. "Especially when money's the great motivator."

Seguin tried to sit up but the paramedic gently, yet forcefully pushed him down. "Okay, you win," the wounded cop said. "So the new regime was to be made from pieces of the old."

Maladrone's words about the need for discipline and order came back to Monk. "There is something to be said for organized crime, Marasco. No random shootings, petty thefts and burglaries stop. Progressive gangsterism."

"Liberal simp," his friend fired back.

"Why don't you two save it for the Brinkley show, alright?"

Ignoring the paramedic, Monk added, "It's the story of big business, Marasco."

Seguin laughed softly.

"Anyway, I think Loco found out about the meeting on Trinity and went there to cap Isaiah Booker," Monk conjectured. "Maybe he figured he'd make himself invaluable to DeKovan."

The ambulance drove along Soto, the street glistening with the clean rain.

"Then how does he get lured over to the apartment in the Crenshaw area?" Seguin asked.

"You said yourself the guy on the roof was a Domingo Trece. Loco couldn't conceive the idea that some of his boys could cross over to the new combine."

"Makes sense." Seguin grimaced as he shifted on his stretcher.

"He probably went over there with one of his supposed homies on the pretense he could get Booker, I bet."

The ambulance hit a pothole. "But you only saw two men enter that night. Counting Loco, there were three in the room," Seguin pointed out.

"Either Blondie or Eddie was already hiding in the apartment. Lying in wait for 2X's return or to spring the trap on Loco."

The ambulance went past Hazard Park, which looked like a lush island newly risen from the ocean floor as its trees dripped with fresh rain. The ambulance got to Marengo and headed on into the hospital.

"The hitters kept in contact by cell phones," Monk surmised. "The plan was probably to do Big Loco at the apartment, and place the blame on Keith. He was on the run 'cause he realized that his own pardner was playin' him, and was in deep. If he showed up, no cop would listen to him, as they'd figure he'd be trying to get out from under the Loco murder beef.''

''All police are not as stupid as you think, Ivan.''

''So I've been told.''

They both laughed and coughed up heavy wads of phlegm. The ambulance wailed to a stop.

Twenty-three

I t was a hot and humid afternoon with few breezes to bring relief. The portable canopies erected on the basketball court hardly rippled. The assembled residents of the Rancho Tajuata sat fanning themselves with printed programs. Latino and black children played tag with each other, the stern looks of admonishment from their parents to cease their running going unheeded.

On the raised dais, also covered under a blue and white canopy courtesy of the city, several officials from the local housing authority squinted with discomfort. Some looked worried to actually be inside one of the ghetto housing projects they only knew by map coordinates.

Also onstage were Henry Cady and Reyisa Limón—sitting on opposite sides of the podium so as not to blow their cover—and a couple of bureaucrats from HUD. Antar Absalla was finishing his speech.

"I don't ask that you pat me on the back for helping to rid our housing project of the bad element. I'm not looking for accolades."

"Then why don't you quit lying," Jill Kodama said loud enough for several rows to hear.

"I ask that you congratulate all the Ra-Falcons who stand side by side with the tenants when I say we're not only here to help keep the peace, but that the revamped security force will also reflect the realities of the nineties." He thrust an arm toward the audience. "I'd like to introduce some of our newest soldiers for peace."

Several young men and women stood up, many of whom were Latino. There was even a Southeast Asian face.

"What a guy," Kodama whispered to Monk. Both sat among the audience.

"Here, here," Monk shouted, tapping his lower leg, in a cast up to his knee, with his cane.

"I guess he ain't gonna mention the kilos of gold, diamond jewelry, freight manifests, and boxes of cash the cops found in that fortified room in the job center." Kodama sucked her tongue against her teeth.

"Don't forget those bills had traces of cocaine on them," Monk said.

"Money laundering, smuggling goods off the books from the downtown jewelry mart, quite an operation they were setting up." Kodama waved at city councilwoman Tina Chalmers, who had arrived late and was making for the stage. "But how the hell were they going to hide all that?"

Monk shifted, trying to get into a comfortable position. "Trentex had taken out permits to rehab the center as an auto parts warehouse. Those old S.P. tracks were due to be utilized again by the Santa Fe Railroad, who bought them out several years ago."

"To-your-door service," Kodama said cheerily. "And I guess DeKovan's not coming back from Switzerland any time soon.'' Kodama could sense the shift in his mood. She looked at his grim profile.

Monk clapped heartily as Absalla sat down, a sardonic twist on his lips. Cady came to the podium to say a few words about the work of the tenants' association going forward, and that he was optimistic that the Rancho would eventually be owned by the residents.

"Seems DeKovan's been maintaining a dual citizenship since the seventies. He's nonextraditable there.'' Monk whacked a leg of the chair in front of him very hard with his cane.

Kodama rubbed his arm. "At least it came to light that it was one of DeKovan's companies that'd purchased the center.'' She looked off beyond the stage, where the hulk of the A. Philip Randolph Advancement and Placement Center shimmered as if it were a mirage. The center should have been a symbol of hope, but instead it had been corrupted into a construct of greedy imaginations.

Monk found little consolation in the fact that the smuggling and laundering operation had been uncovered. For the sad reality was that Efraín Cruzado and members of his family were casualties of war because bastards like Maladrone deemed him a threat, a threat because he wanted to organize people.

Fletcher Wilkenson, another organizer, another threat, was now accepting a plaque from Cady.

"My friends, I would not be so naive as to say the hardest is behind us. But I do know if we can work together, appreciate our differences and emphasize our commonalities, then surely some good will come of that.'' His voice broke and cheers and applause went up from the gathered.

"How's Keith Burroughs?'' Kodama asked Monk, hoping that would get him on another subject.

"He's gonna make it. He told me Eddie Waters had

hipped him to the meeting on Trinity as a way of feeling him out. He wanted to see if his old running buddy was going to roll with the flavor and work for the new crime regime, as it represented the irresistible melding of corporate capital and street muscle. Plus a little mumbo-jumbo had been thrown into the mix for seasoning.

"Oh, check this out," Monk continued. "Keith's hospital bill has been covered by an anonymous benefactor."

"DeKovan," Kodama concluded. "He really is a bent fuck."

"He had enough wherewithal to flee."

The ceremony was winding down. Its purpose had been part dog-and-pony, and part pragmatic. The tenants were feeling good and so Cady, Limón, and the rest of the leadership threw them a bash to aid in boosting morale. The practical aspect was to show the Department of Housing and Urban Development suits that the Rancho was ready and should have the opportunity to work with the federal agency in completing proposals for the loans and grants to convert the complex to private hands.

Afterward, people milled about the dual canopies under which a buffet of sliced meats, strawberries, chunks of melons, and Doritos had been set up.

"I'm sure glad you're back in harness, Judge Kodama." A smallish older black woman looked up at Kodama, smiling. Her wrinkled face was framed by a wide-brimmed sun hat held in place with a long stickpin topped with a teardrop fake pearl.

"Thank you," Kodama said humbly, shaking the well-wisher's hand.

"We sure need more like you." The woman ambled off, holding a plastic cup whose contents smelled like brandy.

"You know what I need right now, baby?" Monk balanced himself on his cane, putting his arm around her waist.

"More codeine, darling?" She pinched his side. "You get the Gorzynskis straightened out?"

"Yes. He finally believed she was only putting away money for an IRA she'd opened up for them when we took him over to the bank to prove it."

"Ivan, come over here."

Monk jerked his head around. Wilkenson was standing in the doorway of the newly reopened rec center. He hobbled over. "Congratulations, Fletcher."

"Thank you. Look at that." He pointed.

On the wide-screen TV, divers in scuba gear were swimming near a Coast Guard boat. "The Gulf of Mexico" was superimposed over the images on the screen. The boat had a crane, and had hauled up in a net an object Monk recognized by the angular patterns engraved on its side.

The newscaster spoke. "Again, at the top of the news, off the coast of Corpus Christi this morning, authorities found an iron lung believed to belong to the missing Jokay Maladrone. The crime boss is wanted for questioning in the murders of several people in Los Angeles. Though his life-sustaining apparatus was found, his body has yet to be recovered."

"Some kind of diversion," Monk said. "He probably just switched machines."

"I don't know," Wilkenson mused wistfully. "It's not like he can just hop out and hop into another one."

"Isaiah Booker has copped a deal," Kodama reminded both of them. There had to be some balance.

"But with no Maladrone, and DeKovan out of reach . . ." Monk stopped speaking; he had a hard time accepting he was going to be denied retribution. "And the real cold part is DeKovan didn't need the money. This whole thing"—his hand swept toward the A. Philip Randolph Advancement and Placement Center—"the murders, everything.'' He spat, air seemingly coming hard for him. "Just a lark for him. One more quirky acquisition in a life of them.'' Monk looked around, but he couldn't figure out what to hit.

Several people came up to chat with Wilkenson and reminisce about the old days. A news crew cornered Kodama to get her comments on Jamboni's announcement that he was going to run for the attorney general's job.

Monk wandered outside and took a seat on a bench, stretching out his throbbing leg. On a corner of the paved area bunched in by newly planted eucalyptus trees, a rooster walked around the tree trunks. The bird turned its head, his red unblinking orb transfixing Monk.

Mesmerized, Monk sat there for several moments. The creature stood sideways, staring at him, still and silent. The thing got on his nerves and he tried to get up, wincing and huffing with effort. He looked down momentarily to see where his bound leg was, and looked up again. The rooster had disappeared.

A blues band began playing on the stage. The woman singer started in on the Robert Johnson number, "Me and the Devil Blues." In the song, a man tells his girlfriend to bury his body along the road. The singer worked the song like it was her own, the crowd having stopped chatting to listen to her delivery. It was as if a shroud had descended upon the gathered, and within its folds, they had been transported to the Delta—where indeed some of their forbearers had left looking for work and relief from Jim Crow decades ago.

She finished with the lyric, "So my evil spirit can get a Greyhound bus and ride." As she repeated the words, Monk was possessed by a mental picture of that rooster's eye boring in on him. He limped off to find the old sister with the brandy.

$5.00 LIBRARY

(H -11/18)